CSI EDDIE COLLINS: BOOK SEVEN

DEATH WARNING

FLINTLOCK YARD

WHO KILLED THE KILLER?

ANDREW BARRETT

Death Warning

Who Killed the Killer

Andrew Barrett

The Ink Foundry

© Copyright 2023

The rights of Andrew Barrett to be identified as the author of this work have been asserted in accordance with sections 77 and 78 of the Copyright, Designs and Patents Act 1988. No part of this publication may be reproduced, stored in a retrieval system or transmitted in any form or by any means electronic, mechanical, photocopying, recording or otherwise without the prior permission of the copyright holder.

Published in the United Kingdom by The Ink Foundry.

For all rights and copyright enquiries, please contact:

permissions@andrewbarrett.co.uk

This book is a work of fiction. Any names, characters, companies, organizations, places, events, locales, and incidents are fictional or are used in a fictitious manner. Any resemblance to actual persons, living or dead, or actual events is purely coincidental.

Contents

Preface	XI
Dedication	XII
Prologue	1
DAY 1	3
Chapter 1	4
Chapter 2	10
Chapter 3	18
DAY 2	27
Chapter 4	28
Chapter 5	36
Chapter 6	41
Chapter 7	47
Chapter 8	56
Chapter 9	58
Day 3	65
Chapter 10	66
Chapter 11	68

Chapter 12	74
Chapter 13	78
Chapter 14	83
Chapter 15	86
Chapter 16	96
Chapter 17	101
Chapter 18	105
Chapter 19	110
DAY 4	116
Chapter 20	117
Chapter 21	128
Chapter 22	136
Chapter 23	141
Chapter 24	148
Chapter 25	153
DAY 5	157
Chapter 26	158
Chapter 27	161
Chapter 28	166
Chapter 29	175
Chapter 30	185
Chapter 31	191
Chapter 32	193
Chapter 33	199

Chapter 34	209
Chapter 35	213
Chapter 36	223
Chapter 37	231
Chapter 38	233
DAY 6	237
Chapter 39	238
Chapter 40	246
Chapter 41	253
Chapter 42	259
Chapter 43	267
Chapter 44	278
Chapter 45	282
Chapter 46	287
Chapter 47	293
Chapter 48	298
Chapter 49	302
Chapter 50	303
Chapter 51	307
Chapter 52	312
Chapter 53	319
Chapter 54	327
Epilogue	329
Acknowledgments	335

About the Author	337
Also by Andrew Barrett	339
Reader's Club	342

Preface

Proud to swear in British English
There is no animal cruelty featured in my novels

Death Warning
is dedicated to Anita Newman

Prologue

IN A PLACE CALLED Beeston on the south side of Leeds, there are people and places that are well worth avoiding. You needed to be tough just to survive around there; only moss and the bad boys thrived.

Sheltering in a doorway to keep out of the wind was a waif who huddled into a puffer coat she'd stolen earlier that day. Despite being used to living outdoors for the most part, she was cold and wet, but was annoyed by a temptation to spend the night inside somewhere. She was considering where might be the easiest place to doss in when she caught sight of a young blonde-haired lass who looked not badly off; her clothes were reasonably tidy, her hair was tied up, she had a good coat and trainers, and she had a phone too. Positively rich. The waif smiled and got ready to jump out.

The blonde-haired lass stopped half a dozen paces short. "Libby," she whispered.

The waif stood up and stepped out of the darkness. "Didn't know it wa' you."

"Are you hungry?"

Libby nodded.

"Want a bath?"

Libby shook her head.

Daisy, the blonde-haired lass, dipped into her pocket and pulled out a crumpled twenty. "I stole it from Vince," she winked, and handed it over. "Why don't you come inside for a bit and warm up. I'll fix you some—"

"Daisy!"

The blonde looked up sharply and didn't say another word, just turned and hurried away towards the man and her house.

"Be safe, girl," Libby whispered.

DAY 1

Chapter 1

Up ahead, the lights were out again. Rain pattered against her hood, and trickled down the apartment windows to her left, and her hurried footfalls echoed off the wet bricks, lonely tonight. The black river flowed almost silently to her right, a gentle lapping at the pilings beneath the path she trod. Shadows of a killer kept her company, flitting in and out of her vision like a hallucination, always just out of reach, never revealing itself.

On the journey home this evening, she'd promised to stop scaring herself, to stop looking for trouble, and just relax, and let her stupid imagination sink into the river and drown.

And that would have been fine if all this nonsense was just her imagination scaring her, but it wasn't. He was back.

Why the hell was he doing this again? She thought he'd stopped, grown up, or found some other person to victimise. She tensed, turned a blind corner, expecting him to be there, and breathed out again when he wasn't. Silly, ineffective up-lighters looked pretty but cast barely enough light to see by. Her jaw ached from clamping her mouth shut against chattering teeth as the final corner came into view. She tensed again, anger daring to make its first appearance in this little production her mind had conjured up, seemingly for its own entertainment.

The last corner was here. Her diminishing bravery pushed her around it, tiptoeing, looking back all the time. And when she looked forward again, there was only emptiness between her and sanctuary. With the cold wind for company, she hurried across the courtyard to her front door, chest heaving, hands trembling. Anger cowering in the shadows of her mind.

Wait. Could she hear them? Footsteps.

The keys rattled as loud as church bells in a library.

She tried so hard not to sob out loud, but there was a pressure in her chest that forced it out. It echoed around the courtyard. Once inside, she slammed the door and locked it; Mia's breath shuddered out of her body, and she dared to climb down from terrified to scared shitless. Anger made a brave resurgence and then passed out.

It turned out the footsteps were real. They came to a halt outside the door and a shadow fell across the frosted glass. She almost squealed, and when the handle turned, she nearly threw up. It felt like being in every horror film she'd ever seen where the victim was alone on the verge of passing out when the murderer appeared at her door. Any moment now an axe would split the door in two.

No one in those films had a phone, or if they did, there was never any signal.

Mia tore her bag open and ripped the phone out just as the handle flipped again.

This time she did squeal, and backed away from the door, trying to unlock the phone and get to the keypad. Her hands shook, and bile spat up into her mouth. The handle flipped back up, and the murderer's footsteps carried away his shadow from her window, and were absorbed by the sound of the rain again. Her breath trembled out, and she blinked away the tears, almost jubilant to have survived. No axe, phew.

Barely a moment passed before she was at the door, eye at the peephole, trying to make sure he was gone.

He'd played this trick on her before. About eighteen months after she met him, she finally worked out what was poisoning her life, and all fingers pointed to him. How he'd manipulated her until she realised she had no friends any more. They'd all taken the volunteer step back and left her front and centre all by herself. Even her mum and dad seemed reluctant to call these days.

She missed them.

Just before she announced that she wanted to split from him, they'd been in a fight, and she'd hit him across the face with her car keys in her hand. They had left a gouge about an inch long and a mile deep. His disbelief, his exasperation, had spun like a vortex into violence in milliseconds. The argument was forgotten in favour of the fight, and Vincent's eyes had turned almost feral. Barely a second had passed before he had her up against the wall by the throat, snarling in her face, shouting, "You'll fucking pay for that!"

Only when Mia had pressed the key into his throat did his grip relax. Eventually he took his hand away and she ran to the bathroom, locked herself in and had sat on the toilet crying into a ball of toilet paper. She could see his feet block out the light under the door. He'd knocked, said, "Mia. I forgive you. It's okay, love. Come on out."

"Go away!"

"Mia. Please. Just... Just open the door. We can sort this out. Like adults, yeah?"

She'd kept quiet, blinking rapidly as though trying to clear her mind.

"Fucking open this door, bitch! Mia? Mia, I'll fucking have you for this."

She hadn't replied to him, and he punched the door. She jumped, and he stormed off out of the flat, shutting off the landing light as he went. She heard the front door slam, and promptly burst into tears. She knew he was too dangerous to live with any longer; thanks to the drugs he'd returned to, he'd lost his loving charm and his good looks, and he'd lost most of his money, too. He'd become too volatile and unpredictable. But worse than that, he was just too scary. One of these days, she'd thought, he's going to kill me.

A full ten minutes later, she tossed the toilet roll in the bin and crept up to the door and placed her ear against it. Silence came back to her – and of course it would; he left ten minutes ago. She wouldn't take the car, because he'd be hiding beside it, waiting for her. She'd grab her bag and purse, and just run, and grab a taxi once she was safely away.

Hurriedly, Mia had unlocked the door and it exploded into her face as Vincent barged in. The edge of it had split open her forehead and blood splashed onto the floor. Before she knew what was happening, he had her by the throat against the wall and he was squeezing the life out of her.

The world was on mute. She'd tried to breathe, looking into his mad, frenzied eyes and quite calmly saw his contorted mouth yell obscenities at her. Eventually, the blackness had come and helped her ignore the spittle flying at her, and the hot blood running down her face. All she became aware of was the slowing beat of her heart. It had grown strained, punchier at each brief boom, until the boom was more of a thud.

She awoke sometime later naked and tied to a dining chair, a tea-towel around her forehead and a dish cloth rammed in her mouth.

She remembered how kind he was to her. "I've got you bound like this," he had said, "because I want to tell you how I'm feeling right now. And I couldn't do that if you weren't bound and gagged because you'd constantly interrupt. I need to get this out, Mia. I like to think we're adult enough to converse and yes, to argue, without resorting to physical violence. You could have blinded me. Okay? Nod, if you're receiving me," he smiled at her. The good old Vincent climbing back aboard, waving at his subjects. "If you agree to let me finish, I'll take the cloth out of your mouth."

Mia had nodded.

He tugged the cloth out.

"Why am I naked?"

"See!" He stood, slapped his leg. "This is why you had a rag in your mouth. Because you can't shut the fuck up!" Vincent had grabbed his hair and sank to the floor, kneeling, head on the tiles, fingernails white.

"I'm sorry," she whispered. "Go on."

"Oh, 'go on', eh? How fucking gracious of you." He'd cleared his throat, and slowly got back to his feet. "You are so hard to live with. Do you know that?" He leaned back against the worktop again, and folded his arms. "I'm prepared to let this go. I know you're under a lot of stress at work and so on, so I'm going to be the bigger party, here, and I'm going to pretend it never happened. I forgive you. Okay?"

She sat there staring at him aghast. "You forgive me?"

"I know," he'd smiled again. "I'm that kind of guy. I'm just an old softy at heart." He was in front of her, staring at her, staring *into* her. "Give softy old Vincent a kiss and tell him you'll behave in future. Eh?" He brought his lips down to hers, testing her, and for a moment she was tempted to bite his fucking nose off. But she was tied in a chair, in a kitchen, where there were lots of sharp things. She kissed him, even closed her eyes, even gave him a bit of tongue.

He had parted from her. "There," he said, "that wasn't so bad, was it? I forgive you."

She remembered how that felt. How utterly lonely he'd made her; how utterly alone. And worse, how utterly helpless and belittled she felt. Now, back in the darkness of her hallway, she stared through the peephole, and listened carefully.

She bit her lip, turned the key, and opened the door.

Chapter 2

"What's this stupid email you sent to me?"

"Hello, Eddie. Do come in." Head of the Major Crime Unit, Detective Chief Superintendent Miriam Kowalski, took a breath, slid her spectacles off and dabbed at sweat on her upper lip with a hanky. "I wondered when—"

"It's an insult to those who keep their craft to themselves."

"They say it'll raise people's awareness of how hard we work."

"Just for the Crown Prosecution Service, commonly known as the Criminal Protection Service, and for the judiciary to fuck it all up again?"

Miriam shrugged, no answer. Then, "It's good for our public image."

"Who gives a shit about our public image?"

"Obviously not you." Miriam pointed to the ceiling. "But they do."

"Who? The typing pool?"

"Typing pool? You do know we're in the twenty-first century, don't you, Eddie? There hasn't been a typing pool for twenty years. You watch too much *Frost*. I'm talking about the ACC."

Eddie's mouth swung open, and he stared in silence as Miriam grew more uncomfortable.

"I didn't have any say in the matter."

He continued to stare.

"We have no choice… Just remember to smile. Okay?"

A thick, spiky sigh bubbled out of his mouth, and then with creaking hinges, his jaw snapped shut.

"I knew you'd be impressed."

He pointed. "You've had your teeth whitened."

Beneath pursed lips, she ran her tongue over her top teeth. "Don't be ridiculous."

"Jesus! I can't believe we're playing games when we're here to care and protect."

"We're not—"

"I can't believe we've been reduced to prime-time entertainment for a nation of braindead Audi-driving morons."

Miriam looked away. She whispered, "It won't be aired at prime-time."

"Sorry?"

"It'll go out at eleven PM."

"Really?" Eddie put his hands on his hips. "So it won't matter if I smile or not then, will it."

"Be pleasant to them, they're here to make us look good."

Eddie growled at her. "Honest hard work makes us look good, not white teeth and bullshit."

Eddie Collins, head of the CSI department at MCU, kicked his way through the doors into the main CSI office, dragging behind him a fury that was tempered just below simmering. The carpet around him smouldered.

Kenny was leaning over recent addition to the team, Mark 'Skid' Strange, pointing at something on his screen and offering advice on his photographic skills. Sid, the admin assistant, was reading *Cosmopolitan* at his desk. Kenny looked up, Sid dropped the magazine. "What's happened?"

"Some bastard is coming along to film us doing our work."

"We all got the same email, Eddie."

"You did?"

Sid sat up straight and checked his nail polish. Kenny smirked, and Skid said, "I'm not happy about it. I don't need the pressure—"

Kenny barked, "No bastard's filming *me* at work. I like my privacy; I don't want the wife knowing what I do."

"Don't worry," Eddie said, "I'll keep them away as much as I can." And then, "Your wife doesn't know what you do for a living? Kenny, you've been a CSI longer than I have!"

There was a knock at the already open door, and a man who wore a blue polo-neck sweater and black-rimmed glasses stood there with a box in his hands and something approaching a smile pushing up one side of his porn-star moustache. "Hello. May I..." He came in. "Come in?"

"Can I help you?" Sid stood, and with the importance of a doctor's receptionist, walked around his desk as though he were the first line of defence against intruders.

"*Your Leeds TV*."

Sid was confused. He held a hand to his chest, "I'm Leeds TV?"

"No, no," the man chuckled. "Not *you're* Leeds TV; *Your Leeds TV*. It's the name, you see. That's what we're called, *Your Leeds TV*."

Sid looked at Eddie. Eddie shrugged.

"It's great to finally meet you all, guys."

"Are you the film crew?" Skid looked petrified, nails digging into the desk.

"Just keep away from me, alright?" Kenny stood up straight, folded his arms in his best aggressive pose. "I'm no one's fool."

Eddie gasped and Sid snorted behind a hand.

"I thought I might encounter a soupçon of resistance, and so I brought a little gift, a peace-offering, if you will."

"You can't buy me, mister," said Kenny.

"Krispy Kreme doughnuts. Top of the range."

Kenny licked his lips. "Got any with chocolate sprinkles on?"

"Deffo. Help yourself."

"Kenny!" Eddie couldn't believe his eyes. "You're so fucking shallow—"

"Can't hurt to hear him out."

Sid grew an extra two inches, and puffed out his chest. "Set them down here," he said. "Might I offer you some tea? Coffee?"

"Sid, you're nothing more than a slut."

"Eddie," Sid admonished, "we have a guest; show some decorum."

"Eddie, please," the man said, "have a doughnut. I've been dying to meet you; I have a feeling we'll get on like a house on fire."

Everyone stopped, and watched Eddie.

The man slid the open box of doughnuts onto Sid's desk, and offered his hand to Eddie. There was a chorus of an intake of breath. Eddie stared at the hand; he'd refused to shake better hands than this. "You're not filming us working in our crime scenes; that," he looked at Sid, "is what decorum is." Eddie closed in on the man, and the hand dropped away. "The people we work for might have had no dignity in life, hell they might even have watched *My Leeds TV*—"

"*Your Leeds*—"

"But while *we're* with them, they'll have dignity worth a thousand boxes of Krusty Kremes."

Kenny nodded vigorously as he sucked chocolate from his fingers. "Absolutely."

"I'm here to show what men of honour you are, guys. I want to show how you treat those poor unfortunates." He shook his head, put a hand on his chest. "I'm not here to make anyone look bad or catch anyone out, and I'm not here to mock the dead in any way. We will behave with dignity, Mr Collins."

"Mr Collins," mocked Kenny.

"No more sugar for you!"

"I'm a producer, and my name is Rupert Nell. I look forward to working with you and your team."

"Nell, you say?" asked Eddie, rubbing his chin.

"That's right. Austrian origin."

Eddie clicked his fingers, nodded, and pointed at Rupert. "I know your brother."

Rupert's eyebrows rose. "You do?"

"Yes. Fooky."

Rupert looked puzzled.

"Fooky Nell."

Kenny coughed chocolate crumbs all over the office, and Skid looked like a walrus when he snorted coffee out of his nose – all because of the confusion swimming on Rupert's face. Sid closed his eyes and shook his head. Eddie headed off to his office.

"I don't know anyone called Fooky Nell," said Rupert. "I don't understand."

"Sid, bring coffee. And heartburn tablets. And the job paper."

This was what they called an Indian summer. As *Wish You Were Here* played on Eddie's stereo, it's what *he* called, "Fucking red hot." It landed in Yorkshire like a lost traveller and set woodland on fire, gave a million people who rarely saw sunlight instant sunburn and a headache, dried up rivers, and caused a wave of domestic violence the police had never seen before.

When you released sunlight and thermometer-shattering temperatures into a Yorkshire diet of teeth-chattering greyness and rain so fierce it could wash away whole villages, you got surprised people wandering around in shorts, vests, and flip-flops. After a few days you got slack-jawed people staying inside with the windows open.

After a week, you got idiots stabbing each other. Fortunately, it wasn't due to last. Forecasters said the hottest period on record was due to end soon – so just another day or so till the lost traveller pissed off leaving carnage in its wake.

He was on his second glass of water, lying on his bed in his boxer shorts, the ceiling fan on full throttle, blowing sweat across his forehead. He'd had his third shower of the day not an hour ago, and now, at – he craned over to see the Devil Clock, so-called because it was the great disturber of his most precious state of mind: sleep, with its ability to keep reality at bay – and now at half-past midnight, he felt as far from sleep as it was possible to get. His father, Charles, had fidgeted so much that he was in the lounge watching a David Attenborough documentary about worsening weather.

In the darkness, Eddie groped for his cigarettes, lit one and breathed it out, watching the smoke dissipate in the light from the Zippo. He switched on the bedside lamp and turned Floyd up just a little bit, just enough to drown out those creeping thoughts that insisted upon bringing real coherence into his room, when all he wanted was to drift – eventually into sleep, he hoped.

The creeping thoughts, like a determined army of ants, advanced anyway, and he was forced into full wakefulness, where he reluctantly gave them consideration, despite closing his eyes and pretending to nod off. The thoughts were these: how long could he, Kenny, and Skid, continue as a team? Kenny and Skid got on well enough, and over the last six months, Skid had become a valuable member of the team. That meant that Eddie was more or less surplus to requirements; an office-dweller. Of course, when Kenny or Skid were on leave or sick, Eddie gratefully stepped up. But it was too infrequent.

He looked down at his belly, and realised he could no longer see his dick because of it. He was losing the battle to stay handsome, was becoming a Homer Simpson character. He brushed a hand through his hair, and was grateful to find it still there.

He tackled his wandering thoughts and steered them away from his shy genitalia and back to the office. Indeed, he was about to tackle the question of stealing jobs from his staff by sending them on unnecessary courses, perhaps, when his phone rang. It scared the crap out of him, and he jerked enough to drop ash directly into the dampness of his belly button, where it hissed.

The phone fell on the floor as he tried to reach for it, and it forced him to sit up, and spin his legs out of bed, bend over and snatch the phone again. The fan blew cold air on his sweaty back and he shivered as he opened the line. "Eddie Collins."

There was the tiniest moment of euphoria as the woman on the other end of the phone spoke those magic words: "We've got a body."

"Where?"

It was still so hot that Eddie had to roll his jeans up his legs, and dry his back with a fresh towel before he could get a t-shirt all the way on. In the lounge, he stopped to look at Charles lying on the sofa with his arse poking out of his red flannelette dressing gown. His mouth was wide open, fly-catcher style, and a throaty snore escorted the dribble over his lower lip and into his chin. He wouldn't have looked out of place with curlers in his hair. On the box, David Attenborough was talking about clouds and freezing temperatures.

While Eddie was in the kitchen fixing a coffee in a dented Starbucks travel cup, he spotted a black marker pen by a stack of post-it notes on the counter. The notes were for Charles to scribble reminders for himself. Eddie looked at the pen, looked into the lounge at his dad, and was tempted. Very tempted.

On the floor in front of the sofa was an A4 notepad. Eddie squinted but couldn't make out anything his dad had written on it – perhaps he was studying to become a doctor. He picked it up and began reading. It was something about an old house where a father and son lived. Wait, there was a hidden cellar. Eddie looked down at the sleeping Charles and took hold of the black marker.

Once finished, he brought the marker close to Charles's face.

Charles opened his eyes and whispered, "I dare you."

Chapter 3

WHILE DRIVING THE LAND Rover Discovery through the sliding gate and into the car park at the Major Crime Unit in Morley, more sweat tricked into his eye, and he vowed to get the AC recharged once and for all.

He collected details of the job, swiped his van keys off the desk and drove it out of the car park, the AC belt squealing like a pig, and headed for a small industrial estate in Rothwell.

Rothwell was an average old English town but older than most, earning a Domesday book mention in 1066 – probably for the Black Bull and the tennis courts, Eddie thought, smiling to himself.

The most interesting thing about the half-hour drive was the weather. If Attenborough could see it now, he thought. It was humid, and the lightning flashed right across the sky in some kind of small never-ending pulse of flashes that enchanted Eddie on a personal note, but pissed him off professionally. "Not looking forward to the rain."

As though waiting for him to arrive, the storm began the moment Eddie closed his van door. The wind picked up, and fat, lazy rain suddenly came to life and travelled horizontally into the back of Eddie's head. The air developed that curious atmosphere that always preceded a storm: it was thick, full like a capacitor ready to discharge.

There were blue lights flashing and the rain looked almost disco-like as it speared through them. There was radio chatter, but not as much as you'd normally expect at a scene like this – coppers disliked the rain on account of it messed their hair up. Eddie found himself smiling again – twice in less than an hour! – at last feeling cool and refreshed.

The 'cool and refreshed' part didn't last long before 'cold and pissed off' shot them dead.

A sergeant, eyes squinted almost closed against the stinging rain, approached him, and Eddie lost the smile. The poor man was already soaked through, and the earlier heat had evaporated, bringing a cold northerly wind that turned bare flesh into goose-pimples. He'd be wet for the rest of his shift, Eddie knew.

"CSI?"

Eddie was going to say what he always said: "No, Mr Whippy," but thought better of it – the sergeant didn't look in the best of moods. "No, Mr Whippy." Eddie winced.

The sergeant blew water from his top lip and continued to squint at Eddie.

"I tried. Honestly, I did, but—"

"You're seven years old? Want to go and build a den?"

"No need to take the piss," Eddie said. And quickly added, "Anyway, what have you got for me?"

"A thick ear if you're not careful."

There was a small and hardy group of onlookers across the road. Maybe five or six people, some wearing shorts on account it had been tropical only a few hours ago, but somehow equipped with raincoats on account of it was pissing down. A strange and perhaps fortuitous combination that snatched at Eddie's attention. One of them had an umbrella, and when a particularly vicious belch of wind almost tore it from her hands, the onlooker folded it away and seemed resigned to being wet.

The sergeant nodded and began walking away from the street, into an alley altogether darker than a politician's soul, and as narrow as a politician's mind. Above the entrance was a name plaque, but Eddie couldn't read it; the glance he took suggested it said Flint Yard or something similar. The wind howled up it, loud as a jet engine, but deep like it had come straight from the set of a horror movie. "Pair of kids found him."

"Why couldn't I get a nice, clean, penthouse murder like they do on *CSI New York*?"

"Aside from the fact this is Rothwell and there isn't a penthouse suite within five miles of here—"

"It was rhetorical. And it was private if you don't mind." Eddie stopped alongside the sergeant, and turned on his torch. "Anyway, what the hell are a couple of kids doing up here. Not exactly romantic, is it?"

"Shooting up, I suppose."

Eddie looked at him, unsure if he was pulling his chain or not. "You said that like it was the norm, like the whole world just *shoots up* when the adverts come on, or when reality looks too fucking dull. Seriously?"

He shrugged, "Who knows. But it's getting more and more normal every day." It was his turn to face Eddie, and took a breath before saying. "You're not going to like this but—"

"Then stop yourself from asking it."

"I have priority-ones coming out of my arse." He nodded over his shoulder at the scene guards. "I need these coppers back out there."

"My murder trumps your P1s. Forget it. End of topic. Nice weather we're having…" Eddie took a few steps forward, and then turned and shone the light in the sergeant's face. "If those kids had been shooting up, how do you know they had nothing to do with this?"

The sergeant squinted again, "Do you mind?" Eddie swivelled the torch away. "I don't. Look, we got all their details, they're known to us as lowlife, bottom-feeders; they're young junkies, trainee shoplifters. This isn't their MO. Okay?"

"Even Ted Bundy had to start somewhere."

"Like I said. We know them, we have their details."

Rain hopped a ride on that howling jet engine and turned Eddie's mood down a few notches, put it into a tailspin that crashed moments later as, over the sergeant's shoulder, a familiar silhouette strode this way. A flick of lightning suggested the whole fucking horror movie was on its way here.

"Eddie," Benson shouted.

"Oh my good God," Eddie whispered.

"I'll leave it with you," the sergeant smiled and edged away.

Eddie's grabbing hand missed him by millimetres. "Hey, don't leave me with him," he whispered to the sergeant, "he touches me in private places."

The sergeant laughed. Benson stopped at the edge of Eddie's torchlight. "Very droll."

"I didn't know you were on call."

"Well now you do."

"Did you bring any anti-depressants?"

Benson pulled his coat's furry hood a bit tighter, and shouted, "I suppose we had summer yesterday, and today's the start of autumn. I can't believe it was red hot only a couple of hours ago. Cracking flags, it was."

"Did it catch you out, Obi-wan? Still wearing the bikini under that coat?"

"Don't be a dick. What have we got?"

"I thought your first question would be the first question everyone asks: How long will you be? They're not bothered about finding out who killed the poor bugger any more – they just want to know how long you'll be an inconvenience to them. That's how superficial the world is these days. Got to get back to *shooting up*!"

Benson stared and shook his head. "You are one sad bastard, Collins."

"It's the truth. You see a funeral cortege travelling down the road, and how many people bow or slow down? None, they honk their horns and yell for them to get a move on because they're going to miss *Steph's Packed Lunch* on Channel 4, or they hit Facebook and complain about an inconsiderate dead person travelling at twenty miles an hour."

"What? Look, I don't give a shit about your views on modern society, okay? Especially now, especially in the rain, and especially at two in the morning. Can we please see what we're dealing with?"

"You have a very narrow outlook on life. You should seek counselling. And you, a police officer—"

Benson yelled, "Eddie!"

In a hasty attempt at some kind of scene preservation, Eddie had laid a large grey body sheet over the dead boy and weighed it down with two bricks and a dustbin. Rain was beating the plastic until it sounded almost melodic, rhythmic even. But the wind had entertainment on its mind and tried to pull the plastic free. It was nudging the bricks aside and getting a better grip with each gust.

After trying and failing to put scene suits on over wet clothes, they shuffled the scene tent up to the alley entrance and discovered it was too wide to fit.

"This is a dumb idea," said Benson.

"Yes, it is, but have you ever tried working out in a rain storm? All my trace evidence has been washed away."

Because the alley was so narrow, they had to unclick the tent frame, allowing it to collapse a little, like the umbrella Eddie had been captivated by earlier, and so making it narrower. Eddie, Benson, and two police officers dropped the tent, and took stock. "We've no chance of getting it up there with all this shit in the way." He pointed at wheelie bins and piles of rubbish that had collected in front of those bins like drifting snow against a building, and the incessant wind was adding to it all the time. "Let's get the weights on the tent's feet before the wind takes it."

From out of nowhere a pair of headlights lit them up, and stopped at the cordon tape. Eddie heard the sound of a sliding van door and chatter, hurried voices, muffled yelling, and a van door slamming shut again. A minute later the scene guard shrugged and admitted them. Eddie watched, and his heart fluttered precariously on a ledge.

"Mr Collins?"

Eddie whispered. "Fuck me."

Benson's eyes went wide. "What is it? I daren't look round."

"Film crew."

Benson's eyes closed. "I told Miriam this was going to be a nightmare, and here I am, dreaming it."

The producer called, "Mr Collins?"

Eddie peered around Benson at them. "You're not allowed in here, Fooky. There's a cordon tape that says crime scene, do not enter."

Rupert laughed. It sounded like a sink emptying. "You're supposed to call me when you attend a murder scene, guys."

Benson cringed. "He *is* allowed, that's the problem."

"I never agreed to that," Eddie began. "This is a crime scene. I don't want you interfering with it or with us. We are professionals trying to do our job in very difficult—"

A blaze of crisp light atop a shoulder-mounted camera over-exposed any wrinkles Eddie might have had, and shone through the thin hair at the back of Benson's head to create a glare all of its own.

"—circumstances."

As they were taking stock, a particularly strong gust of wind took hold of the tent and dragged it twenty yards before an even bigger gust turned it into a kite and launched it across the road and through a fish and chip shop's window. The chip shop's alarm sounded, and Eddie didn't know whether to laugh or cry.

The film crew caught it all.

A moment later a large grey plastic sheet flapped from the mouth of the alley and slapped Benson in the face as it chased after its brethren.

Eddie made up his mind. He laughed. "Bit late with the tent weights, eh?"

"You were saying," Rupert called, "how professional you were."

A wheelie bin scooted down the hill on its belly spilling rubbish as it went, and the rubbish it spilled became airborne and pretty soon the whole scene was a hazardous place to be.

Across the road, the person who seemed resigned to being wet, got wetter. And they continued to stare at Eddie and Benson and the dark mouth of the alley.

Benson shouted to Eddie, "What are we going to do?"

Eddie gave it some thought, looked at the fish and chip shop. "Can you work a deep fat frier?"

Benson jabbed a finger, "This really is no time for jokes. Come on. I need to make sure this body is done right."

"'Done right' was possible an hour ago, 'done-ish' is about as good as it gets right now. And for your information, this is the perfect time for jokes."

"I want you to know that the public will be on your side, guys," the producer shouted. "These are awful conditions, and no one could blame you for laughing when there's a dead body exposed to the elements."

Eddie's nostrils flared. "If I hit him in order to protect the scene—"

"It's still assault. Sorry."

Ten minutes later, and working behind a screen made up of a discarded decorating table on its side, held in position by a really pissed off sergeant, Eddie and Benson hauled the body into a body bag that was almost an inch deep in water as they zipped it closed. The only thing Eddie noticed on the corpse were faint scratch marks on his forearm. And that was all. No time to notice anything else.

Sometimes, you lost. Sometimes, there *was* no scene preservation and chucking a dead kid into a bag just to get him out of the elements was about all you could do.

The mood was sombre; the weather was mostly to blame, but not wholly so. The camera crew were pushy, insistent, no respecter of private space, and Eddie didn't know how much that microphone on top of the camera would pick up, but it had the effect of lessening anything they said to whispers – no way to communicate on such a sensitive job as this.

The scene, the alleyway, would yield little now that Armageddon had farted all over it. Eddie stared at the ID card he'd yanked from the kid's pocket before the zip sealed him away. "Marshall Forbes." He squinted and read the date of birth in torchlight. "He's twenty." He dropped the card into an evidence bag, sealed it and handed it to Benson. "Your exhibit."

Benson stuffed it into a pocket. "What are we doing about him?" He nodded at the bag being buffeted by winds.

"Was he certified as life extinct?"

Benson nodded. "An hour ago. Paramedics did it."

"Okay then, get the body snatchers, and I'll arrange for a PM in the morning."

The onlooker trudged across the road, and drew Eddie's eyes away from Benson.

Eddie let encroaching thoughts of a cooked breakfast escape, and his expression changed to one of defensiveness. It never ended well when a concerned citizen approached a crime scene. This citizen wasn't some kid getting kicks out of taunting the coppers, he had an interest and that was always trouble. Eddie tried to shield his eyes from the rain and from the spotlight, and nodded at the man. "You okay?"

The man stared at the alley, and as Eddie and Benson approached, cleared his throat. "They say there's a body in there."

"We can't give out any details, I'm afraid," Benson said.

"I understand." He took a step closer, looked Benson in the eye and asked, "Is his name Marshall?"

Benson glanced at Eddie, and that was enough for the man to take the first of many sobs.

The camera kept rolling.

DAY 2

Chapter 4

IT SEEMED WRONG SOMEHOW to even think again about breakfast after the father of the dead kid collapsed and wailed into the night. Eddie got on his knees to hold the man, and after a while helped him stand again. It sucked any remaining black humour out of the job – left it tight and sombre, claustrophobic and tense.

It was still an hour away from daylight when Eddie swapped the van for the Discovery and headed home, resigned to being something less than effective, resigned to leaving a scene that might never yield an offender – ruined by the fucking weather!

Once home, he discovered the lights were still on and when Eddie closed and locked the front door, his father, was still snoring on the sofa. It was as though the last few hours had been a dream, that he'd stepped outside, turned around and stepped back in again – a time slip. Eddie let sleeping dogs lie, grabbed a fresh towel from the airing cupboard, dried off and closed his bedroom door. He was asleep in moments.

At seven-thirty, just three hours later, Eddie was shocked awake by a horror he thought he'd never witness. His eyes opened to see Charles hunched over him, with both hands around his neck, and his scrawny claws clamping his windpipe shut. Eddie tried to shriek but nothing came out. His lungs screamed for him, and Eddie grabbed Charles's arms and pulled.

"You little bastard!"

Eddie ripped the claws from his throat and gasped fetid air. "Have you been eating garlic again?"

"I ought to have drowned you at birth!"

"What's the matter?"

Charles pulled back, and Eddie scurried away up the bed as far from the old freak as he could get.

"This!" He thrust the A4 pad into Eddie's face.

Eddie rubbed his throat and started to smile. A laugh followed quickly, and all the shock and pain in the throat was gone. "It's just a bit of fun, dad!"

"I won't forget, I'll get you back, you little prick."

"Seriously, Dad, it's just a penis and a set of hairy balls. Banksy would be proud."

"These are my notes. My private notes. Never, I repeat, never, touch them again." Charles pointed an angry finger at Eddie, and Eddie flinched. "Moron."

"Morning."

Eddie flinched. It was nine-thirty, and on his way into the kitchen, Eddie peeled his eyes open and saw his father, wearing his favourite pinny, cracking eggs into a pan.

"I thought you might like a hearty breakfast to get through the day."

Eddie stopped, looked at his dad.

Charles smiled at him, resumed cooking. "Bacon too. Black pudding. Mushrooms."

"Okay. I give in, you're going to spit in it, aren't you?"

"Don't be vulgar."

"After drawing on your notes? The penis? You said you'd get me back, remember?" He stopped at Charles's side. "Going to chuck a load of salt on it?"

"No, what? No, look, forget about the penis. I forgive you, okay?"

"You forgive me? You were set for strangling me two hours ago."

"I was tired. Fretful."

"What do you want?"

"I don't want anything."

"Okay. What have you done?"

"And I haven't done anything, either. Ungrateful swine."

Eddie put his hands on is hips. "Listen, you never get up to make me a cooked breakfast. Ergo, you're up to something."

Charles stopped, delight on his face. "Ergo," he said. "That's a great word, don't you think?"

"Eh? Oh bollocks." Eddie led Charles out of the kitchen, spatula still in his hand. "Come on and sit down."

"Hey, what the hell are you doing? Get off me!"

"Dad. How many fingers am I holding up?"

"One, you dirty bastard! Now let me go."

"Mushrooms! That's it; have you been picking your own again?"

"What? No, I haven't; they're from Sainsbury's."

"I've told you before about foraging."

"And I've told you before I'm too old for all that nonsense. That's a young man's game."

Eddie was confused. "Are we talking about the same thing?"

"The bacon is burning, you turd."

"Are you having a stroke?" Eddie let him go, and watched Charles shuffle back into the kitchen, mumbling something under his breath. "You sure you don't want me to call a doctor?"

"Why? Aren't you feeling well?"

Eddie shook his head, and whispered to himself, "I should go back to bed, get up again. Today needs a reset already."

"First signs of dementia, whispering to yourself, you know. Now come and get this inside you."

Eddie slurped some coffee, stuck a forkful of mushrooms into his mouth after sniffing them first.

"Nice?"

"Dad, seriously, are you using something? You can tell me; I can get you some help."

Charles smiled. "Tell me about blood. Pools of it. I've heard you mention slugs before."

Eddie looked at the mushrooms, at the slime on them, felt how they slid over his tongue. And for a second, he gipped, then swallowed. "What the hell's got into you?"

"What? Nothing. Just interested. Slugs, they like blood, don't they?"

"Erm, yeah, they do."

"And the jugular, is it easy to cut, say, with a penknife?" Charles wiped his hands on his pinny and put the kettle back on.

"All this for drawing a dick on your notes? I'm sorry, okay, I won't do it again."

"I said that was behind us now. Forgotten. Dead." He cleared his throat. "So, jugular. Penknife. Is it easy?"

"I'm not Google, dad." Eddie put down his cutlery. "Okay, this has gone too far, what's with all the silly questions?"

"I'm just taking an interest in your job."

"Why?"

Charles shrugged, avoided eye contact. "Nothing to worry about, son. I just feel like I hardly know you, like I should try and understand you, and the best way to do that is by understanding your job."

Eddie grabbed his coat and his car keys. "You know I think you're full of shit, don't you? You know I think you're up to something."

"I'm not!"

"You're ill, aren't you?"

"No, I'm fine."

"If you're dead when I get home, there'll be trouble. I mean it, dad."

Charles listened to the Discovery driving away, and reached for his dictionary. He flicked through the pages. "Erectile... eremite... Aaah, ergo: therefore." He looked to the ceiling, feeling surprised and delighted, but a little cheated. "Ergo. Must remember that one."

The gates rumbled open, the wire welded to their frames rattled as the wheels trundled on the rails and hypnotised Eddie. It took the blow of a horn from the car behind to stir him from his lethargy. With a single digit, he waved his thanks, and drove into a spot away from anyone else's car, stopped the engine and lit a cigarette.

His problem was his dad, and Eddie suspected his near death at the hands of a crazed maniac last year was telling on him. She'd had her arm around Charles's throat, and Eddie had been a little slow to react; it was this slowness, this reluctance to step in and save his dad immediately that had thrown Charles into a bit of a conundrum: if Eddie couldn't bring himself to save his old man, did his old man belong in the same house as Eddie?

They'd had it out several times. Argued about it, shouted and sworn, cursed each other, and they'd talked about it like two almost civilised people, and yet they'd not come one inch closer to understanding each other, let alone forgiving each other.

It was the grain of sand that had found its way into a new hip joint, it was the smell of cowshit spoiling a family picnic, or it was a drunken yob vomiting on your anniversary meal. Close, but it was actually someone trying to kill your father when you hadn't decided whether he deserved to live or not yet. And from Charles's point of view, it was watching your son have an internal debate about saving you while some mad bitch was choking you to death. It tainted their relationship.

Eddie could see it from his dad's point of view, sure, but things had changed because of it – understandably – yet no amount of apologising had changed Charles's mind, it seemed. Did he trust Eddie any more? No one knew.

And no one knew if that choking action, suffering through the process of being strangled almost to death, had flipped a few switches inside Charles's head, and now he was Charles Version 2. In other words, Charles was mentally unstable, and it was Eddie's fault.

What on earth was he writing something about a lost cellar for?

"Do slugs like blood, indeed," he said and opened the car door.

Charles sat in Eddie's window seat, a cooling cup of tea on the shelf beside him, and he watched the road. Ahead it went straight down to an old opencast coal mine that had since been turned into a landfill site, and subsequently returned to farming. Sounded idyllic until you learned the farmer had died and a consortium had bought the farm and the land with the intention of turning it into a live music venue. Charles gritted his teeth.

The road also veered right, and that way went to the main road and civilisation. And it was from that direction that a bright orange pizza delivery van limped into view.

"Amazing!"

Charles watched it, his nails digging into the back of Eddie's chair. The gravel crunched under its tyres, and Charles staggered to the door and swung it wide as the youth got out from behind the wheel, a pair of earphones keeping him insulated from reality, his eyes half closed, his head dipping in time to some bass rhythm.

When the kid looked up, large box in hand, to find Charles standing on the doorstep, almost salivating, hands out, waiting, he almost shit his pants, "Oh, Jesus," he yelled.

Charles looked at him. "Maybe you should concentrate on your job then you wouldn't need fresh underwear after each delivery."

"Morning, Mr Collins."

"Come on, hand it over."

The kid looked at the box as he walked to Charles. "Wow," he said, "this is just packaging, right? They don't actually make these things no more, do they?"

"It says pizza on the side of your van, right? Yet here you are delivering parcels."

"Driving's driving, Mr Collins; don't matter what Ethel carries."

"Ethel?"

"Me wheels. She's my Ethel – named her after me granny."

"That's nice, Connor, I think she'd like that."

Connor nodded, handed it over. "Will you be ordering pizza tonight?"

Charles felt the weight of the box, almost revelled in the delight inside, and he smiled at the kid. "Do you know, I think we might just have pizza, yes."

"Great, I'll see you tonight, then."

"You work long hours, don't you?"

"Driving's driving, and money's money. I need money, don't matter how I earn it, so long as I do."

An admirable quality, Charles thought. "Okay, keep safe."

Connor slid his earphones back on, slid back into his own world, and drove away into oblivion.

Charles closed the door with a foot and hurried into the lounge, his heart tripping and his slippers sliding on the carpet in his haste. He put the box on the coffee table and stood still for a moment, hands on hips, staring down at it, soaking up the feeling it gave him.

Although it was a long time ago, he could remember Christmas as a kid, and the feeling of anticipation, hot and tingly as he tore through the paper. This time, he prolonged that feeling by refusing to open the box, even though he knew what was inside. It was lovely, eagerness; it was somehow purer, richer, even at this age.

He sat, bent his fingers back, and slid a knife through the security tape. With reverence, he opened the box and peered inside at The Magic Machine.

Chapter 5

Things didn't look much better. Eddie stood by the front of his van and burned his fingers on his latest cigarette. He lit another, and turned to face the fish and chip shop. The tent had been removed by the council apparently, long before Eddie showed up. It had been shredded, said the scene guard. The frame was twisted, and "It was only good for scrap," he'd said without an ounce of care.

"We only had three tents," Eddie said. "Eight hundred quid each."

The guard looked at him, shrugged. "Pay for them yourself, do you?"

Eddie sighed, "Nah, but still, it was an expensive kite." The rest of the scene had calmed substantially thanks to the drop in wind – it was barely a breeze now. The sun tried and failed to evaporate the clouds, and when their reinforcements arrived – the black kind – it inevitably bowed out of the competition, and people drew on extra layers. The recent heatwave, despite it being unbearably annoying, was missed already.

Eddie waited for the bastard rain to start up again.

A team of men hoisted a board into position and a couple more screwed it over the broken window frame.

Still without a suit, Eddie walked towards the alleyway, flicking the cigarette away as he went, and ducked under the second and final stretch of scene tape. All eyes were on him now – him being the only one inside the cordon – and it was possible to hear voices hush, see elbows nudge and heads nod.

Eddie ignored it all. He looked briefly at the spot at which Marshall Forbes's father had collapsed last night under a weight so massive it crushed spirits not bones. Eddie felt sorry for the man – there was nothing so frightening as watching the effects of death on those still living. Instant demolition of the human psyche. Whatever was left was just ash, and at the mercy of the lightest breeze.

A rat ran across Eddie's field of vision and snapped him out of his reverie. He blinked, concentrated, and followed it into the mouth of the alley. This time when he looked up, he could read the whole of the sign, and it proclaimed: Flintlock Yard 1792.

He could see where the feet of the ill-fated tent had gouged through the silty mud that had gathered near the mossy walls, and there was rubbish from the escaping bin that was lodged in a cast iron fall pipe so rusty it looked like a brown lace tube. After a few yards, maybe twenty, the arched ceiling was gone and the whole area was only slightly lighter but considerably wider – a proper yard, indeed; the ground a mixture of flags and cobbles, and tall brick buildings either side stole what extra light there was.

The brick walls and the cobbles glistened with rainwater, and the noises of dripping water and a door banging somewhere nearby knocked his concentration. A belch of starlings screamed overhead and was gone.

He stared and he listened, and he tried to absorb the remnants of some poor kid's death. He could imagine how he felt; how lonely and afraid he must have been, and then, when the fatal blow was delivered, how fucking terrified he must have been.

Eddie chastised himself: how could he claim to be able to imagine how he felt – of course he couldn't. "Poor kid."

What the hell was he doing in a dark alley late at night by himself? His father was distraught, and that was a sign Marshall came from a family who cared for their own – just as it should be. So, maybe it stood to reason that Marshall was a good kid, not liable to curse at a funeral procession. And if that were true, these circumstances confounded Eddie even more.

He had lain here, just to one side of a small industrial wheelie bin, the type Americans called dumpsters. And though it was difficult to be sure because of the ferocity of last night's weather, Eddie would lay odds on that the lad had been stabbed in the chest and dumped here.

Had he been killed here or just dumped here?

Why had he been killed? Had he been robbed? Did Marshall have a secret life that might have involved drugs or sex? In the gutters, and in the silt by the walls, were old condoms like a smack of jellyfish run aground and perished.

Eddie squatted where the kid was slumped last night, and he looked. Despite evidence popping out to land in Eddie's lap on a few previous occasions, this time, he got a big fat nothing. The weather had ruined anything that might have been here and washed it down the drains, and so the poor kid's family would have to rely on the detectives at MCU, and their methods of tracking killers via lines of enquiry they liked to call 'police work', and then sugar-coating it in the word 'intelligence'. "Good luck with that."

When Eddie stood, his own words slapped him in the face: down the drains.

He was staring down the nearest one when a rather large shadow fell across him. He didn't look up. "Anything from the PM?"

There was a tut. "How did you know it was me? How did you know I'd been there?"

"Because you smell like death. Sometimes it can be a very cloying, lingering smell."

"Still could have been someone else."

Eddie tried not to smile, and kept inside just how large that shadow had been. This was the new, shiny, caring Eddie, the one who considered others' feelings. They called it Empathy. And he was now Eddie the Empath.

Eddie stood. "So? What was Doc Steele's conclusion?"

"Stabbed in the heart."

He faced Benson. "And we paid him how much to work that out? Three grand?"

"Seriously, how did you know it was me?"

"You've got a real complex, these days." Eddie sighed. "What the fuck is going on with you?"

"Do you think I smell?"

Eddie closed his eyes. "Of dogshit and curry, yes."

"Seriously!"

"Stop saying 'seriously'. I don't believe I'm having this conversation with a fifty-eight-year-old teenager! *And* right where a kid was killed last night. So compassionate."

Benson breathed deeply. "Okay, okay, enough." He composed himself. "Can you get anything from this scene?"

Eddie stood and arched his back. "It's not a scene any more. Really, the weather killed any chance of recovering anything useful. It's just a shitty back alley in the arse end of the city – same as a thousand others, covered in rat droppings, old condoms, and puddles."

Benson sniffed. He nodded, "Fair enough."

"I'll take some scene photos and then you have something to refer to, but," he shrugged, "honestly, there's nothing else I can do in daylight."

"In daylight?"

"Yup."

"That says there's something you can do overnight?"

"It's a long shot, but if you keep the scene guard on, I'll come back tonight and give it a once-over with the Crime-lite."

"And what's that likely to give us?"

"If it gives us something, it's more than we've got now, eh? I don't know. I just don't know. But it's worth a look."

"Okay. What time do you want me here?"

He grunted across at Benson. "It's a one-man job; stay home and play with your bellybutton fluff, maybe take it for a walk." Eddie was about to duck under the tape when his phone rang. He reached the van door, and answered, "Eddie Collins."

Chapter 6

It was a dispatcher from a local Leeds Control Centre, a Divisional Control Room. "Eddie, it's Youssef from Leeds South DCR, can you speak?"

"Yes," Eddie said, "I've done it before."

"Pardon?"

"Never mind, go ahead."

"We have a suicide in Hunslet, and I wondered if you'd be able to lend a hand."

Eddie opened the van door and reached in for his cigarettes. He lit one and asked, "Lend a hand?"

"No staff available. I know it's outside your remit because it's not a suspicious death, but we have officers guarding the scene and it'll be hours before divisional CSI can attend…"

He left it hanging there, and Eddie dutifully picked up on it. "Indoors or outdoors?"

"Indoors. Hanging."

Eddie checked his watch. It was half past ten. It would take twenty minutes, maybe half an hour, to travel there, and probably no more than an hour to process the body. That meant he'd be finished in perfect time for lunch. "Give me the address."

He was there in under thirty minutes. Hunslet was the old workhorse of Leeds. At least it used to be. Come five o'clock and the whistles sounding at the dozens of factories around here, the streets would be full of flat-capped workers spilling onto the streets and heading home – thousands upon thousands of them.

The River Aire would have been heaving with vessels, oil-rainbows shimmering on the dead water as boats loaded and unloaded at the mills and factories alongside the crammed docks. The skies would be black with smoke and the cobbles would be loud with clogs and segs and cartwheels.

That was then, and now Hunslet was turning chic. There was glass and chrome everywhere, new houses, apartment blocks, and even old mill conversions that made the shithole look like something from a holiday brochure straight out of Naples or Venice. Kind of. Either way, the Hunslet of old was long dead, and the new investment meant the wealthy and the glamorous were crammed along the dockside counting their money and laughing at poor people.

As he drove along the pristine new streets, marvelling at the silk purse that had once been a sow's ear, Eddie was surprised at how beautifully things had turned out. They'd even planted trees, and there was real grass, too.

The whole place was so beautiful it was almost a cliché, and for the first time in his life, Eddie understood why people turned to vandalism – vandalism against perfection. He'd never understand people vandalising a shite city centre with ridiculous tags and overbearing illustrations, but yes, he could understand someone taking a small bulldozer and driving it right through the centre of this oil painting – it was just too perfect, too nice, it set your teeth on edge. It had no story to tell, there were no imperfections; it was the kind of place you'd tip-toe through in case the sound waves from your shoes broke windows or damaged a millionaire's train of thought – you could get jail time for that!

Eddie made a note of his arrival time and then lit up a cigarette. He'd parked behind two police vehicles – a marked car leaning on the driver's side, and a plain car – still obviously a police car.

The sky was the same colour as the rooftop slates. He slid from the van seat and slammed the door as loudly as he could, and watched all the designer curtains twitching up and down the road as servants took notes for their masters. The scene tape across a wide driveway fluttered in a breeze that smelled of lavender – 'Crime Scene, Keep Out, Sir, If You Don't Mind'. It couldn't have been a bigger contrast from his previous scene – this one was actually pleasant.

On the steps of a local pub – did they still call them pubs? – The Malham Tarn, three people, one smoking a cigarette and two puffing on vape machines, simultaneously nodded – a universal sign of hello when a wave of the hand is either not possible or might be seen as inappropriate. Eddie nodded back, and for a reason not known to him, mouthed, "Wankers."

A local copper, just slightly taller than he was round on account of the hat, wobbled out to greet him. "Now then."

Eddie sighed, and took another drag. "No prizes for guessing which is your car."

The copper paused, unsure what Eddie meant, but then couldn't be bothered working it out anyway. "And you are?" He tapped a pen against a clipboard. "Already got CID here."

"Oh goody," Eddie said, annoyed that they could make any job twice as lengthy as it needed to be. "There goes my early lunch."

"Sorry?" It wasn't the copper's day for understanding Eddie's comments.

"Don't be, it's not your fault; I'm too cryptic for this kind of beauty." Eddie took another drag, sad to see he was half way through already – how time passed so quickly when you're contemplating death, he thought, and said, "CSI. I think you're expecting me."

"Call-sign?"

"Bravo-Seven-Two."

The officer wrote it down, made a note of the arrival time and then said, "If you'd like to follow me." He ducked under a length of crime tape across the street and walked between two buildings, lost to sight in seconds. Eddie watched him go and felt the muscles in his neck relax. The building was one of three huge mills at the riverside that had been converted into swish apartments that normal people could afford. That way they could look up the road and see the millionaires pointing and laughing at them.

Around them, a hum of traffic noise was a constant companion, gracing them from an overpass a couple of hundred yards away; a huge concrete snake on concrete stilts. Huge LCD advertising boards erected to subliminally create buyers from tired drivers, Eddie could see them from here, and wondered how the insurance companies would take it if a driver walled his car because he was watching an advert for perfume.

He was still smoking the same cigarette when the copper returned peering at him like a meerkat. "When you're ready," he called.

Eddie lifted the cigarette so the copper could see it. "I'm not ready yet."

Raised eyebrows and a loud tut, preceded, "I think we could do with getting this sorted sooner rather than later. If you catch my meanin'."

"She's dead, right?"

The officer nodded, and the three smokers outside The Malham Tarn got comfy. Eddie did not nod at them.

"Then she can wait another minute."

The officer shook his head.

This infuriated Eddie – instantly, like someone had slapped his face for no good reason. He was here doing him and the local CID a favour. Would it kill them to leave him the hell alone for one single minute while he finished his hard-earned cigarette? "No it would not, yet he seems perturbed." Eddie stared at him and took another drag. He was almost sure the officer tutted again. He flicked away the smoked cigarette and bent under the tape, a camera bag swinging from his shoulder.

Eddie was reminded of Alice, gullibly following some strange white rabbit she'd only just met. And here was Eddie, doing the same thing. The uniform bobbed up and down as the copper's little legs scurried along, and Eddie found himself smiling as he followed between two buildings, emerging moments later into a courtyard of sorts that took Eddie's breath away – equally beautiful and cheap.

The officer was standing beyond a second stretch of scene tape by an open doorway of an apartment in the far corner of the courtyard, his rabbit whiskers twitching. Eddie blinked and the whiskers disappeared.

"Have you ever met someone for the first time," Eddied asked, "and wanted to buy them a toaster for their bath?"

The officer looked even more confused. "I'm not sure what you mean."

"Of course not," Eddie smiled.

He approached over the cobbles and a female, arms wrapped around herself in some strange embrace, appeared from the door into the daylight and stood alongside the officer. She looked too posh to speak to the likes of Eddie Collins, but bless her, she gave it her best shot. "I shouldn't be here. I don't do bodies." She shuddered.

Chapter 7

"You don't do bodies?" Eddie asked.

"Nope."

Eddie liked her accent, Southern; it had a twang, a verve lacking in the almost flat Yorkshire dialect around here. "Then why are you here?"

She took a couple of paces away from the entrance. "My Inspector is a knobhead who thought this would be funny on account of he knows I hate bodies and he's a spiteful bastard. So here I am. Last time, though."

"Oh?"

She looked at him. "Oh, what?"

"I mean why is it your last time at a body?"

She thought about it for a while, and her eyes drifted to the dead woman. She took a breath and turned away, facing Eddie. "We argued for the last time, and he's transferring me out."

"Where to?"

She shrugged. "Don't care, darling, so long as it's away from him and dead bodies. I won't miss the place, and I won't miss this stink. Now, thanks for coming, love, but shall we get on," she said. "I know it's not exactly in your remit…"

And there it was again, someone else incapable of finishing a fucking sentence. "My pleasure," Eddie lied. "I must remember to visit once all this is over. Do they do tours? Postcards? *English lessons?*"

The officer and the female looked at each other.

Eddie was enjoying himself already. "Eddie Collins," he said.

"Regan Parker. Appreciate you coming out." She held out her hand and Eddie pretended not to notice. The hand crept away again. "Come on, let's get this shit out of the way."

Eddie heard the hum of traffic disappear as he followed her through into a hallway that was sparsely furnished – minimalist, he believed it was called. There were the exposed stairs with a chrome railing at each side; the balusters disappearing from view as the staircase ascended through the ceiling. The floor was carpeted, and there was a coat rack, no, two coat racks – a coat on each, he noticed – and a shoe rack. The only real adornment was a vase with some plastic flowers in it, and a framed picture on the wall showing an elephant in the red, white, and blue of the Union Flag, wearing a bowler hat and carrying an umbrella in its trunk. There were the obligatory spiders' webs in all the corners, but the stand-out feature was a woman suspended by her neck from a baluster half way up the exposed staircase.

"Ah," Eddie stepped forward, and stared.

Regan folded her arms and wrinkled her nose up. "Gimme a burglary to deal with any day. Or a Section 18 wounding. A stabbing. I like a good stabbing; domestic stabbing, I mean, not a stranger stabbing."

Eddie had the feeling she was waiting for something. "Something wrong?"

Her teeth were almost white, like Miriam's had been, and at first Eddie distrusted her for it. White teeth were for the vain, he thought. You couldn't get through life with white teeth – only toddlers and salesmen had white teeth – oh, and celebrities; everyone else had off-white – magnolia – teeth, because coffee, tea, and smoking did that; y'know, *life*. Those who wanted to appear aloof from life, bleached them. Regan's though, well, they were slightly off-white. Good. "What's up?" he asked.

She giggled, and that was usually something Eddie didn't tolerate, either. Giggling people were imbeciles, and he didn't really accommodate imbeciles unless they worked for him, and he was able to control them and their tendencies. "I've heard about you." She held her hand out before her and her fingers writhed like a medusa hairdo, "You see it. The murder, I mean. You see it happen."

"I what? I *see* it?"

She shrugged. "It's what they say."

"Who's 'they'? Wait. No, let me guess. Clueless idiots?"

And now *she* laughed.

Eddie was warming to her; it was refreshing to talk to someone who had a spark, a bite, and wasn't afraid of banter. "I don't 'see' anything. I just try to work out what happened. Any idiot could do it. You could do it."

"Touché." She stopped smiling. "I think it's a load of bollocks, m'self."

"You do?"

"Illogical. Timewasting nonsense. Let's get on with it; do your thing, whatever floats your dinghy, darling, and let's get the hell out of here so I can get in the queue at Subway."

Eddie didn't. He turned front and appraised the dead woman.

"I can see you enjoy a good body," she said.

"Well, I couldn't eat a full one."

"The mystery, I mean, the puzzle. I bet you love working it out. Look at her, why did she top herself?"

Eddie took a step back, "Please," he said, "be my guest."

"What? Nah, love. You got the wrong end of the stick. I'm not interested in bodies at all; I was just making small talk, yeah? Just to pass the time, while you do your... whatever it is you do."

Eddie stared at her. "Well, I can't do my... whatever it is I do while you're blabbing in my ear. Darling."

She palmed him away, "Look, I'm sorry, I've offended you—"

"You haven't offended anyone. I just need a couple of minutes to decide—"

The White Rabbit cleared his throat, and Eddie turned to stare at him. "Shouldn't you be guarding the scene?"

"But, I..."

"But, I... what? For Christ's sake."

"He wants to watch," Regan said. She came in close, "This is the highlight of his year. Nicked bikes and burglary sheds are pretty major stuff to him. This," she nodded at the dangling woman, "will stay with him forever. I mean *forever*."

Eddie nodded, he understood, and while he appreciated how important the dead lady was to the White Rabbit, "What's your name?"

The White Rabbit stood taller. "Colin Halley. Halley – like the comet."

"Not Hali – like the tosis?"

Colin's face crumpled, "Not sure I follow."

Regan snorted.

"It doesn't matter," Eddie buried the smile that wanted to explode on his face. "While I appreciate how important this is to you, Colin, I'm going to have to ask you stay as scene guard for the time being, okay?"

"Is this because I was impatient with you?"

Yep. "No, don't be silly; I'm a professional, and I don't take umbrage when someone's rude to me." Eddie smiled wide. "Now go stand outside. We'll call you if anything juicy happens."

"You will, won't you?" Colin looked between Eddie and Regan.

She nodded, "Ain't nothing juicy here, sweetheart."

"Speak for yourself," Eddie said.

A face full of regret led Colin away from the scene and back into the greyness of the courtyard, his shoulders slumped and his arse dragged in the dirt behind him.

Eddie turned to Regan, "Hope you're hanging around – pardon the pun – but I'll need a hand cutting her down."

Regan, yelped, "I don't think so, love. I already told you; I don't do dead people. Christ, I don't really do live people, come to that." She shuffled back towards the doorway. "No, you carry on, do your thing. I'll get Colin to help you cut her down."

Eddie glanced at her over his shoulder. "Hey, you okay?"

"This is my last day, working for CID."

Eddie returned his attention to the body, determined to do his bit for her rather than indulge some slightly self-centred woman who was already reminiscing about leaving the force. "Whoopie-doo," he whispered.

"I can still hear you, y'know."

Eddie sighed. "I don't care. I'm here for her not to listen to you whine."

"Hey, no need to beat about the bush, come right out with it."

"How many women do you know who have hanged themselves? I mean apart from those you bored to death." Eddie was already grinning at Regan as her head snapped around, ready for an argument.

Regan laughed, looked away from the body again, and stood watching Colin's arse jiggle about through the archway. "No point asking me."

He fished in the camera bag, slid the flash unit into the hot-shoe and turned everything on. "Why did she kill herself?"

She shrugged. "How should I know?"

"Aren't you supposed to be looking into why she killed herself; y'know, boyfriend problems, bullying at work, bad parents, that sort of thing. Isn't that what a detective would be doing about now?"

She shuffled from foot to foot. "Hurry up, eh. Do your thing and then I can get the hell out of here; the stench is doing my head in."

"But she's still fresh."

"Not her, you!"

Eddie grunted, but inside he was laughing. He took the initial shots, including one of the prominent scar running vertically down her forehead. It wasn't a recent scar, but it warranted recording. Then he took out a long metal tape measure that he positioned next to the body, and fired off more shots showing how high from the ground the ligature was, how high the baluster was, the details of the knot, and where the stool had ended up.

He found it strange that the stool she'd stood on had ended up underneath other items in here. "It should be on top," he said to himself. "But she's not even off the floor, so why would she need a stool in the first place?"

"It's so fucking spooky when you talk to yourself."

"It's the only way I can get a decent conversation or the right answer."

She shook her head, and tutted. "Love yourself, don't you?"

Eddie straightened, "Look, how about you fill in the blanks concerning her, eh? It would be helpful if I knew who she was and what she did for a living… you know, things that might help us understand why she killed herself."

"Does it matter?"

Eddie lifted the camera off his neck, dropped it into the case and walked across to her. She didn't move – she couldn't have looked more cool if she'd been chewing gum and blowing bubbles with it. At that moment, she reminded Eddie of Rizzo from *Grease* – all bravado, all antagonistic, but soft as melted chocolate under the bubbling hatred. "Yes. It fucking matters; you can't just fill out your Form 49, inform the coroner and piss off to Subway. You must learn something about her."

Regan shook her head, raised her eyebrows.

"Even if you don't care, you have to find out these things for the sake of the family; they need to understand what happened to their daughter, why she took her own life."

She stood up straight and pulled a notebook from her jacket pocket. "Her name is Mia Chandler. She's a teacher at St Bartholomew's Academy, and has been for five years. She's twenty-six, lives alone in a flat in a riverside complex in Hunslet, one of the posh ones – this one. Parents live in Horsforth."

Eddie picked up the camera. "In among that lot," he circled his finger in front of Regan's face, "is the reason she did this. Which one is it? The reason, which is it, Regan?"

"No idea."

"What about her parents?"

"Dad's a mobile mechanic, works from a small garage in Kirkstall; mother works somewhere in the General Infirmary – don't know where yet."

"You told them yet?"

"I ain't spoiling their afternoon till we confirm identity. Made that mistake before," she laughed, "*they* weren't exactly happy with me, know what I mean?"

"I can imagine."

Eddie carried on with his examination, oblivious to Regan's presence, concentrating on the body, and running things through in his head. He used a pair of plastic tweezers to pull her bottom eyelids away from her eyes and peered at the petechiae there. She had bright green eyes, very striking, like they'd been made from a slice of the Northern Lights.

From behind him, Regan coughed.

He blinked, summoned back here, and dropped the tweezers into a bag for later destruction. He moved onto her throat and her neck, marvelling as always how far the ligature would bite into the flesh, almost consumed by it.

Her hands were white porcelain, some muck in the ridge detail of her fingertips, but there was redness, too – blood. And now he was confused. Why on earth would there be blood on her hands? There were no obvious wounds anywhere, not even any on her neck where the ligature had cut in. Sometimes with hangings, you'd see scratch marks on the neck where the fingers had dug in as death crept in from the curtains, stealing across the stage to claim them.

He stood back from her, taking her in, imagining what she was going through when that ligature bit and sealed her throat closed. What drove her to it? Did she regret it and try to come back, try to reverse a bad decision, but failed, destined to die because of an ill-considered thought. "Poor kid," he whispered. Surely someone could have helped her.

And then he arrived at the handbag, slung over by the wall, its contents spilled out across the carpet like vomit from a drunk. He photographed everything, and opened out the sheet of paper that didn't belong folded up in her bag. That paper belonged in her hand, or poking out of her jeans pocket – it should have been with her, her last connection to this world. He opened it and gasped at what he saw.

Chapter 8

"*I'm sorry. I can't love you any more, Marshall.*" Eddie peered at the words, photographed them, and read them aloud in a hushed voice: Still kneeling, he looked up at Regan. "It was good to meet you, but I think you can go now."

She took a step forward. "What? What have you found?"

"I thought you didn't care?"

"Stop fucking about, love, and tell me."

She read the note, and looked at Eddie, confused. "I don't get it, why have you gone all hyper – lots of suicide notes say sorry to people."

"This person, this Marshall, was a twenty-year-old male found dead last night in an alley in Rothwell. Stabbed in the chest."

"Ah. Shit." She looked up, seemingly considering her stance now, her sudden redundancy at this job. "So, it changes nothing; this is still a suicide. I'll finish this one last job—"

"But it's part of something bigger."

"Not from my point of view. I want to finish it; I want to put a final full stop in my report. My final report for CID—"

"She's involved in a murder, Regan. This stops being a simple suicide right now. So if you have people looking for Mia's parents to give the death warning... well, you should call them back in till we know what the hell is going on."

"I haven't. I already told you that." She nodded, pinched her lips, and left the house already bringing a phone to her ear.

Eddie sealed the note into a tamper evidence bag, and gasped for the second time in five minutes – a new record. In among the debris that had cascaded from her bag was a knife, heavily blood-stained, and the blood shone in places as though it was thick, as though it was still wet.

"Fuck me," he whispered.

Chapter 9

"You want to tell me why she's still dangling?"

Eddie, now in white scene suit and overshoes, recorded the ambient temperature. Hearing Benson's voice torpedoed his mood, and as he watched it sink, he looked at the dead woman, then stood up and approached him. "Took your time."

"I've been here twenty minutes already listening to that DS, whatshername—"

"Parker."

"Yeah, that's her. Anyway, she was practically crying because she's been pulled off this scene."

Regan cleared her throat. "I'll be going now, Eddie, love." She was at Benson's shoulder.

Benson closed his eyes and exhaled through his nose, deflating.

"Nice working with you," she smiled.

"Hope your new inspector's kind to you," Eddie said.

"Can't be any worse than this one." She patted Benson on the back and walked away.

Benson opened his eyes, licked his dry lips. "She gone?"

Eddie covered his mouth but still managed to laugh at Benson. "That was fucking awesome. You want sauce on that foot?"

"Yeah, yeah, very funny. Now give me the lowdown."

"Twenty minutes crying? I thought *she'd* have done that."

"I want *your* lowdown," he looked behind him, and whispered, "not hers. What's this about her knowing Marshall?"

"Go get a scene suit on and then come and look at this."

* * *

Eddie leaned against his van, smoking a cigarette and laughing while Benson sprayed a scene suit on. "I can't bend down to put the overshoes on."

"Don't look at me, I'm not obliging."

"I'll go without then."

"Fine. The floor's shit anyway." Eddie flicked away his cigarette. "Can't believe you didn't bring coffee."

"Call it an incentive. The longer you're without coffee the faster you'll work."

"Regan was right, her inspector couldn't be any worse than you. I thought you'd have sent Khan out here, anyway. How come you've climbed down off your ivory swivel chair?"

They walked back through the courtyard, Benson more staggering than walking, over the cobbles and back towards the hanging woman. The scene guard, PC Colin Halitosis glared at them.

"Khan is being a cock. He's just after my job."

"So let him have it. You're always complaining about being an inspector, anyway."

"Just like you complain about being a CSI, you shouldn't listen to me." Benson flapped his arms. "I couldn't do anything else. Not qualified to do anything else. Wouldn't want to, anyway."

"So ship him out to another inspector's position somewhere. This is a pretty big force."

"God I hate these damned suits. I've got one testicle down each leg."

"Thank God for that; I thought you'd shit yourself."

"It's all in hand, watch this space is all I'll say." At the entrance to Mia's house, Benson asked, "so what makes this a dodgy suicide?"

"It's not a suicide."

"You're kidding. You've got form for declaring murders."

Eddie was taken aback. "Yeah, because they *were* murders. And this one is too."

* * *

"There's a shitload of discrepancies with this scene, but it took me ages to work them out."

"Like what?"

"The stool, for one thing, it's under other junk."

"She's kicked it. She's practically kneeling on the floor, anyway. That junk could have fallen on—"

"Yep, I'd worked that one out, but it still struck me as odd. Anyway, there's other stuff too. Come have a look at this." Eddie knelt by her side.

"Don't expect *me* to kneel."

"I would laugh so hard I'd vomit. Go on give it a try, please." Eddie laughed, and Benson just shook his head.

"Get on with it."

"If you could get down here, you'd see a red stain on her fingers."

"Christ, why can't you just call it blood?"

"I haven't tested it yet. Till then it's a red stain."

"Okay, okay," Benson said, "so what's so strange about this red stain?"

Eddie stared at her fingers and tried to imagine what her last moments were like – how frantic they would have been – if this scene was genuine.

"You ever read Plato? I bet he was a CSI."

"Well there's no chance he was a fucking inspector, is there?"

Benson sighed, and his shoulders slumped. "Look, my balls are screaming at me. And I'm disinclined to take a lesson from Eddie Collins CSI today when he could just tell me so I could leave the scene and go pull my bollocks out of my socks. Please, if you'd be so kind."

Eddie looked at the beads of sweat on the sides of Benson's nose, and relented. "So far as I can tell there shouldn't be any blood on her fingers."

"So where's the blood— I mean the red stain, where's the red stain come from?"

"From the knife that killed Marshall Forbes." Eddie raised his eyebrows, waiting for the gravity of that statement to punch Benson in the guts.

For a moment, Benson was silent, and Eddie thought he looked like a kid trying to force out a particularly stubborn poo, when it was just Benson dragging up a name from the near past and linking his scene with this one.

"I know it's hard to comprehend it—"

"How have you linked them?"

"In her bag is a suicide note..." He stopped, eyes searching the ceiling as if looking for, "The pen. I don't remember seeing a pen."

"You were talking about the note."

"Oh yes, the note said, and I quote: *'I can't love you any more, Marshall'*. Fairly uncommon name, don't you think?"

"Just a minute..."

Eddie smiled.

"...Marshall Forbes... and *her* were an item?"

"As I said, it's a fairly uncommon name, wouldn't you say?"

"I would, yes." Benson looked even more confused. "Does it mean she can't love Marshall any *longer*, or does it mean she couldn't love him any *deeper* if she tried?"

"That's your department; I'm not good with people and their ambiguities. But I would say the first, seeing as she's now dead."

"Or, is it from him, Marshall? *'I can't love you any more'*, signed Marshall?"

"He's what, twenty? And she's twenty-six. There's something a bit unnatural about that."

Benson said, "Rubbish. Anyway, it depends on whose viewpoint you're seeing it from."

"Hmm, suppose. Are you saying she killed him because he was breaking off their relationship?"

Benson slipped into a moment of thought, and then said, "So, we need to be thinking—"

"Wait, work that out later; that's not the interesting thing."

"It isn't?"

"Well, it's interesting, but it's not *the* interesting thing. *The* interesting thing is the knife in her handbag. It has blood on the blade and handle, and it also has ridge detail in that blood. I haven't yet photographed it, but I'm willing to bet your knighthood those marks will belong to Mia, there."

"The *blood* on the knife, did you test it?"

Eddie blinked. "Ah..." he held up a finger. "Bastard, you got me."

"I did, smart arse. So are you saying she killed Marshall?"

"The red stain on the knife. If that stain is so thick and coagulated that it's stayed wet in its centre, coating her fingers and her palms..."

"Can't you finish a sentence? What's wrong with you?"

Eddie blinked. "It must be something in the air," he mused.

"I sense a 'but' coming."

"The 'but' is, why bring a bloodstained murder weapon with you? Surely, you'd have chucked it away, dropped it down a drain, or slung it in a pond? Hell, there's a fucking big river right there!" The question wasn't aimed directly at Benson, it just hung in the air between them, up for grabs by the first who could develop a theory.

"It strikes me as a bit amateur," said Benson. "A bit convenient, and bit too easy to solve. It's blatantly been put there – possibly by her, I grant you – as a way for us to sew up these two deaths nice and easy, file them away, forget about them; no need to begin looking for a third-party murderer."

Eddie liked Benson's theory. He nodded. "I do see your point, that it looks too easy to be true, but what else have we got? It's either a shit cover-up, or it's totally genuine, and that's just how her mind worked."

"We'll have more once we've interviewed a few people." Benson stared at her. "Waste of life." To Eddie he said, "Better go and shake a few trees."

"If she didn't kill herself, then someone wanted it to look like she did, and they wanted it to look like she killed Marshall too. I mean, even the rest of her fingers, and her palms don't have blood on them. The killer just dabbed her fingertips in the wet blood on the knife, and expected me to fall for it." Eddie shook his head. "That's almost a fucking insult. We'll take her clothing, and send it off to the lab for them to search for Marshall's blood on it. But there won't be any of his blood on her clothes because she was never there; I bet you. I also bet that's not her handwriting on the note."

Benson stood in thought for a moment or two as Eddie took more photographs, took measurements of the stool before carefully dropping it into a large tamper evident bag. "What's with the stool?"

"Sending it for chemical fingerprinting."

"If it shows her marks on it, what would you conclude."

"Don't know yet; let's not get ahead of ourselves. If you don't try, you don't get."

"Anything else?"

Eddie swivelled and looked at the entrance. "We'll examine the door for prints. The handrail is chrome, so we can check that for prints, but the baluster is bare wood; I'll have to saw it out and send it off for chemical treatment, maybe superglue."

"Worth a try."

"Yep, okay," Eddie said, and knelt before her again, mesmerised by the slim rivulet of blood that had trickled from one nostril and the single drop, like a crimson tear, that landed on the toe of her right shoe, "I want to have a close look at her neck when she gets to the PM."

"Still think someone killed her?"

Eddie stood and faced Benson. "I'm on her side. I don't believe she killed herself."

"I'll get Khan to do a CCTV trawl around here, and I've arranged a PM for tomorrow morning."

Eddie said nothing, just stared at her. Eventually Benson wobbled off to peel himself out of the scene suit and repackage his testicles into his boxers, but said, "See you at the mortuary. Nine a.m. sharp," before he left.

Eddie stared at her. "What aren't you telling me?"

Day 3

Chapter 10

CHARLES HAD LAIN AWAKE for what seemed like the entire night dreaming of this moment, and feeling the power of his characters speaking their lines to him, the director choosing camera angles, deciding what to describe, and deciding what to show and what to tell. It was exciting. It probably wasn't the entire night, but it certainly felt like it, listening to the ticking of the Westclox on the bedside table.

And now he was here, sitting in front of The Magic Machine, a cup of Yorkshire Tea on the table by its side and the remains of a well-buttered crumpet on a tea-plate next to it.

He stared at it – a genuine 1967 Imperial 66 typewriter. He'd used one exactly like it when he worked at an accountant's in the early 1970s. He couldn't help smiling at it, and for a moment enjoyed being whisked back to those days, seeing the cigarette in the ashtray, the girlie calendar on the wall, and the pile of papers to type out, a fresh ream of foolscap on the side table along with a box of Blue Swallow carbon paper. Good days, shit days. And then, as if by magic, he was sitting in his son's house, fifty-some years later. And the only constant was the typewriter, the Magic Machine indeed.

He spooled in a sheet of A4 and spun the wheel, bringing it up in front of the keys. He bent his fingers back, preparing to get the old typing muscles back in action. The story was there, teetering on the edge of a precipice inside his mind, and he could see the house, the characters and what happened to them, all ready to flow like a movie out of his mind, through old fingers, and onto the pristine white sheet via his new old friend.

He licked his lips, readying himself. He stared at the paper, ready to inflict ink on it, and then went to make a fresh cup of tea.

Tea half drunk on a coaster beside the old '66, Charles prepared himself and… absolutely nothing happened. And nothing for another hour. He looked at his watch, and hoped Eddie wasn't expecting a hearty meal when he walked through the door, because there was none. He was writing, dammit. Well, he was *thinking* of writing, which amounted to the same thing.

He decided to bludgeon his way into the story rather than creep; he was going to do the jive across the page instead of prepping his points. The juices began to flow, and he summoned his apprentice story-teller's voice and, like Beethoven at a Steinway, hit the keys.

Nothing happened again.

He prodded them and there was no arm shooting up through the little triangular window to strike the ribbon against the paper and leave a letter on the page. He tried again and again, and went through the entire alphabet and got nothing more than a hollow clunk. "Bollocks," he said. "I was literally on fire, then!"

Chapter 11

SHEILA CHANDLER ANSWERED THE phone approximately two-hundred times a day – well, it certainly felt like it. And they were all important calls. You didn't work for one of Leeds's main group of heart consultants at the General Infirmary, and not take important calls all day. It was her job, and had been for fourteen years – and she was damned good at it.

She was hard-nosed but full of empathy; she had a knack of seeing the world through the eyes of people who were desperate, who were sometimes clinging onto life by the skin of their teeth, so it was hard not to feel for them. But she was pragmatic, and her consultants had a heavy workload where tough decisions were a great factor in her life and theirs – factors that depended upon the time they could allot to certain cases. And sometimes, that time was zero, none at all, zilch... goodbye, it was nice knowing you, we hope you have a great send-off. But while this happened, and while Sheila was sympathetic and cried with them, the tears were plucked from a box she kept in her top drawer. She couldn't afford to be genuinely emotionally attached, so she never was.

But this time the phone call was different.

This time the phone call wasn't a desperate old man wanting another few months to see his son married, this was a call from an old friend of hers, one with whom she shared a Starbucks and a doughnut quite regularly. This friend, Christine, was just a few breaths away from being hyper, maybe a wrong answer from being hysterical, even. She got Sheila's attention immediately.

Sheila stared at the wall, a spot – possibly a dead fly, just beneath the clock. Her eyes did not blink, they did not stray, and apart from a gasp, Sheila did not breathe.

"Just answer me one thing," Christine said. "Have the police been in touch?"

That fly was the centre of her universe. The world slammed on the brakes. That was the last thing she expected to hear today. Questions fired through her brain, and all that happened was her mouth went slack. "No," someone on her behalf said through her mouth. "Why?"

Christine whispered, "I don't know if I should say." Her voice was unsteady.

Sheila wanted to scream at her, but instead looked at the dead fly and said, "Tell me."

There was a considerable pause, even a nervous swallow, but eventually, Christine said, "Have you heard from Mia lately?"

That call from a friend asking if she'd heard from her daughter wouldn't normally elicit such an extreme reaction, but that friend – Christine – worked in the mortuary. Sheila found herself racing along corridors, down stairs, through doors, knocking into people, and all without even noticing. Her vision was waterlogged, her judgement soggy, and the desperation an easy match for some old guy wanting to see his son at a wedding; her desperation was made up of two things:

Christine was wrong about the name, or there'd been some clerical error.

And like it or not, Sheila had to get to the bottom of it, and fast.

But as the blank faces and the bland décor blurred past her, the upsetting thing she realised was that Christine wouldn't have made any such call unless she was totally sure of her facts. Christine didn't just work in the mortuary, Christine was a mortuary technician, she worked with pathologists, and she carried out the post mortem examinations alongside them. There *was* no clerical error.

At the end of the corridor she ran down, nerves sparking off her fingertips and hot air tearing new grooves in her throat, Sheila saw a figure standing at the other side of a glazed door. The door opened, and Christine stood there with her hand outstretched and mascara streaking down her cheek.

"I can't believe no one's been in touch yet."

Sheila didn't slow down, she ran straight past Christine, and felt the temperature dive and the smell soar. Christine cried out after her, but Sheila recognised a sign that simply said theatre, and blundered through a pair of black rubber doors with echoing voices beyond them.

The whiteness of the room exploded in her eyes.

The people in there stopped talking, the echoes faded, and they all turned to stare at her. There was a man in black with a camera around his neck, another man in green wearing a pair of white wellington boots, and a man in a suit and a woman in a brown leather jacket with a shiny top lip. Both had notebooks.

"Sheila!" Christine ran into the room behind her and stuttered to a halt with tears glistening on her cheeks. From somewhere nearby a fly was zapped by a purple light. Christine looked at the police gathering, and at the pathologist. "I'm... I'm sorry," she said.

A man in a suit turned to see what was happening, and within milliseconds, grasped the situation and walked towards her, hand out, mouthing distorted words, "Mrs Chandler," he said, "we have people on their way to see you."

It was all just echoes to Sheila. White echoes, like waking up in a mad place, a Juniper Hill place. Beyond the approaching man, and slightly to his right was a row of three stainless steel tables, each with their own complicated shower setup, squeegee leaning against the metal plinth at the head, and each with its own overhead lighting cluster on an arm – the same type you might find in a dentist's surgery.

On the nearest table was the naked figure of a young girl. She looked about twenty-six and eleven months old (it was Mia's birthday next month), and she had dark curly hair that always looked unruly, hair that refused the attention of straighteners, and she had a tattoo on her upper right arm – a sword piercing through a monster's skull – something the mother had probably gone berserk over. And there, as Sheila approached the body, she noticed another tattoo on her right thigh, a flower, and a clock face, beautifully entwined. And this tattoo was something the mother knew nothing about, perhaps because of the fuss the mother had probably made of the first tattoo?

"Why didn't she tell me?" she asked. *I am out of the loop, off the need-to-know list, below the radar.*

"Mrs Chandler, please..."

There was a clear plastic bag over her head, and one on each hand and one on each foot. But didn't she know it was dangerous to play with plastic bags. "Shouldn't put them over..." There was a deep black line around her throat and a slug of blood coming out of her nose, and Sheila's world stood perfectly still. She didn't hear the men stutter how they'd tried to call her, she didn't hear them cooing as they tried to usher her out of the room, she didn't hear Christine sobbing. She didn't hear anything except the zap of another fly.

"It's a lovely tattoo. I would have liked it, Mia." She blinked as if just waking up. And she looked at the men with pride in her eyes. "I want to say goodbye." The pride was being washed away.

"Out of the question, Mrs Chandler," they said, and Sheila howled.

The blackness came for her, and pride fled.

"Wait!" Eddie grabbed Benson by the arm and turned him round. Benson looked confused, but was happy to let the others lead the hysterical woman away.

"You can't do this."

"Do what?"

"Drag her away like this." Eddie pleaded, "Let her see her daughter."

"Her daughter is a crime scene. Who is it that always goes on a lecturing spree when—"

"Fuck that!" The mother was almost at the black rubber doors. Eddie took the camera from around his neck, thrust it at Benson. "Hold that."

"Eddie! Think of the contamination!"

"Stop," Eddie went to the woman. "Come on," he said, "let's say our goodbyes, eh?"

"Eddie, what the hell are you doing?"

Eddie looked at the pathologist. "Go and cover her up."

"What?"

"Now! Go on."

The pathologist hurried back to the body, and Christine was there holding out a white blanket, tears in her eyes as she helped pull the blanket into place. This time Regan looked at him, caught him gently by the arm. "This isn't a good idea, Eddie."

"Move."

"In fact, it's probably a very bad idea."

The stunned mother, the woman whose face was wet with tears, who was speechless by the news, shocked that her baby was dead, stood there utterly immobile, incapable it seemed of processing anything more complex than sobbing and shaking. She stared at Eddie with eyes so deep and so pained that he'd break every rule in the book just to give her one last minute with her daughter. "Come on," he whispered, and held her shaking hand.

Benson whispered as they passed by, "I'm warning you, Eddie."

Eddie ignored him, guided the woman to her daughter's body. "Touch only her hand, okay? And if you're going to kiss her, kiss her cheek. I'm... I'm sorry about the plastic bags."

Benson shook his head, growled at Regan. Regan stepped up, "Please don't do this, this will end badly, Eddie."

Eddie looked up at her, smiled, and said, "It doesn't matter." As he went past her, he nodded at the mother, and whispered, "This matters."

She approached her daughter's body. She stood with Eddie at her side, and almost collapsed, then shuffled, with Eddie holding her, to Mia and bent. Sheila leaned forward, lips ready to kiss her daughter for the last time. And when she did, she blubbed. "Cold... My baby..." She began to slowly collapse, like a drunk who couldn't coordinate her legs any more, and she almost deflated to the floor, but Eddie had her under her arms and lifted her up, supporting her. "You bastard, Vincent Lightowler."

Chapter 12

Eddie thought she did very well, much better than he would have done in her situation. She cried, of course she did, but she was restrained with it, dignified. She held her daughter's right hand and she only kissed her cheek, and stroked her hair. He didn't look around at those who stood watching, shaking their heads in disbelief at what he'd just done.

And what *had* he just done? He'd taken all the rules on contamination, dropped them into a keg of gunpowder, surrounded it with a ton of TNT and then blew the bastards to bits.

But he watched her, the mother spending a few precious moments with her daughter – their *last* moments, moments that she'd replay until she too died.

He felt no regrets.

It took a lot longer to get going again than anyone thought it would. Sheila, who'd eventually become hysterical, left the theatre with Christine supporting her under one arm and a green-faced security man under the other. It had clearly been his first time down here in the bloody bowels of the hospital, well out of everyone's way, and he didn't appear overly impressed with his first visit: too cold, too clinical, too bloody, and too many dead people around.

And even then, once the mother of the deceased had left, things didn't immediately jump back on track. No, Benson, and Steele, the pathologist, both had another go at Eddie, when all he wanted to do was start the examination.

Eddie was itching to get at the ligature, and once he'd completed another round of images concentrating on the ligature and the knot, Steele took a sharp scalpel to it and peeled it out of the furrow in her throat, handing it to Eddie as though pleased to get the thing out of his way. Eddie put it on brown paper and photographed it in great detail, ignoring Steele who was now waiting for him.

"How much longer, Eddie?"

Eddie looked up, a smirk already in place. "How long is a piece of string, doc?"

"Droll. So very droll. Look, can't you finish that off later, whatever it is you're doing with a length of old rope, and let's get on with her neck."

"In a minute."

"You were the one who wanted to take a look."

Eddie got to his feet. "Okay, okay, you wore me down."

"Well, really," said Steele, "I'm trying to get on; we've had enough delay already."

Eddie merely tutted and got a light into that furrow. It was possible to see the imprint of the rope, of each strand even.

Then Benson appeared. "You know I won't be able to keep what you did from Miriam, don't you?"

Eddie peered at the wound, squinted, and brought the light a little closer.

"Nothing I can do for you now, mate. You screwed up big time."

"There," Eddie whispered, and pointed.

"We did try to tell you it was a bad idea."

"Look. What do you think those are?"

"I'm trying to talk to you, Eddie."

Eddie swivelled his head around to face Benson and stood up. "I know you're trying to talk to me; all I hear is Charlie Brown's teacher: *Wah, wa, wa, wah* in my fucking ear when I'm trying to concentrate." He sighed, said, "What did you want? Me and the doc are busy people, we don't have the time for you malingerers."

"What have you found?" Benson asked and then bit his bottom lip.

"UV."

"What?"

Eddie left the theatre, and then poked his head back in through the big rubber doors. "Back in a minute. Don't touch her."

Benson, Regan, and Steele all looked at each other, perplexed.

The UV Eddie mentioned turned out to be ultra violet light, and when Eddie shone the UV torch onto Mia's neck, he was well rewarded.

"What the hell is that?" asked Regan, who'd crept forward from the corner of the room, meekly, shyly, and with a green face, to see what was exciting Eddie so much.

"How does it work?"

Eddie looked at Regan, surprised she'd want to be included in a discussion this close to dead meat, but pleased to assist.

"Ultra violet light has a much shorter wavelength, so a much higher frequency than visible light, and so it's able to penetrate the upper surfaces of the skin and show us what lies beneath."

"Like an x-ray?"

"Yes, sort of. UV is somewhere between visible light and x-ray on the spectrum. It can penetrate, but nowhere as far. It's why you can get UV protection in your sun tan lotion."

"And in this case, what *does* lie beneath?"

"Two thumb marks," he said. "If we flipped her over there'd be four finger marks too, there to counteract the force applied by the thumb as it squeezes. Trouble is, each digit would have only twenty-five percent of the force applied by the thumb – so I'll stick with thumbs." He pulled a DNA mask over his face and bent down to look at the marks again, but this time through a small magnifying glass.

"Anything?" Benson asked.

Eddie shook his head. "No, nothing. We'll have to go the DNA route and hope it gives us a profile."

"What if the murderer was wearing gloves?" Regan asked.

"We might be lucky. If someone's had the gloves on for a while, they get blasé, they scratch their forehead or their neck or their ear. And each time they do that, they pick up skin cells. When they strangle someone, they transfer their own cells onto their victim. So, in principle, catching the murderer will be a piece of piss. We'll see how much that principle applies to real life, eh?"

Chapter 13

"Look, I'm not going to argue with you; you were wrong to allow her near the body, you know you were."

"I'd do it again."

Miriam looked up. "I can't say I'm surprised by your attitude."

"It's not an attitude; it's called doing the right thing."

"No!" Miriam stood, fists on the desk and back bent so her head was closest to him. "The right thing was to let her spend time with her daughter after the post mortem, after she'd been made to look pretty again, not while the pathologist was preparing an examination of her. And no amount of your, frankly, ridiculously misplaced empathy can make up for the fact that you could have compromised any forensic evidence from that girl."

Eddie the Empath, indeed. He said nothing.

She shrank back a little, her face returned to its normal pale colour, and her hair stopped bouncing around her shoulders like a million tiny coiled springs. In a much calmer voice she said, "I'm dismayed to hear you say you'd do the same thing again."

Eddie was about to reply, but decided he was in enough trouble without adding to it.

She sat, deflated, blew a sigh through puffed-up cheeks, and looked up at him. "This isn't a Hollywood movie where you're the fucking hero, and the audience loves you for breaking the rules and being a maverick, so you can 'do the right thing'. It's romantic bollocks, Eddie. You've compromised—"

"You already said that."

"Watch your mouth!" She leaned forward, elbows on her desk and cheeks throbbing as she clenched her teeth together. She lowered her voice, "I need someone I can trust to do the right thing, Eddie; I mean *the* right thing, not his own perception of what that might be. I don't need someone to be a gallant hero, okay? If I can't trust you, then I want you to resign, go back to being a CSI somewhere else. I'd rather struggle on with just Kenny and Mark till I can recruit someone who's prepared to stick to established rules." She cleared her throat. "Is that crystal?"

Eddie nodded.

"So what's it to be?"

"I'll play by the rules."

She nodded; relief showed as her shoulders relaxed slightly. "Glad to hear it. I hope there's not a next time, but in case there is, consider this your final warning for such a breach. Next time, you're out."

"One thing, though. She confirmed a name you were already convinced was the murderer. I consider that a validation of your suspicions by a woman who should know what she's talking about."

"Vincent Lightowler?"

"That's him."

"We have seven entries for domestic violence between Mia Chandler and Vincent Lightowler, Eddie. And all without compromising evidence." She stared at him for a moment to emphasise her displeasure. "A lesson learned, I hope."

He knelt on the desk with the window open, blowing smoke through it, and watching the headlights passing on the motorway some quarter of a mile away. The traffic noise was just incessant, but it had a soothing quality, one that allowed him to drift away on a thought bubble that could take him anywhere.

Someone knocked on the door. Eddie jumped and instinctively shouted, "Fuck off!"

The door squeaked open anyway.

"I said fuck off."

"This is the best coffee in the building. And I have some wonderful pecan pie."

Eddie tossed the cigarette and closed the window. He didn't turn around. "I hate pecan pie."

Sid put the plate on Eddie's desk. "Liar. It's the last slice, so you'd better eat it before Kenny notices. I might have stolen it by mistake."

Eddie said nothing for a while, then nodded, as though hoping to be left alone. "Thanks. Close the door—"

"I heard what happened."

Eddie tutted. "Fucking grapevine."

"No, no, Melanie in CID admin told me. She practically had her ear to the door. Miriam's not quiet when she goes off on one, is she?"

Eddie just sighed, stared out of the window.

"I'll er… I'll see you tomorrow, then."

Eddie nodded. When he heard the door close, he turned and jumped. "Fuck!"

"I'm still here. I didn't want Kenny to see the pie on his way out. Sorry."

"I thought you'd gone."

"Ha."

"Look, what do you want?"

Sid nodded at the coffee and the pie.

"Thanks, Sid. You can go home now."

"I worry about you."

Eddie sat in his chair, leaned it all the way back, and ran fingers through his hair. "She was right. I messed up."

"That's good. Admitting you're wrong, I mean. It's good – helps you get over things more quickly, able to get back on the horse." Sid stared at him. "Are you not going home?"

"Soon. I have to go back to that boy's scene with the Crimelite, see if I can find anything." Eddie sighed. "You know what the stupid thing about all this is?"

Sid shook his head.

"I'm a contamination factor. I've been to both scenes, and now I'm going back to the first again."

"But you couldn't have known that, couldn't have avoided it."

Eddie thought about it, nodded, and said, "Yeah, you're right."

Sid nodded. "Don't forget to phone Rupert; he'll want to be there."

"I've already forgotten. And you're only interested in him because you think he can get you an acting job."

Sid held his nose high. "Nothing wrong with wanting to better oneself."

"What's up? You're being more abnormal than usual."

Sid wrung his fingers together, "I can see where you'd get that impression, but I assure you—"

"Spit it out."

"Okay. Two things, really."

"Right. Go on, then. Number one is..?"

"Yes, yes. Number one is something I *did* hear on the grapevine, actually." Nervously, he licked his lips. "Mark is leaving."

"What?"

"There's a white envelope in his tray addressed to you."

Eddie put his head in his hands. "What an utterly shit day. What's number two."

"I'm doing a sponsored walk and wondered if I could put you down for a tenner?"

Chapter 14

"Cheers, Connor," Eddie said.

Charles froze halfway through getting the plates out, listening to Eddie.

"What?" There was a pause. "Typewriter? Don't know what you're on about, mate. Catch you next time, yeah?"

Eddie closed the front door and, in the kitchen, slid a pizza box onto the counter. "Connor—"

"I heard."

"Typewriter? What's he on about?"

Charles split the pizza sixty/forty and shoved a napkin in Eddie's hand. "I ordered a replacement iron from eBay, and it came delivered in an old typewriter box." He shuffled into the lounge. "That kid needs to mind his own beeswax."

Pizza eaten, Eddie scrolled through the channels and looked at his watch. "Oi, come on, I don't have long and then I need to get back to work." Eddie turned off the TV, and tutted. "Can't believe the shite on that thing. Four hundred channels of grade-A shite." He tutted again, and looked across to Charles. "What do you have lined up for tomorrow?"

Charles looked up from his book and slid his spectacles up onto his forehead. "I'm going to Garforth library. Lovely place, Garforth.

Did you know there used to be a school directly opposite on Church Lane?"

"Yes. Of course I knew – I went there, Dad!"

"I knew that! No need to get cross; I was just teasing." He swallowed tea, smacked his lips and said, "Garforth Parochial School."

"All I remember of it was the gardens and the weeping willows swaying over the little stream that ran through it. Oh, and playing Top Trumps! And seeing who could pee highest up the wall round the back." Eddie smiled at the memory. "I won."

Charles watched him. It was good to see him smiling. "I'm doing some research into this place."

"Our home? Why?"

"Well, I mean, it's old, isn't it? Leventhorpe Hall was built in 1774, so this place won't be much younger."

"So?"

"So, it's history, Eddie. It'll be good to see what she's been through in all those years."

"She? It's a pile of stone, Dad."

"You act like you don't care."

"Erm, it's not an act, Dad."

"This was all very posh once upon a time, you know, lad. There was us and Leventhorpe Hall, Swillington Hall, South Lodge… All listed buildings, now."

"Shit. Better rip out that fancy bathroom I put in last year, then."

"I mean, South Lodge," he raised his eyebrows at Eddie, "you know what happened there, don't you?"

"It was built on an Indian graveyard?"

"No, it was—"

"It's where the Zombie apocalypse began?"

"Was it?"

Eddie laughed, lit a cigarette.

"You can be flippant, boy, but there's some real history right on our doorstep. I'd like to look into it."

Eddie eyed him. "What are you up to?"

"Up to? Me?" Charles stood, and shuffled across to the kitchen. "Want a coffee before you go?"

Chapter 15

BENSON SAT IN HIS car in the school car park, not sure how to proceed with this at all. This was the kind of situation where having a deputy along for the ride was a good thing. He would miss Khan for one simple reason: he did not think. If he were here now, he would get out of the car and get on with it; tact was a stranger to him, and so whatever response he got from his question was usually a complete shock, and very often an insult.

A smile touched Benson's lips the same way a Mars bar did on the way over here, but unlike the Mars bar, it left no pleasant aftertaste and provided no stimulant to this current problem. The current problem being who to choose as his sergeant, who to offer encouragement and wisdom to, who to turn into his protégé?

Morse had DS Lewis who went on to become a thoroughly good inspector. Benson nodded. And there was Frost with DS Toolan – died unfortunately. Who else, he thought. Ah, yes, The Sweeney! DS Carter, a very good protégé to…Benson snapped out of his daydream, shuddered, and whispered, "Come back, Khan, all is forgiven."

Before his thoughts could insult him again, he climbed out of the car, aware that he was getting noticed, and probably for all the wrong reasons, seeing this was a school and he was an old man watching people. There would be no beating around the bush, he'd have to come right out with it.

An old man, he thought. An old man. When the hell did that happen?

Before he could sink into a depression, he spotted the sign for reception, and walked into a cool foyer with a girl chewing gum behind the glass screen. She looked up briefly to discover Benson was a stranger to her, and pointed to a TV to the left of the room. "Sign in, please." And then she was back in her magazine, job done, instructions given.

He hadn't even told the young lady he was here to see the headmaster. He looked at the contraption. It was not a TV. He pressed buttons, and his picture appeared on the screen with an option, simply: okay?

Benson took a deep breath and a step back. Chewing-gum lady still had her head down, masticating. He hated people who chewed gum, they were so rude. "Excuse me," he said. She didn't move. "Excuse me," he called. Still nothing. "Hey!"

She looked up, gum chewing suspended.

He pointed to the screen. "What the hell do you want me to do with this thing?"

Benson saw the distinct roll of the eyes but didn't catch the exchange of words with an unseen co-worker as she stood and flopped through the door to the side. She appeared behind him, placed him on a line on the floor, reached around him and pressed Okay?

"Type your name in there."

"Look, I'm here to see your headmaster. I'm Detective Inspector Benson."

She continued to chew, arms folded, unimpressed or possibly just detached.

Benson was losing his cool. "Are you on drugs? I just want to go and see the bloody head! What the hell is wrong with you?"

Her name tag proclaimed her as Andrea Neal, and Andrea's eyes welled up, and the bottom lip curled out like she'd just grown a slug on her chin, and she heaved a sob out like she was throwing up.

A male wearing a suit designed for a mod in 1963 appeared on scene. He had black hair and looked like a Beetle wannabe. "Everything alright? Andrea, what's—"

"I have been clean almost two *fucking* months, Jake!" She turned to the man, whom, noted Benson, wore black eyeliner. "Tell him!" And then she stormed off and slammed the reception door.

Benson asked, "You are?"

"I'm the headmaster, Jake Simpson. What's the problem with you; don't you have any empathy?"

Benson took another breath. He stuck out his hand and made himself smile. "Mr Simpson, my name is Detective Inspector Benson."

Simpson looked him up and down, hands behind his back.

Benson flipped open his wallet and displayed his Tesco Club card.

"That's not helpful," said Simpson.

Benson checked, and closed his eyes. "Ever had one of those days?"

"Where I make staff members cry? No, not really."

"Here," he showed the warrant card. "Can we speak somewhere private please?"

"Yes, of course. You'll need a visitor pass. I think Andrea was busy helping you with one when you called her a drug addict."

I wonder how Eddie might deal with this, Benson thought, and pictured him grabbing Simpson by the throat and throwing him through the reception window.

"Please," said Simpson, "take a seat." He closed the door and sat opposite Benson.

Benson creaked into a chair and attempted to cross his legs, failed, and abandoned the idea. He wished he could get back out of his car again and start over, but instead, this crude little man with a pointed nose and a sharp attitude, seemed intent to punish him. However, Benson tried to put that aside, there was important business ahead.

"How can I help, Detective Inspector?"

"It's about one of your staff members, Mia Chandler."

Simpson took in a breath and then just stared. "Mia?" He adjusted his tie, licked his lips, and continued. "I reported her as missing yesterday. She's been absent two days. Not like her at all."

"I'm afraid I have some bad news, Mr Simpson. We found Mia dead yesterday morning at her home in Hunslet."

Simpson gasped again, his eyes went wide, and he peered past Benson as if lost in a daydream. Benson had seen this a lot, and he'd managed to find out what it was: people were trying to remember the last time they saw the dead person alive. It was their first reaction. Their last association. "I only saw her as she was leaving school on Monday... I can't... Are you sure, Inspector? I mean, Mia had... she was so... Really, are you completely sure?"

"We're sure." Benson fidgeted as the news sank in, got comfortable, ready to send in the next question.

"But there's been nothing on the news..."

"There will be. But for now... we're keeping it discreet. A need-to-know basis."

Simpson stuck out his chin – happy, it seemed, to be on that most exclusive of lists.

He Khan'd it: "Was she having an affair with anyone here?"

Simpson's eyes focussed tightly on Benson, and he closed his mouth. "You need to work on your empathy, inspector. You really are appallingly bad at dealing with people."

"I'm sorry you feel like that, and I appreciate you're shocked by the news, but I'm trying my best to deal with Mia's death as quickly as I can."

"Have something important lined up?"

"What? No, you misunderstand, Mr Simpson. It's very important I gather as much information about her as early as possible."

Simpson stopped breathing, a second shockwave thundered through him, and his eyes lost their focus again and stared through Benson as though he wasn't there. And then, "Are you telling me she was murdered? Is this why you need to act fast – the golden hour, is it, before the case turns cold?"

"I beg your pardon?"

"I watch *Cold Case USA*, Mr Benson. I know all about the golden hour."

"The only golden hour I know about is Tony Blackburn on BBC Radio 2."

Simpson leaned forward, aiming his pointy nose squarely at Benson. "Do we have any suspects?"

"We?" It was Benson's turn to be shocked. "What were you saying about empathy?"

"Well, come on. We need to put grief aside and move forward. We don't have much time, Inspector."

"Let me come back to that, but in the meantime, are you aware if she was having an affair with anyone here at school?"

Simpson plunged backward in his chair, eyes fixed on the ceiling, a pencil tapping against his top lip, deep in thought. Eventually, he leaned forward again, and whispered, "No."

"Does she have a best friend here, a confidant, who she might have shared that kind of information with?"

Simpson tried to mime it, but it came out as a hushed whisper anyway, "With whom she might have shared that kind of information." He looked up, smiled at Benson. "I said that out loud, didn't I?"

Benson sighed. It was like being with an Eddie Collins on grammar steroids – just has to point everything out.

Eyes on Benson, Simpson pressed an intercom button on his desk. "Andrea, would you be kind enough to hasten Marilyn Stroud to my office? Thank you."

"Of course, Mr Simpson. Is everything alright?"

"Nothing to worry about. But do hurry, we don't have long left."

Benson sighed again and looked to his fidgeting fingers in his lap. A new sergeant was an urgent issue.

The minutes trickled away in an uncomfortable silence that effectively stretched each one to something approaching infinity. Somewhere, children screamed and laughed, an adult screamed and cried, and Simpson smiled politely. "Do you have children, Inspector?"

"Christ on a bike, no."

Simpson nodded.

"You?"

A shadow appeared and cut through the slice of light under Simpson's door.

Simpson shuddered. "Perish the thought. I am blessed with almost four-hundred stand-ins, though. That's quite sufficient, I think."

Benson's stomach grumbled. Simpson raised an eyebrow. "Might I offer you an After Eight, Mr Benson? They're left over from the Christmas party, but they're still in-date." He took them from the drawer, opened the flap, and said, "Oh, my goodness, the whole pack is mouldy."

The door opened and standing there was a pale middle-aged woman with redness creeping into the whites of her eyes, and radial wrinkles surrounding dry lips like the drawstring around a duffle bag.

"Mrs Stroud, come in. Sit." Simpson looked at Andrea, "Thank you, please close the door."

Andrea almost bowed in retreat and stared hatred at Benson as the door closed.

"There's no easy way to say this, Marilyn, so I'll just come right out and tell you." Simpson cleared his throat, and Benson raised a hand, hoping to stop him. "Mia Chandler has been murdered."

Marilyn gasped, put her hand to her mouth and closed her eyes.

Benson thought she might swoon and fall sideways from her chair. "This is like a bad episode of *Hetty Wainthropp Investigates*."

Simpson said, "There were *good* episodes of *Hetty Wainthropp Investigates*?"

On the other side of the door, the owner of the shadow tripped and fell, spat chewing gum across the reception, and as Andrea climbed to her feet, shouted, "Mia Chandler's been murdered and she's already mouldy!"

"You are kidding?" Benson glared at Simpson. "That rumour should be stamped on before it spreads through the school. Last thing needed is a riot."

"Passive sentence," Simpson whispered as he stood. He reached for the door, and turned to Benson and Marilyn. "You'll wait, won't you, until I return?"

"Of course."

Simpson left, closed the door, and screamed at Andrea.

Benson turned to Marilyn, and smiled his friendliest smile. In a low voice, he said, "I'm Detective Inspector Benson. I'm desperately sorry you found out like that. Were you and Mia very close?"

Marilyn nodded. The redness in her eyes deepened as they filled with water, and when she closed them, the tears squeezed out and flooded the wrinkles. "She was a lovely girl. Is it true, that she was murdered?"

"We think she has been, yes."

"Who would do that to her? She was a smashing lass. Really good-natured, wonderful with the kids, a delight to the other staff members."

"This might sound insensitive, but do you know if she was close with anyone here, I mean in a romantic way?"

Marilyn thought for a moment and then shook her head. "No, she was very professional at all times, and wouldn't dream of getting involved with other teachers in a romantic way. And I'd know if she were, we were very close friends, she would have told me. I taught her to knit."

"We found a note, and it mentioned Marshall. Do you know a Marshall?"

Marilyn looked confused for a moment, and then it dawned on her. "Marshall. He was one of her students until a couple of years ago."

"Why, what happened a couple of years ago?"

"He left school."

"Ah, right, I see. I'm just bouncing ideas around at the moment, trying to get a feel for the way she lived her life, but do you suppose it's possible that Mia and Marshall were... that they were seeing each other?"

"Romantically, you mean?"

"Yes."

"Definitely not, Inspector. A student? No way."

"You sound very sure."

"I am."

Just then the door burst open and Simpson entered, a sheen of sweat across his face. He looked between the two as he slackened his tie. "You started without me, didn't you?"

Benson smiled. "And we finished, too. I'll make sure our liaison colleagues keep in touch." He stood, thanked Marilyn, and said to Simpson, "Thank you for your time; I hope Mia's death doesn't create too much of a storm for her pupils to deal with."

Simpson held the door open for him, and whispered, "With which to deal."

The door slammed behind Benson, and he found himself in the foyer. It seemed the news had seeped out already, for there was a new electricity around the place, a new vibe: hushed conversations, open tears, kids comforting kids, teachers crying and hurrying out.

Across the room, behind a glass screen, was Andrea. She was chewing gum again, on her phone, busily texting someone. She stopped as Benson approached, wiped an imaginary tear from her face, and then sniffled. She reached for a tissue from a nearby box, and dabbed at her dry eyes. Benson aimed his face at a gap at the bottom of the glass, "I hope you're okay, Andrea."

She blew into the tissue, dabbed at her eyes again. "Grief brings people together. I don't hold your insensitivity against you."

"That's very kind. I am a bit of a—"

"Arsehole? Yes, you are."

"I was thinking more bull in a China shop, but I see your point."

She looked around, then leaned closer, "How did she die, Inspector?"

"You scratch my back, Andrea, if you know what I mean."

"I'm listening."

"Was Mia romantically involved with anyone here?"

"No, not that I know of. And I know everything that goes on here."

"Do you know about a student called Marshall?"

It took her a moment, but her internal Rolodex system spat out a nod before any computer system could. "Marshall Forbes? Left a couple of years ago. Was she and—"

"You mean, you don't know?"

That put doubt in her mind, and she looked confused, hesitated to say, "I usually know of any liaison between staff and student, and I don't remember anything featuring the saintly Mia Chandler."

"But you're not sure?"

Andrea bit her bottom lip, and then, as though she'd remembered something, her face glowed. "There was definitely nothing going on between her and Marshall." Her voice hit whisper mode and she leaned closer to the gap, peered at Benson through the tops of her eyes, and made sure the foyer was clear before saying, "Marshall Forbes is gay."

"So? There's no chance he might have been playing for both teams?"

"She was having some issues with…" She clicked her fingers, "I can't remember."

Benson tutted. "Shame."

"But if you leave me a card, I'll make some discreet enquiries."

Benson liked Andrea after all – she was easy to read. He was glad she'd quit the drugs. "You need to be *very* discreet, okay?"

"Count on it. Now, how did she die?"

Benson slid a card under the gap. "Hanging."

Chapter 16

It wasn't properly dark, not at this time in the evening, but even if he'd waited until two o'clock in the morning it wouldn't be much darker than this. It would have to do.

Eddie climbed from the van, gave his details to the bored-looking copper manning the scene tape, and warned her not to look around at him while he was working. She looked at him quizzically, unsure if he was taking the piss.

"I work naked, and I don't want you taking photos of my bum, okay?"

She appeared a bit shocked, but one thing she didn't appear was happy, nor to Eddie's displeasure, did she seem amused. Oh crap, another member of the PC Brigade, he thought. "I'm kidding, okay? You remember what a joke is, don't you? Or did they extract that from your soul when you swore your oath?"

"I am tired, and I need the toilet. So no, I'm not finding anything funny right now."

Eddie blew a sigh at her. "I'll be using a Crimelite, and if you stare at it directly, it'll melt your retinas and burn through your iris. Okay?"

"Seriously?"

"Yes, seriously."

"Shouldn't you put a screen up, then, in case someone walks by."

"No one will walk by, because you will stop them and turn them around. Won't you?"

She didn't like that idea, but she nodded, "Okay. How long you gonna be?"

"Depends if I find anything."

"Don't find anything, okay?" She held the tape up so he could duck underneath it.

"Try not to." Eddie trudged past her and she let the tape go. He put the camera and tripod down, and set up the Crimelite, using a 480Nm wavelength to begin the search. He pulled a pair of goggles from the case, made sure they were the 490nM ones and slid them on, noting how disgusting the rubber seals smelled, and how quickly the bastard things fogged up. He took out the torch, something that was a good solid weight, but was no bigger than a banana. It had a deep lens at one end and a switch next to it. The warning signs along its length had worn away.

From somewhere not too far away, a dog barked. And he noticed traffic noise, voices, another dog. All these things rudely invaded his thoughts, and he resented them for pulling him back to the here and now.

He concentrated, and blocked out the sounds, peering into the darkness of the alley with its industrial wheelie bins, cobbled ground with a gulley running up the centre, and who-knew what shit lurking among the debris. The smell was enough to knock out a bull elephant and Eddie breathed it in deeply, trying to get accustomed to it so it wouldn't disturb him, so he could concentrate on the scene rather that working out where he was going to vomit.

The Crimelite emitted a narrow cone of strong blue/violet light that caught hold of contaminants in the alleyway and turned them a dazzling yellow to his eyes. It was good with body fluids – especially with semen at rape scenes – but it also came in handy for jobs like this where who knew what might be at a scene.

It was what he called a speculative search – a suck it and see kind of scenario. He decided to do it methodically, beginning on the right side of the alley, the side the dead kid was found, and he'd do the ground first, then the wall, working his way twenty yards in. Then he'd do the same on the left side.

He began by pointing the Crimelite at the ground, quite close to it so the beam was maybe eight inches across, and he walked very slowly tracking the beam left and right as he did so. All he found were smears of the kid's blood embedded in between two dirty cobbles. He lifted the beam; crouching down he aimed at the lower part of the wall and began slowly walking along again. There were plenty of stains, mostly old semen higher up, maybe a few squirts of dog piss lower down, some mustard splashes, and possibly something that looked like tomato sauce next to one of the bins.

Nothing of any value.

He reached the end of the alley, sighed, and pulled off the goggles, allowing the cool breeze to clear the lenses, and for it to dry up the sweat on his face. The scene guard still had her back to him, and there was no foot traffic to be wary of.

He was desperate to find something to help the case, and to help the dead kid, and the poor father, but he was also desperate *not* to find anything. It had been a very long day indeed – certainly longer than any he'd worked in recent memory; it had been hard physically and mentally. And, he thought, it had been a bastard emotionally, too.

No one ever expected a CSI to admit to that. Of course he wouldn't, either. Ever. CSIs were made of granite and reinforced concrete. They saw all manner of deaths, all manner of deprivation, callousness, cruelties, dealt with body parts and endured grieving families, snotty people, argumentative coppers, entitled media people, disrespectful youths, ungrateful detached gaffers, and ridiculous rule-makers... it was a long list, and there were plenty more things too, but you were expected to rise above it, trample those feelings and emotions until they were part of the road you walked along to get to the next scene.

But emotions had got the better of him today, and he'd flouted the rules to grant them the freedom they needed – yes, he'd let a mother have a moment with her dead daughter. "How could that be wrong?" he whispered, listening to the breeze playing in the alleyway behind him. "But it was. Let it go," he replied to himself.

It was a great pity that dog shit didn't fluoresce. If it had, he might have avoided stepping in a pile of it the size of a dead man's fist, and the smell was strong enough to make him gag. He lifted his foot and a piece of that fist-sized lump peeled off. He retched again. "You dirty bastard!"

Some way behind him, the scene guard was laughing.

"I thought I told you not to look!"

"You didn't say anything about smell, though."

"Picture a waterfall," he shouted back, "maybe a toilet flushing, or heavy rain."

"Not funny," the scene guard said, "I am literally peeing my leg off."

"So it *is* funny." Eddie laughed as he scraped the remainder of the dog shit off on the corner of the building and along the kerb. He then went away from the scene and found a stretch of longish grass where he could finish the clean-up operation.

Once back in the alley and back inside the sweaty and now cold rubber goggles, Eddie flicked the switch, turned off his mind, and went hunting. The hunting lasted only two minutes before the battery in the Crimelite died. Just as it did so, something caught his eye. A quick blast with his regular torch confirmed it, and Eddie took a breath.

"Might be a while before we can relieve you," Eddie called to the guard.

The guard screamed.

Chapter 17

THERE WERE EIGHT PEOPLE in the crowd. Miriam had hoped for more, but she'd take everything she could get. She cleared her throat, and thought of Eddie Collins as she began her address. She thought about him in the mortuary helping a mother, and she thought of him at the dead daughter's scene, kneeling down beside the body and gathering his thoughts, putting them into some kind of order and trying to work out what had happened to her, or at least trying to come up with a place to begin his examination.

She swallowed and looked at their solemn faces, knowing the cameras were rolling. Her mouth was dry, her eyes were wet. And that in itself was unusual – Miriam was detached entirely from the physical aspects of the investigation – only those on paper or on the screen interested her. Her backside usually stayed in her chair from beginning to end. Except for moments like this.

At her side, and in front of her at the far side of the room, capturing the reaction of the assembled members of the press, were a couple of cameramen working on their documentary. They all stared at her, pinning her down, slicing information – slicing emotion – from her.

She began:

"A murder investigation is underway following the death of a twenty-year-old male who was found stabbed in Rothwell two days ago.

"And it is with great sadness that I advise you of a second murder investigation in the space of a few days. This investigation concerns a twenty-six-year-old female who was found deceased at her home in Hunslet.

"Detectives from West Yorkshire Police Major Crime Unit are leading the investigation into the murders, and both scenes remain in place while they undergo forensic examination and specialist searches.

"Our investigation into both murders is still at an early stage, and we continue to carry out extensive enquiries to establish the full circumstances surrounding these deaths.

"We recognise that incidents of this nature will cause considerable shock and concern in each community, and ask that people engage in tolerance and understanding at this most difficult of times. Our colleagues at Leeds District are increasing their presence in each area to reassure people and to keep them updated as our investigation progresses.

"We have already identified a number of avenues of enquiry to both incidents, but would still like to hear from anyone who has any information that could assist the investigation. Please contact MCU detectives via 101 or go online to the West Yorkshire Police website."

She stood there for a moment or two after the final words evaporated on her dry lips, and wondered what she should do now. They all looked at her, and she looked at them. As though something took over, she found herself smiling, nodding, and saying, "Thank you, ladies and gentlemen; you've been very kind."

As an officer held the door for them to exit, Miriam, stood quite still, unable to move as thoughts of Mia Chandler's death took centre stage.

She had a few hand-held notes, but struggled to see them clearly because her hands were shaking, and because of the anxiety eating away at her peripheral vision with such ferocity that it wasn't long before her tunnel vision was being altered – like having a migraine where part of the picture is warped, and disappears entirely. And because of this new anxiety, this new impaired vision, she began panicking and found herself breathing quickly.

Faces stared at her, and after a few moments, those faces began looking at each other – searching for confirmation that this was not normal. DCI Miriam Kowalski had frozen.

At each side of her, the documentary film crew were staring at her, too. For some reason she brought an image of Eddie Collins to mind and focussed on it. She knew that he called the producer Fooky Nell. He called people names he could remember, names that better suited them rather than their own name, names that were memorable to him. It made her smile... Fooky Nell.

Smiling during a press conference about two recent murders was not best practice, but the images of Eddie had spun the wheels again, and got her moving. Anxiety put aside for moment, Miriam looked at them all. "Any questions?" She began breathing again, and her fingers, up to now curled around the notes, relaxed, and her vision returned, and the onset of stomach cramps abated.

"Are you treating these deaths as linked? Do we have a serial killer in the community?"

"We believe these are totally unrelated deaths." She knew she'd go to hell for lying to them, but right now – there was no sense in revealing their cards to the killer, and also there was no point in frightening the public.

Chapter 18

THE SCENE GUARD WAS talking to someone. Only 'talking' was possibly the wrong word, she was getting ever more forceful, ever louder. Eddie threw the goggles into the case and walked out of the alley. The guard's colleague was also approaching her, and Eddie could see the same man who had stood in the pouring rain last night, arguing with her.

When the man saw Eddie, he stopped arguing, stood silently to one side, and waited for him. All three people watched him, and Eddie had the overwhelming desire to check his flies weren't undone. But none of them were smiling at him; more importantly, none of them were pointing and laughing at him.

The man held out his hand as Eddie approached, and his face was eager, his posture desperate. "Hello, hello," he said. "Do you remember me?"

Eddie did, and reluctantly nodded.

"My name's Stan," he said. "I'm sorry to bother you again, I know you must be very busy." There were tears in his eyes still, and they clung to the eyelids as though terrified of falling.

"Eddie, I'm a CSI. How are you holding up?"

He let go of Eddie's hand, stood alone like a withered rose in the depths of winter, beauty eaten away by coldness, just a stem with thorns and anger, and he shrugged. He swallowed, and it was easy to see that he found talking difficult; it was liable to turn into a sob, despite clearing his throat. His chin wobbled and he avoided eye contact and so avoided embarrassment.

But there was no embarrassment as far as Eddie was concerned. He looked at the two scene guards and said, "You okay to give us a minute? This is the father of the person we found in there last night."

There came two long nods, an 'ah, I see' kind of nod, and a shuffling of feet gave Eddie and Stan a couple of yards of privacy.

"I'm back just looking for anything we missed because of yesterday's weather."

The tears finally fell, and Eddie wanted to hold him.

"You're very kind, I appreciate what you and your… what you're doing for us, sir. I had a visit from some colleagues of yours today. CID they said, I don't remember their names." He smiled across at Eddie as though apologising. "They asked us all kinds of questions."

"They're just trying to find out—"

"I know, I know, it's alright. You expect it, when… you know, when there's a death in the family." The lower lip trembled but he persevered, "They asked what Marshall was doing here, and I said I didn't know, and the wife didn't know, either. But I've been thinking about it, dwelling on it, as you're apt to do. I can't sleep, Eddie. It's as if I've forgotten how to, y'know. Not too sure how to do most anything, now. I can't… We can't function, sir. See?"

Eddie nodded. "There's no need to call me sir."

A smile, "A habit. And I'd bet you are a sir, anyway."

He gave Stan some time.

"He was after cash, I think."

Eddie nodded again.

"We'd had a bit of a barny."

Eddie interrupted, "I wonder if you'd be better speaking with someone from CID about it, Stan. I'm just—"

"The man who's trying to find my son's killer."

"I'm just CSI, mate, that's all."

"That's all? You're not a pen-pusher, you're not a Family Liaison Officer who is so patronising that I want to yell at him. I want to tell *you*, Eddie, and if you tell your CID colleagues, that's fine. But right now, at this silly time of day, after I've had a long time to think about it all… right now I'm standing with you, the man who is at the crime scene trying to find evidence. Is that alright?"

"Course it is. Carry on."

"Thank you, sir. We'd had an argument. He's such a clumsy lad, you see. He had a cup of tea in one hand a plate of sandwiches in the other… I'm going back a week, maybe ten days, I'm not hundred percent. But anyway, my laptop is out on the coffee table, and he bumbles in, trips over the rug, knocks the darned thing onto the floor and steps on it. Breaks it. Kaput, no laptop.

"No laptop, no job, see?" He shifted on his feet. "I do copy for adverts, that sort of thing. I do a lot of work from home, and begin writing them by hand, but I need to finish up by using a laptop… You get my drift. So I was angry with him, and we argued."

Eddie swallowed, wondered what the hell was coming his way and prayed the scene guards could still hear all this.

"I confiscated his money. I went into his room, opened his sock drawer, and took out his pocket money, his savings, the whole lot. There was nearly three hundred quid there. He worked hard for that money, long hours at a restaurant and at a car wash during the day. He was twenty-one, sir; it takes a lot of hard work to prove your worth in this day and age. He worked really hard." The eyelids filled up again, and this time a slow slug of clear snot cruised towards his top lip. Eddie tried not to look. Stan cleared it with a sleeve and an apology. "I put his money toward another laptop. I had to teach him a lesson, I had to let him know there were consequences."

"I'm sorry you had—"

"That's not it, Eddie, that's not the worst that happened. The money he'd saved was for a concert in London; one of his favourite bands. It was for a weekend stop-over with friends, taking in the sights, the museums, the London Eye, you know the kind of thing. I'd... I'd ruined it all for him.

"You know what? He was right. All along he was right – he'd argued that my laptop should have been on my desk in the back office." Stan sobbed, and Eddie closed his eyes. "If I'd worked at my desk, none of this would've happened." He stared at Eddie. "It's all my fault. He was here trying to make more money so he could still go to London.

"I suppose this is where the local... the local sex workers congregate?"

Eddie felt like saying, 'How the fuck should I know?', but refrained. "Not really my patch. Have you ever been in here, seen inside, I mean?"

Absently, he shook his head, "No. I don't even know where my son died. Shameful. I am such a coward; a better father would have found another way. When it all ends up like this," he looked around at the scene, "you'd do anything to change it, to take it back. Who gives a damn about a fucking laptop, excuse my language."

"Are you going to be home all day tomorrow?"

Stan nodded.

"I'll let the investigating officer know what you've said, and someone will visit you, okay? Are there any times they should avoid?"

Stan shook his head.

"Leave it with me, I'll get someone to come and see you, to make a note of everything you've told me, okay? Don't worry, I work with some smashing officers, they won't patronise you."

"Thank you, thank you, sir."

Eddie did something he rarely did, and held out his hand. "Go home now, and try to relax. I promise I'm doing my best for your boy."

Stan only smiled, a kind of gratitude in his eyes that was so deep it looked almost painful. He bowed his head, and as he walked away, Eddie could hear him crying.

Eddie looked back at the alley. It held a pull for him, but that pull – a gut feeling – could be used to help someone else as well as Stan Forbes. He turned and watched him walking away, a cloud of dejection drizzling over him as he went, slouched over like a man twice his age. Eddie swallowed, he stared at the alley again.

"You done in there?" asked the scene guard. "Can we wrap it up now?"

Eddie looked at his watch. It was eight o'clock. "I have just one more thing to try first."

Chapter 19

He'd done well.

Eddie glanced at his watch and discovered only forty-five minutes had elapsed since he made the call. He climbed out of his van, ignored the scowls of the scene guards who were eager to get something to eat, and one in particular who was standing cross-legged, and met him as he opened his own van door.

Mark stood there, arms folded, cheeks throbbing as he gritted his teeth.

"Wow, you look like something I drew with my left hand."

"I was having a bath."

The dishevelment wasn't lost on Eddie, but his smile persisted through all the signs shooting his way. "Thanks for coming, Skid. I really appreciate it."

"How many times have I asked you to stop calling me Skid?"

Eddie shook his head, "I lost count months ago. Listen, never mind that now, I have a special assignment for you. Come with me."

At the entrance to the alleyway, Eddie cast an arm across it, and said, "There was a dead lad found in there a couple of nights ago, could have been last night, actually – I'm so tired I don't know what day we're on. Anyway, the weather was extreme, and I guess any evidence that might have been there has been shot to shit by it."

Skid nodded. "And..."

"Well, that's a fair question. I want you to see if you can find anything."

Skid turned to Eddie. "Listen, Eddie, I know you think you're helping me, but really—"

"You're a great CSI, kid. You have really great potential."

Skid smiled, "Thank you. It's nice of you to say so—"

"No, no, it's not." There was no smile on Eddie's face. "This isn't a pissing competition, you know. A kid was killed in there, this is about as important as this job gets. I need your input, I need your skills."

"I don't have any skills. At least I don't have any skills compared to you."

"Bollocks. If you think I'm giving you a pay rise for that pathetic attempt at a compliment, you've got another think coming."

"I know what you're trying to do, Eddie."

"What? What am I trying to do? Enlighten me, why don't you." Now *Eddie* folded his arms.

"I... You want me to go in there and find some evidence that was missed last night to prove what a wonderful scene examiner I am."

"Shit," Eddie said, "that's amazing; how did you know that? Are you clairvoyant?"

Skid looked at the pavement, shuffled his feet. "I don't think I'm cut out for this job, Eddie."

"What? Nonsense. I know a waster when I see one, employed one or two, actually, and you're not a waster. Mate, you're doing great – you just need a confidence boost to prove it. I know you're good at your job, you've just got to convince yourself of that."

"I've tried, really I have. But I mess up so much, I still daren't go to anything decent by myself, the paperwork is a complete nightmare... I don't think I should ever have applied."

"Stop it, you're going to have me in fucking tears in a minute."

"I'm serious."

"Don't be ashamed of who you are."

"What?"

"That's your parents' job."

"I'm not ashamed—"

"That you think you're not good enough proves to me that you are. You'll keep trying, you'll keep looking, you'll keep improving. I don't want some knobhead who thinks he's perfect. I want you."

Skid looked confused. "Was that a compliment?"

"Who cares?" Eddie closed in, looked at the scene guard to make sure she was out of earshot. "Remember the words you said to me in the interview, how you wanted a job you could actually make a difference at, something that was a challenge?"

"Yes."

"Good. This is your chance, now get your arse in there and find me something."

"Find what?"

"I've been up eighteen hours, and I'm worn blunt, okay? I've looked. I cannot find it, whatever it is, but I know the bastard thing is in there. Go and find it. Now."

"I can't!"

"Why? You missing *Britain's Got Talent*?"

"No, but—"

"Well then what? What is more important or exciting in your life right now, this evening, this minute? Huh, what is standing between you and finding that kid's killer? Got a hot date? Got some knitting you must catch up on? Got to shave your legs, what?"

Skid sighed into the evening. "Nothing."

"Thought so. Mind the dog shit, four yards in, left hand side."

"Eddie—"

"Go get your torch. Hurry, I'm getting cold here – nipples like chapel hat pegs."

"Eddie—"

"Look, don't make me ignore you again." Eddie closed his eyes, held out a hand, palm towards Skid. "Stop fucking talking." He pointed to the alley. "Go."

"I don't even know anything about the case."

Eddie sighed. "Kid found stabbed to death. Knife wound to the chest. Found next to that wheelie bin."

"That it?"

"That's it. Go on."

"I think I ought to tell you something."

"I'm not paying you overtime so you can stand here gossiping and talking bollocks. Now move it, Skid, before I put you on your arse and drag Kenny out here."

Each time Skid went to open his mouth, Eddie filled the air between them with some verbiage or other, until he gave up, and wandered into the alley like a lost pig. Eddie smiled to himself, convinced the lad would turn out to be a success at his job.

Despite the faltering steps he was taking this evening, Eddie knew he had a certain drive, a motivation to succeed, to excel at it, and to wring everything out of a scene. Eddie knew this man worked for the victim, and that was all Eddie cared about; it was all they both cared about.

He was on his second cigarette, standing by the van admiring the PCSO's arse when he heard, "Eddie?" It was Skid, standing by the entrance to the alley. He was smiling.

Eddie grinned, breathed in deeply and walked over to him, the PCSO's arse completely forgotten about. "Found something?"

"Come and look."

It turned out that the dog shit Eddie had stood in wasn't the only dog shit in dodge. "I was losing hope of finding anything," said Skid, "until I saw this." He crouched, shining his torch on one of the large rubber castors poking out from the side of the red industrial wheelie bins. The wheel had travelled through a mound of dog shit and, just like Eddie's boot, a huge dollop of it clung on to each side of the wheel. On the centre part, the bit that contacted the cobbles as the wheelie bin was pushed along had a thin smear of shit across its width. Embedded in that thin smear was a circle of gold-coloured metal.

"What the hell is it?"

Skid got down on his knees, his face dangerously close to the wheel, so close that it would have taken only a slight shove on the back of his head for Skid to get a mouthful of second-hand dog shit. Much as he was tempted, Eddie checked himself, reminded himself that he had grown and matured recently, and there was no need to be so juvenile any more.

"If you push my head into this shit, I'll get my own back, and it won't be pleasant."

"Jesus," Eddie said, "you really *are* clairvoyant, aren't you?"

"You know what this is, don't you?"

"How could I know?" Eddie asked. "I've never seen it before."

Skid craned his neck, peered up at Eddie, and it was all he could do to look confused, to eliminate the smile that was creeping through.

"So? What is it?"

"It's an earring."

"Really? Wow, that's some find." Eddie stood. "I hope we can still get wearer-DNA from it, and that it's not been ruined by Fido's shit."

Skid stood, smiling too.

"See, you *are* good at this job. You *are* cut out for this job. Okay?"

Skid nodded.

"Now, what did you have to tell me?"

Skid looked away. "Oh, it was nothing."

"Listen," Eddie said, "we can score a few brownie points here. I'll get Fooky Nell up here and he can fill his boots filming you zapping the Crimelite around the alley. What do you say?"

"I'm not a fan of being filmed."

"You don't have to do anything different than you've been doing for the last half hour. It's not as though you have lines to fucking remember."

Skid gave it a moment's thought before reluctantly saying, "Okay."

"Good lad. Your mum would be so proud."

DAY 4

Chapter 20

He flicked away the cigarette end and focussed on the glass cube of ugliness in front of him, with Beelzebub sitting behind her reception desk, sharpening her tongue and nibbling brimstone.

The door creaked closed behind him, and he found the air conditioning uncomfortably cold.

She stared at him, just her eyes visible over the top of the reception desk. Eddie watched her; a human crocodile waiting to piss him off.

Despite it nearly cracking his face, he smiled at her. "Cold in here, don't you think, Beelzebub?" He squeaked across the foyer floor, the shiny tiles beneath his feet screamed with every footfall, and Eddie felt a new heat in his chest.

Her eyes tracked him as he passed in front of her.

He paused in front of her desk, sniffing the fiery air. He said, "Can you smell sulphur?"

She growled, and Eddie ran the rest of the way, holding in a child's laughter.

Half way up the stairs and his mind zoned in on Charles again, on the word 'ergo' specifically. What the hell was going on with his dad? Why had he suddenly turned into Mr Weirdo? "Rewind," he said to himself: *suddenly*? Eddie grinned as his feet dragged him through into

CID where they paused. For a moment he didn't know why they'd paused, but he soon came to understand.

Eddie approached the desk. Her head was down, her arms were folded across the desk in front of her. She wore a brown leather coat with brass buckles at the cuffs, and now he could see her chewing gum, a knee buzzing up and down in tune to a song cruising through her mind.

His smile grew before his attention was captured by movement to his right. It was Benson standing behind the glass in Miriam Kowalski's office. Obviously, he couldn't hear their conversation from here, but whatever it was, it was juicy enough to hold Eddie's attention and the attention of those around him. Benson's arms were flapping. In fact if they flapped any quicker, there was a danger he'd take off. His finger was pointing, and if Eddie were to put money on it, he'd say Benson was shouting – definitely not happy about something.

Benson saw the whole office staring at him, saw Eddie grinning at him, and slapped the blinds closed.

Eddie stared at the reason for the outburst, and couldn't help himself. "Hey if it isn't Nosey Parker."

She peeled her head from the desk, her leather coat creaking like Benson's knees did, and looked up, but kept on chewing gum, kept on buzzing the knee. "Oh," she said. "It's you. Peter, is it?"

"Close. Eddie."

She clicked her fingers, "Ah that's right, Eddie. Well you're about thirty-five years too late in calling me Nosey Parker; it's been done to death. Cliché." She smiled at him – not a nice smile. "Choose another name, love; that one was boring when it was born, okay?"

"Regan," he said.

"You got it! Give that boy a fish."

"Your old fella liked *The Sweeney*?"

Her eyes sparked, and then they shied away, perhaps embarrassed by a memory, or sucker-punched by a childhood sadness that almost caught her again. "My old lady did. Was her fave show." She paused. "Not many folk these days know of that show."

"She had good taste. I'll call you Sweeney."

"You have trouble calling people by their allotted names, don't you? Regan is just fine, thanks."

Eddie sat beside her, wheeled his chair a bit closer. "Your old inspector must really hate you."

She winced.

"To send you here, I mean, when you don't like bodies."

"It's a shitter, right? Wish I could say it was a trap and he walked right into it."

"Well, *he's* okay, at least, Benson, I mean. Not vindictive." She swivelled her heard toward Miriam's office. "Just a bit... vocal."

"I think it's because he wasn't consulted."

"Hmph, join the fucking club, darling. We truly are numbers."

"Khan was his last sergeant, and he..."

"Liked him?"

Eddie looked to the ceiling and thought about that for a moment. "Tolerated him."

"Oh boy, this should be fun, then."

Miriam's door opened and closed, and in between both events, Benson appeared in the main office, his face a shade of beetroot, and a tremble in his fingers that you could see from Regan's desk.

She unfolded her arms and took off the leather jacket.

"I don't like gum-chewers," he said as he sat next to Eddie.

"Boss," Regan spat it into her hand and then looked around for somewhere to dump it.

Benson sighed.

"Sounds like you're already pissed off with me, and I've only been here ten minutes."

Benson rose so he could talk down to her. "Don't mouth off at me. I have people above me and have people beneath me. Seems those beneath me can do as they please without so much as a by your leave, and those above me..." he glanced to his right, to Miriam's office, "and those above me treat me in a similar way. So no, I'm not keen on the new status quo."

"Great old band, they were," Eddie said. "Loved *Rockin' All Over The World*."

Benson sat back down and stared at him. "Shut up or leave me alone."

"But—"

"I mean it. I'm not in the mood for you or her."

Regan stood up and leaned over Benson. "Well, with due fucking respect, Boss, I'm not delighted by this situation, either. My old inspector is my old husband and he's done his best to screw me over for the last eight months, not content with screwing me over for twelve years before that. And now he's finally got his fucking wish!" She was pointing her finger at him. "And I'm at my wits end. I'm a bloody good copper and I deserve some respect, and until you are dissatisfied with my performance as a cop, I expect you to treat me *with* that respect. Is that clear?"

Eddie's jaw hung open and his eyes flitted left and right as they tried to get a look at Benson and Regan all at once. The office was silent. Miriam stared at them from her open office door.

"Tom. Regan."

Both looked at Miriam.

"A word."

Eddie watched them both enter Miriam's office, and decided to come back in ten minutes after they'd hugged and made up. Right now, there was coffee with his name all over it – actually, it had Kenny's name all over it. But who cared?

"Aha!"

Eddie stopped dead in the CSI office. The door closed behind him, and Sid stood before him. "I need to put up the tea fund contribution."

"But I don't drink tea."

Sid closed his eyes, and took a minute. "You know what I mean. Anyway, I'm incorporating a weekly treat of Krusty Kremes to keep morale up."

"Krusty Kremes? Is this because Fooky Nell bribed you all with them?"

"Well," Sid shrugged, "they were very nice indeed. And everyone perked right up afterwards."

"Kenny won't stand for it," Eddie said, peering around Sid, looking for him. "Tight as a duck's arse, is Kenny. Where is he?"

"Wife's poorly," called Skid from across the office.

The phone rang and Sid danced across to it. "Good morning, Major Crime Unit CSI, Sid speaking, how—"

Eddie stood in the middle of the office, aghast. "Cannot believe you've not shortened it to hello. Or even what?"

"I'll tell him. Thank you." Sid hung up and said to Eddie. "That was Inspector Benson. They want you at a briefing now, main briefing office."

"Fuck me," Eddie said. "I'm not paid enough for all this shit."

"Here, take your coffee, make you feel better."

"Going home would make me feel better."

He'd lost count of the number of briefings he'd attended over the years, and at each one the SIO would sit near the front absorbing all the info and issuing new actions, and Eddie would sit there with the urge to fart and leave. Occasionally he could be found at the back of the room snoring.

He entered the main briefing room, some large office with a semi-circle of chairs and top table that he never knew existed until he saw a tidal wave of shirts syphoning through a door. It smelled of newness in here, and Eddie nudged one of the DCs out of his chair because it was at the back and as far away from the top table as it was possible to get. The DC stared at Eddie and Eddie growled back.

Benson saw and shook his head. "Child," he mouthed.

Eddie stuck out his tongue and rubbed the side of his face with two fingers. Benson looked away.

Miriam closed the door, swigged on a bottle of water and took the chair not behind the top table, but next to Benson. "Okay, settle down, people." The room hushed and Eddie felt like nodding off. "First bit of news for you all is the appointment of Detective Sergeant Regan Parker. She's here as Ram Khan's replacement, but she's here because she's very good at her job, too. You might have heard DI Benson welcoming her this morning. Let me reassure you that the volume of his welcome was because I failed to appraise him of the move, and is in no way an attack against Regan personally or professionally." She turned to Regan, and said, "Welcome aboard, Regan; it's good to have you here." And then she offered an inaudible round of applause with just her fingertips. Others joined in. Eddie did not, and neither did Benson.

After that, the very first thing she did was face Eddie and ask, "How did your search go last night at Marshall's scene?"

Eddie dried up. There were twenty faces all staring at him expecting some professional to stand and give a detailed account of some forensic procedure or another. He swallowed, shrugged. "It went okay, thanks."

"Did you find anything?"

"Did you not read my report?"

"Yes. But not everyone else here might have. So, please…did you find anything?"

"Not really." Eddie sipped coffee.

"Eddie, tell us about the earring." Benson said.

"Oh yeah," he said, "we found an earring."

There was a pause and then Miriam and Benson shouted, "Eddie!" at the same time.

"No need to shout," he said. "It was gold, round, had a blue enamel outer surface. And we found it in dog shit stuck in a wheelie bin wheel."

"Was there a name on it?" This was from Regan.

"Fairly certain they don't christen wheelie bins."

Regan nodded, squinting at him. "You know what I mean."

Eddie shrugged, "Here in Yorkshire we don't give our dogshit names, either." Eddie was disappointed in her. Bitch. "Could call it Richard if you want. Richard the Third, maybe?"

"No, I mean was it like Gucci, or Maria Black?"

Benson tutted, "He's not—"

"What?" shouted Eddie. "How the fuck should I know? Do I look like a Mr T sort to you?"

Laughter in the room, and Eddie felt himself go red, and was on the verge of getting the hell out of there – it suddenly felt two-hundred degrees and rising.

Benson was glaring at her.

"It's no problem, Eddie. Get me an image of whatever you found later, would you?" Miriam smiled at him, and she had the effect of calming him. The temperature subsided along with the laughter, and Eddie nodded.

He surprised himself by speaking up without being bidden. And this would normally be something he'd share just among Benson and Miriam, but he'd not had the chance with Regan and Benson scrapping this morning, and now this bastard briefing. To let this briefing end without mentioning it would be silly, and possibly a bit negligent, so he swallowed more coffee and said, "You remember when Stan Forbes turned up on the night we tried to erect a scene tent?"

Benson nodded. "Yeah, poor fella."

"He turned up again last night."

Miriam took notice, looked directly at Eddie.

"He said CID visited him, and he didn't like them. I said he should try working with them. Anyway, they asked him why Marshall would be in Rothwell at that time of night. He told them he didn't know why, but then, he says, he'd had time to think on it.

"Marshall had accidentally ruined his dad's laptop. His dad, Stan, took his savings as a punishment, to go towards buying a new one. But Marshall needed that money for a trip to London."

Several 'awwws' around the room.

"So someone'll need to go back," he said, "to get it statemented, get it cleared up."

"What's your impression of Mr Forbes?"

In all the years doing this job, that was quite possibly the first time anyone had sought his opinion concerning another living person. Usually, people didn't care less what he thought – and Eddie didn't hold that against them – he knew he was a poor judge of character. He took a breath, thinking back to last night and how the man repeatedly called him sir, and how he was grateful to him for working his son's scene. "I liked him. I had time to chat with him; didn't feel the need to piss him off just so I could get on with the job."

Miriam and Benson nodded. Regan looked confused.

"He came through as genuine. The first night he broke down and wept, and last night he was very polite tried to offer this new information he'd overlooked because of his confused state of mind and lack of sleep.

"I said I'd get someone new to come and visit him so he could talk about it properly, get it recorded, you know."

Miriam looked across at Benson, and he nodded as though replying to a request.

"Even though the Forbes investigation is just a couple of days old, it has all the hallmarks of a case going tits up very quickly." Miriam took another sip of coffee and continued. "No witnesses, no CCTV, no forensic input of any value. And then a twenty-six-year-old female, Mia Chandler, is found dead in her home in the docklands of Hunslet.

"These deaths were miles apart, not obviously linked. But this apparent suicide was to have a severe impact on Marshall Forbes's investigation. There was a considerable amount of forensic evidence from *that* scene, and… Eddie, if you wouldn't mind?"

Eddie stood up, patted his stomach and left the room, mouthing his apologies as he went.

Benson cleared his throat. "I can fill in for him, I think?"

Miriam nodded.

Eddie walked into the CSI office and Sid looked up from his copy of Elle. "That was quick. Briefing finished already?"

"It has for me," Eddie said. "Parched, Sid. Absolutely parched."

Sid bookmarked the page and closed the magazine, putting it on the edge of his desk, perfectly in line with it, just as Eddie insisted. They both arrived in the kitchenette and Eddie leaned back on the doorframe as Sid got busy with mugs and biscuits.

"I don't bother with biscuits at home," Eddie said. "Only here. I wonder why that is."

"Comfort food. You're stressed-out here, all the pressure of being a CSI Supervisor," he shook his head, "must drive your blood pressure through the roof. And there's nothing quite like a Garibaldi to bring things back to calm again. That's what my old mum used to say."

Eddie nodded. "Speaking of old women, Dad made my breakfast this morning."

"Ah, well, that's nice."

"Isn't it? He was acting very pickled cucumber, as well."

Sid paused, kettle en route to the mugs, "Did you ask him why?"

"He said he wanted to take an interest in me and my work. I think it sounds dodgy as hell."

Sid added a drop of milk, closed the fridge door, and stood with his finger on his bottom lip – something right of out of a Scooby Doo cartoon. "Do you think he might be entering the male menopause?"

"I think he entered it about twenty years ago and can't find the way out. Judging by his pinny, I'd say he's got lost and is now heading towards the female menopause." Eddie dunked a biscuit, ate it, and asked, "And he's taken an interest in local history, visiting the library and such. Why is he so interested in words as well?"

"Words?"

"I said ergo a couple of days ago, and he nearly wet his pants."

"He isn't ill, Eddie?"

"It's difficult to tell with my dad; he's always been a bit... eccentric."

Sid raised an eyebrow.

"I brought boiled rice and mackerel for lunch."

Sid raised the other eyebrow.

Chapter 21

It was a semi-detached house on a dead-end road called Knightsbridge, where there once was a stone mound believed to be a cholera or a Black Death grave. Knightsbridge had a narrow alleyway leading towards the arse end of Rothwell – which was a South Leeds village old enough to warrant a mention in the Domesday Book of 1066 – and the church of The Holy Trinity. It was said the graves of the Holy Trinity cemetery had a small area called dissenters row where all the non-Christians, the Catholics, and agnostics, were buried, well away from the Christian part. It seemed that even the dead had to be kept apart from each other.

Benson pulled the car up outside and cut the engine. He turned to Regan and was about to speak when she interrupted him, "Keep my mouth shut, right? You'll do all the talking, eh?"

"Something like that. And stop being so…"

"Southern?"

"Yep, stop being so Southern."

They climbed out and slammed the doors, and stared at each other over the car's roof.

"Are you pissed off because you didn't get to choose me, or because you lost Khan?"

"Khan was a good fellow," he began, "but he was too head-strong for my liking, would go off on his own, thinking he knew what he was doing, when all he was really doing was wasting police time and annoying me. You, however, have been forced upon me, whether I wanted you or not, and it turns out that you, like Khan, are also head-strong. I do not like that in a sergeant of mine."

"Why not? Surely, it's better that a sergeant thinks for himself—"

Benson held up a finger, "There is the problem exactly. If I wanted someone to think for themselves, I would stay back at MCU and send you out willy-nilly to complete these tasks, *my* tasks, whereupon you'd report to me on your return."

She shrugged, "So what do you want from me?"

"I want..." Benson closed his mouth, and thought about that for a moment. "I want you to do what I tell you to do. Nothing more, nothing less."

"Okay, Boss. So what do you want me to do?"

"Accompany me, that's all. And stop calling me boss – it really gets up my nose."

"What should I call you?"

"To my face, you may call me sir, or Tom or Benson. Behind my back you may call me anything you like so long as I don't get to hear about it. Understood?"

She only nodded, accepting defeat easily it seemed, or not risking him blowing his top to Miriam again. Either way, he thought, she gave in too easily, and he didn't like that; he preferred a fighter. Khan was a penis – there was no denying it – but he had spirit, and would argue.

For the moment, before both began walking to Stan Forbes's house, he appraised her, and found himself profoundly jealous of her. She was young, had verve – even if she had temporarily suppressed it for an easy life – and she had wit and temerity. All Benson had these days was creaking bones, irregular bowel habits, bad breath, bad temper, and a longing to go back and do it all again. To feel fresh and vibrant again… to wake with your face still on the right way round each morning would be such a blessing.

"Where's your radio?"

She looked shocked. "I… I haven't brought one."

"Why not?"

She hesitated, shrugged, and said, "Don't really use them any more."

"And what happens if you need to shout for assistance?"

She looked away, an embarrassment bunching up her lips.

"Don't forget in future."

It felt altogether too calm for Benson's liking.

"Come in, sir, come in. Young lady."

Benson said, "I'm DI Tom Benson, this is my sergeant, Regan…"

He looked at her, was about to click his fingers, when she said, "Parker."

"As in nosey," the man smiled.

"Never heard that before; how very original." Regan smiled in return, but Benson could see it riled her.

"Please, come through."

In the lounge, the net curtains fluttered like a lightweight flag against a window that was letting in fresh air and faint traffic noise, and letting out a grief that was heavy with silence. There were family portraits on the wall, and a couple of small school photographs of Marshall on a glass-fronted sideboard by the small TV unit.

Benson sat at one end of the sofa, Regan at the other with a pen and notebook in her hands, and opposite them, sat Stan, who smiled all the time. "Might I offer you some refreshments? Tea, coffee? We even have Red Bull. It's what the youth of today drinks apparently."

"That firmly rules me out, then." Benson waved a hand. "We're here, Mr Forbes, because our CSI told us you'd remembered something important."

"He was a smashing chap, your CSI. Very amiable, and very keen, doing a smashing job at the scene last night. I mean, it was well past dark, and he was there working away. Such a joy to see someone who takes pride in their work, and takes their job seriously, don't you think?"

Benson didn't return the effervescent smile – he thought it might prolong things unduly if he turned himself into the friend that Stan obviously wanted him to be. He chose to keep things professional, cool. "What did you want to tell us, Stan?"

"Oh, it's a silly thing, really; you'll laugh! Your colleagues from CID asked why Marshall—" his voice cracked, and he coughed, "Excuse me. They wanted to know why he might be up at that alleyway at that time of night. It must have been quite late on, I suppose, maybe eight o'clock. Maybe half past. Well, I couldn't for the life of me think why he'd be up there." He went silent for almost a minute, and Benson and Regan watched him trying to bring his face under control.

And suddenly, like he'd had fresh batteries installed, he was off again, smiling through his words. "I have an office in the back of the house. It's nothing special, no more than a broom cupboard really, something like Harry Potter's cupboard under the stairs," he laughed, "but it's where I usually work from. I'm a copywriter you see."

Benson nodded. "Go on."

"That day, maybe a fortnight ago, I'd decided to do work in between watching a bit of the rugby on telly. So my laptop was just there on the coffee table, wire trailing to the plug point over there. Silly boy walks in with his headphones on, a drink in one hand and a plate of sandwiches in the other, knocks into the laptop, and then stands on it. Broken. Smashed, it was."

Benson watched him take a break, watched him breathing hard as he stared down at the rug and carpet, at the coffee.

"If only…" He placed his hand over his mouth, looked away again.

Benson had been around hundreds of relatives of dead people. It was easy to spot those who grieved against those who pretended to grieve. It was just as easy to spot those who grieved against those who felt guilty. But what was difficult, what would always be difficult, was separating those who felt guilt as a natural emotion because of the death of their loved one, and those who felt guilt because they'd killed the loved one. Benson squinted; it remained the toughest part of his job.

"I should have worked from the office. I could have recorded the rugby and watched it later." He smiled again. "I don't know why I didn't."

"So why was he up at the alleyway?" Regan asked.

"Yes, yes, why indeed. Are you sure you wouldn't like a drink?"

Both shook their heads, and Stan looked almost insulted.

"I feel ashamed to admit that I took the lad's savings to buy a new laptop. He'd worked hard to save up that money, and I took it. I told him it was punishment for breaking my laptop, that without it, I wouldn't get paid, we'd lose the house, and so on. You know, to illustrate the consequences of being clumsy."

"A guilt trip?"

He absently wiped a tear. "He said it wasn't his fault." He blinked, stared between Benson and Regan, hoping for some support, perhaps. "And it wasn't. It was mine."

"And why was he—"

"Ah yes," he smiled again, "I get waylaid so easily, these days. He had saved that money for a rock concert in London, a weekend stay-over with his friends, sight-seeing, that sort of thing. And this money was for that, you see. So he needed money and fast." He swallowed, rubbed his hands together, elbows on knees. "It's no secret, really, that a person can make money around that area if they're prepared to… if they don't mind performing favours. If you see what I mean. Would you excuse me?" Stan got up and trod carefully out of the room, closing the lounge door quietly after him. A waft of curry smell curled into the lounge, and Regan's stomach rumbled.

Benson and Regan looked at each other, and though it was tempting to talk about what they'd just heard, neither spoke. Both waited patiently for Stan to return.

He did return, five long minutes later. His eyes were red, and he carried a tissue. He closed the lounge door, smiled at his guests, and took his seat. "Forgive the wait, I just checked on Mrs Forbes. She's not taking this terribly well, sir. I took her a cup of tea, but she's still out of it. Could I interest you in some tea, Inspector? Sergeant?"

"We're fine, thank you," said Benson. "We'd like to ask a couple of questions about people he knew. Specifically one person called Mia Chandler."

Confusion pulled Stan's eyebrows most of the way down, and the smile became a frown. "I've heard of her." And then his eyes widened in realisation, "Yes, she's his teacher. Well, I mean she *used* to be his teacher, a few years ago." He drifted away in thought, "Nice lady, if I remember rightly."

"You don't happen to know if Marshall was seeing Mia, do you?"

"Romantically, you mean?"

Regan nodded.

He shook his head. "Not that I'm aware. He hasn't got a girlfriend, never mentions any girls, anyway. He's into his music, always listening to music. And he likes computer games, *Call of Duty* and such. He's not one for going out and socialising, really. But I could go and wake Mrs Forbes if you like? She picks up on these things much better than I do. It's a failing of mine, really, well, it's a failing of most men, I think; can't see what's under their noses, eh, Mr Benson?"

"Ask her when she's good and ready; no rush."

Stan nodded.

"One last thing before we go," said Benson. "I know my colleagues have already taken away Marshall's phone and computer, but do you mind if we take a look in his room?"

Stan positively bounced to his feet, "Oh of course, no problem at all. It's like Columbo, getting an insight into the victim's life by standing in their room." And then he seemed to hear what he'd just said, and how he'd called his murdered son a victim in the most flippant way, and the tears cascaded down his cheeks, and the tissue he carried was soon wet. "Forgive me," he croaked. "I don't know what I was thinking. Please, follow me."

The stairs creaked as the three of them ascended, and as they neared the top, the snoring grew louder.

"Forgive Mrs Forbes," Stan whispered, "she's been given a little Valium to help her relax. This has hit her very hard."

They nodded and ignored her, stepped through into Marshall's old room. It was cramped with three of them in there, so Stan excused himself, stood out on the landing, staring at his feet, catching tears.

Benson and Regan poked and prodded their way through drawers, through books and magazines, computer games and *Star Wars* figurines, but saw nothing that gave them any such clue, certainly nothing that even Columbo could use. There were no condoms or condom wrappers, no sex toys or porn magazines or DVDs, no evidence of drug use. He was a clean-living lad, thought Benson, whose last act was to prostitute himself to go and see a rock band in London.

When they reappeared on the landing, Stan almost stood to attention, smoothed out the creases from his shirt. "The ironic thing," he said, "I haven't been able to type a single word on that new laptop. Not a one. It's like it's cursed."

Back in the lounge, the smile slid off Stan's face and he stared in earnest at them both. "Now," he said. "I've answered your questions as best as I can, and I've seen first-hand the hard work your CSIs are putting into my son's case. But I want a straight answer to a straight question – one I put to the family liaison officer daily, and one that is answered with platitudes." He stood tall, took a breath, and said, "Who killed my son?"

Regan slammed the door and hooked her seat belt under her thumb, dragged it over and clicked it in place. She looked across at Benson and asked, "Truth or lie?"

"Every time I looked at him, I wondered about Mia Chandler, and who killed her. He stalked her a few years ago, and I don't like that kind of behaviour in a victim." Benson stared straight ahead, took a big breath, and said, "But I think he was telling the truth."

Chapter 22

THERE WAS A BEDROOM at the back of the house. It looked out over the garden. And you didn't need to look too carefully to see the ruins of the old swing there, and the slide right next to it. He'd even concreted in a Swingball post for the girls to play tennis against each other.

He could imagine them, *remember* them, squabbling over who was hitting it too hard, usually Mia, who refused to be beaten at anything; so competitive that it caused more rows than enough. He smiled at the shouting he could hear right now, Mia calling Clara a wimp, Clara storming off, throwing the bat into the bushes. He was usually too busy with the barbecue to do anything about it other than laugh. It was no big deal – happened every Sunday throughout the summer months, and it always got resolved over the burgers and hotdogs.

But the garden was deserted now. Abandoned. And the bedroom was empty. Silent.

Mia had moved out a couple of years ago, and though Sheila wanted it kept just as Mia had left it, Mike said it was a waste of a good room. But each time he opened the door with a box of junk to put in the corner, he stared at the bed, pictured Mia in there snoring, or watching some shit on her iPad, earphones in, oblivious to the world, and he couldn't do it. It would be like some kind of desecration. He always closed the door after him, found somewhere else for the box of junk.

She had her own place across town looking out onto a swanky little courtyard with the River Aire flowing past her lounge window. Nice view from her bedroom, too. But she should be with her family.

It had almost killed him when she left, but she was outgrowing the family home, and he could tell she wanted to begin a family of her own. Teaching was still good, she'd said, she was enjoying it, and because of the move, commuting was easier. But he knew there was something wrong, well maybe not wrong, exactly, but there was a change in her. It was like she didn't want to come and visit any more, and whenever he turned up to visit her, she'd make an excuse so he couldn't stay, or even make an excuse so he couldn't come in.

Eventually, Mike had found out what was at the core of all the excuses. A man called Vincent Lightowler. With a name like that, he'd said, he should be in a fantasy movie, maybe *Lord of Rings* or something. Mia hadn't found it funny, and that in itself was a shock because she always laughed at her dad's jokes – it was an arrangement they had, like how she howled whenever he started singing.

Mike was smiling now. The barbecue, the laughter, the howling. All wonderful memories. All in the past.

It was cold. He stared at the dashboard and found his face was wet again and his eyes were stinging again, couldn't breathe through his nose. Everything felt full, pressurised like a tyre ready to pop – his head ached and actually hurt; the pain there was immeasurable, but if a doctor had asked him to give it a number from one to ten, he'd have chosen infinity.

Just being alive was painful.

No father should ever bury his daughter. And to think she suffered like that, without her family there to... if not prevent her death, then at least to ease the path towards it. Tears dripped into his overalls, and he didn't even notice.

He couldn't believe that the cops thought she could kill herself. Lined up alongside everyone else on earth, she'd be in the Would Never Kill Herself row. She was always so positive, so focussed, so competitive. She would never dream of hanging herself, of giving in like that, and yet the police gave the impression they didn't believe him when he told them that. How could they not? If they found her hanging, it was murder. Simple as that. And that's what he'd told them.

They nodded and made notes, and left. They didn't believe him.

Later, when he sat down and cried with Sheila, and she'd told him what she overheard in the mortuary just before they cut… just before Mia's examination, Mike knew that had to be it. There really was no investigation needed, was there?

The police already thought it was suicide, and yet if they contemplated the alternative, a certain Mr Lightowler had already occurred to them.

He squinted, unsure of their course of action.

"What did it matter?" he mumbled. "Even if they thought Vincent was responsible…" Even if they thought Vincent Lightowler had killed Mia, what would they do? Sheila had asked this very question earlier as they both emptied another box of tissues and cried at their loss.

They might catch him. They might get a confession out of him, or they might be able to prove he did it. But they might not. He might walk. Free. Laughing at their pain, at the police incompetence. If they *did* catch him, yes, he might go to prison and serve eight years for manslaughter with diminished responsibility. You see, Vincent Lightowler had a mental incapacity – Vincent Lightowler was a drug-taking sociopathic narcissistic bastard with ADHD or whatever they fucking called it, he didn't know. He didn't care. It didn't matter.

What on earth possessed Mia to get mixed up with a cretin like him?

The point was this: he did it, and that made him a murderer, didn't it? And no amount of prison time was punishment enough for killing Mia. Sheila had looked across at him, offering him a tissue, and she'd said, "I know where he lives, Mike." There was no ambiguity in her meaning, either.

Mike's eyes filled up again, and he sobbed in the darkness, still not wholly believing two things. He found it incomprehensibly difficult to believe that Mia was dead. And he found it impossible to believe he was going to take care of the police's and justice system's problem for them. No expensive eight years inside for Mr Lightowler, pain free, living as not even number one on the doctor's scale. No, for him, Mike had something interesting planned – he wanted to see if he could get Lightowler's pain intensity to match his own – infinity was asking a lot, but he had tools to help him get somewhere near.

He blew his nose, wiped his eyes, and then studied a movement through the windscreen; it was him. It was Vincent crossing the road in front of his car. Mike's heart kicked again, and all he wanted was for it not to pack in before he'd finished administering his own justice.

It was eight-thirty, plenty dark enough, and Mike had been sitting here in the van for almost two hours prior to Lightowler arriving home, just to make sure no one else was likely to pop around and interrupt them. The house had been in darkness when he arrived, and he'd seen Lightowler hang up his coat in the hallway, then go through to the lounge, and disappear from direct line of sight, but saw a light go on at the side of the house – the kitchen. Lights went on and off upstairs before he reappeared in the lounge, wearing different clothes, then drew the curtains. He saw Lightowler's shadow dip as he headed out of the room. The light at the side of the house in the kitchen changed, maybe he'd drawn blinds or something.

Mike swallowed, looked at his hands trembling, and gave himself the option of quitting while he still could, while he was still this side of the legal line, and while no one was in any pain.

But wait, someone *was* in pain. Him, Mike, was in pain – and Sheila, too. And this was the only way to rinse it all away – with that bastard's blood – all of it.

He started the van and without turning on the lights, crept forward and parked outside Lightowler's house. He turned off the engine again. It was time.

Chapter 23

"I think it was a stupid display of your immaturity." Benson sipped and wiped froth from his top lip onto his shirt sleeve.

Eddie finished his doughnut and licked his fingers. "Not especially bothered what you think. The point is I don't do people any more. You know, all my life I forced myself to endure situations that I found stressful. I saw those situations as normal – that everyone hated them as much as I did – as much as I *do*. But that's not the case at all; some people love being the centre of attention, they love giving presentations and talking to audiences. I don't. I can manage a one-to-one, but that's about all. Anything more than that stresses me out – and I don't need more stress in my life. I'm the back-room boy, the grey man in the corner of the room – and that's where I'm happiest."

Benson sighed. He picked up the remaining doughnut, licked his lips… and then put it down again.

"What's the matter? Why didn't you just buy three doughnuts to begin with?"

"Because I'm trying to be good." He sighed again. "Christ, I'm beginning to sound like you, sighing all the time."

"You're allowed to. I don't have a monopoly on it, and let's face it, there's a fucking lot to sigh about."

Benson smiled. "I'm fat. I'm old."

"At last, you found a mirror that works!"

Benson marched on, regardless of Eddie. "And I don't like it. Time is travelling past me faster and faster. When I was a kid, a week would last almost a month, and now it lasts about two days. Does that make sense?"

"Perfect sense. It happens to us all, especially when we're so occupied with everything in life: time passes fast not necessarily when you're having fun, but it passes fast when you're busy. And we always are. But yes, you are fat. That said," he pointed a finger at Benson before Benson could begin shouting, "I haven't seen my own dick for months. Not even sure if it's still there."

"Not as though you use it, is it?"

Eddie's face clouded as he thought about the last time he was on par for using it. Her name was Miss Moneypenny. It didn't end well. For her. Nor him, actually.

Benson twigged what was happening in Eddie's mind. "I'm sorry, I didn't think—"

"It's fine. You can't go through life apologising for all the bad things that happen. Shit, you'd never get out of bed."

"We're all getting fat and old."

"You have a pretty good head start over me, though."

"Funny."

"Is that why you're so pissed off with your new sidekick?"

"Don't know what you mean."

"Come on," Eddie said, and grinned. "You've been a mean old bastard to her ever since she was appointed your sergeant. And really, apart from the gum-chewing, and the constant talking, and the…" Eddie slipped into a short silence, and then said, "Actually, I can see your point."

"She's okay. She has the makings of a good copper, actually. But I do resent her," he shrugged. "She's young, got it all ahead of her, whereas I spend most of my time looking back, these days, as though everything in front of me is suddenly a long way behind me. It's the time speeding up thing, all over again. I feel like I don't have a lot left in front of me."

Eddie stared at Benson's stomach and was about to remark, when he saw Benson shaking his head. He decided it might be better for his health if he said nothing. "She does have nice eyes, though," he said instead.

Benson lifted the last doughnut, and put it down again, "Leave her alone. She's had a shitty time with her ex. I don't think there's room for more disappointment in her life."

The door squeaked open and groaned shut, and it reminded Eddie of a conversation with his dad. But this wasn't his dad; he looked up as Miriam slid into the third seat around the table, the one with an untouched latte on the table before it.

"Sorry I'm late," she said, and took a mouthful of lukewarm coffee. "Is that last doughnut for me? Starving."

Eddie watched the reluctance on Benson's face as he nodded, almost drooling, and barely kept from laughing about it.

"You'll spoil your dinner," Eddie winked.

"You can't spoil a microwave lasagne. It's already as bad as it's going to get."

"You haven't tasted my dad's cooking."

Miriam smiled, then closed her eyes and swallowed. "Divine. Anyway, what have you two been talking about?"

"He can't see his dick," said Benson.

"But I *can* see you. Same thing," Eddie said, grinning again.

Miriam laughed, dabbed at sugar in the corners of her lips and said, "Update me on Mia and Marshall."

Eddie said, "The fingerprint in blood on the knife in Mia's handbag came back as hers."

"No surprise there."

"And the blood comes back as—"

"Marshall Forbes."

Eddie nodded.

"So on the face of things," Miriam said, "it looks like Mia stabbed Marshall and then took her own life by hanging herself."

"On the face of it," agreed Benson.

"But we all know that's total bollocks," Eddie said.

"Because?"

"Because she didn't kill Marshall."

"Can't put that to a jury, sorry. I need more."

"No way did a lass with such a slight build like her kill a stout twenty-year-old male, built like a barrel."

"Hardly *CSI New York*, is it?" Benson said.

"But if she was having an affair with him, she'd be able to get close, use brains to overpower him, not brawn. And stab him when the time was right."

"I know you're playing devil's advocate, Miriam, but it doesn't feel right to me."

Benson cleared his throat. "I spoke with someone at Marshall's school today, asked about a bit, seeing if he was having it off with his teacher—"

"Tom. Please, a little decorum."

Benson looked at her as though he'd stepped on a puppy. "Romantically engaged."

Miriam nodded.

"Turns out that Marshall was gay. Not even bi-sexual. He was gay."

Eddie blinked. "Casts new light on the note, then."

"I also spoke with Stan Forbes today, he's Marshall's father. And the last thing he asked me was who killed his son. I couldn't answer him, but I have a good inclination who killed Mia, and the knife links both crimes—"

"And the note," Eddie said.

"And the note, yes. So if a lad called Vincent Lightowler used to date Mia, and he is a nutjob by all accounts, I think we should begin looking there."

"Explain 'by all accounts'."

Benson looked at Miriam, then at Eddie.

Eddie said, "At the mortuary, when Mia's mother turned up, she was calm and then flew into a rage, and she was screaming Vincent's name, saying he was the killer, that he'd tried before."

"What does Marshall have to do with Vincent, though?"

Eddie shrugged, "The note suggests they were poking each other."

"Eddie, please."

"Sorry, romantically engaged in shagging."

Miriam tutted, "There's no hope."

"I know, right. Teachers shagging students."

"No, I mean... Oh, never mind."

"Vincent finds out they were an item, kills the kid and kills Mia, tried to shield himself by planting her prints on the murder weapon in the victim's blood."

"But they weren't..." Eddie stared at Miriam, unable to bring to mind a suitable word.

"Shagging?" she said, smiling.

"I prefer romantically engaged, but I see your point, Miriam."

She laughed. "You're impossible."

"Anyway, Vincent thinks Mia and Marshall are together and doesn't like it, kills them; maybe he doesn't know Marshall is gay.

Maybe he didn't care – any male attention might have been a trigger for him, a no-go."

Miriam sipped and looked at Benson. "And what does Mr Lightowler have to say for himself?"

Benson shrugged, still mourning the doughnut. "Not found him yet."

"Have you spoken with Mia's parents?" She asked Benson while looking at Eddie. "Since that day at the mortuary, I mean?"

Benson smiled at Eddie's sour face. "No. They've been interviewed; I've read the notes. I'm happy."

Eddie looked confused. "You haven't spoken with them? They might be able to tell you about this Vincent fella, maybe shed light on any new boyfriend, problems at work."

"It's all in the notes, Eddie. Keep your nose out."

"Sounds like my nose needs to be in, mate."

"Do I tell you what fingerprint powders to use at a job."

"Only because you haven't got a clue – you're a typical gaffer, you; no idea what you're doing, but happy to hand out shite advice to those who do the fucking job!"

"Boys!"

Both stared first at Miriam, and then at the other customers who'd interrupted their own conversations to listen to Eddie's.

"Sorry," Eddie said. "But sometimes he can be a complete—"

"I said enough."

Everyone took a minute, slurping at drinks and nibbling biscuits, and around them the volume steadily grew back again.

"How are you getting along with Regan?"

Benson finished a mouthful of biscuit, spat crumbs as he said, "She's alright."

"I marvel at your in-depth appraisal—"

"Shut up, Eddie. At least *I* can give in-depth appraisals. I don't walk out of a briefing because I'm shy."

Eddie stared across at Benson, and was about to speak when Miriam said, "Glad to hear it; you can nip out and speak with Mia's parents."

"Are you kidding?"

Miriam leaned forward. "I bet that stunning interview technique of yours could glean more info from them. Show Regan how an old-timer does the job, eh?"

"Less of the old-timer."

"Yeah, watch out," Eddie said, "he's having a pre-retirement mid-life crisis. Gets tetchy if you mention age or fatness."

Benson pointed a finger, face enraged, ready to spew hot words at Eddie, but Miriam stepped in once again.

"If you can't be civil, we'll stop having our little natters here and we can have them back at the mill with bad coffee and droopy biscuits. Is that understood?"

Both nodded, and when Benson sneered at Eddie through the tops of his eyes, Eddie stuck out his tongue.

Chapter 24

There was something almost delightful about the name Daisy. It always coalesced as an image of a cow chewing cud, a large Disney-type bell around its neck, and big fluttering eyes, and a pleasant disposition. But today, Daisy was a girl who had anything but a pleasant disposition. She was arrogant, had an inflated ego, and thought she was better than him, when in fact, she was scum under his Rhinestone Design boots. Suede boots, if you don't fucking mind. He'd seen one of the royals – not the top echelon of royals, but one of the more junior members, might even have been a hanger-on, or a peer, perhaps, wearing them. They would suit Vincent Lightowler, he thought.

And so they did.

One might say those boots were not for men who lived in places such as Beeston in South Leeds; more suited, perhaps, for men who lived by the river in some swanky apartment in Hunslet. But one might also say that of Vincent, too. He spoke well, acted with decorum, and with manners befitting a modern gentleman. They were as out of place on Vincent's feet as he was as out of place in Beeston.

The houses here were ten a penny. They were so cheap because they were fucking lousy. They were back-to-back, meaning they only had one entry/exit door, a lounge and a kitchen on the ground floor, a bathroom and one bedroom on the first floor, and a single room on the second floor with a ceiling that sloped to the centre of the building.

But they had one important facet that Vincent fully exploited. They had cellars, or basements, if you were that way inclined.

Either way, they had somewhere where one might keep a certain Daisy while one taught her how to behave with respect and with compassion, and where she might learn to appreciate her betters and fucking well kneel when kicked.

Work had been lousy today. Arguments with people he didn't like the look of, didn't like being in the company of, arguments with people who refused to see common sense. By the end of it all, he was tense, he was fragile, even, and beneath the sparkling exterior, Vincent Lightowler was fucking angry.

He'd been looking forward to this all day. In fact, when he'd had the time to contemplate it fully, he'd developed quite a little happening in the nether regions, and had to excuse himself for ten minutes. Vincent smiled and unlocked the front – and only – door, locked it behind him and turned on the lounge light. The high ceiling made him feel small, cold, and isolated. He turned on the standard lamps either side of the chimney breast and shut off the big light.

The room darkened, and warmed simultaneously, and Vincent allowed himself to shudder at the prospect of tonight's entertainment. "It's wrong to call it entertainment," he chided. "It's education. And you must remember that." If you grin – like you're doing now! – while you're passing on your lesson, she's not going to take it seriously, she's going to think it means nothing to you, and so... "And so she won't absorb it; she'll rebel against it." Yes, he thought, I must try to engage with her on a serious level. A low IQ level.

He went upstairs to change out of his working clothes and into something more suitable for the task at hand. On the way back down stairs he put his mood into serious-mode, and made himself think of Mia, of how she'd tricked him, how she'd been downright awful to him, refusing to listen to any of his advice, refusing to take it on board, refusing to forgive him whenever he overreached himself and damaged her. Childish cow!

Things were wholly different with Daisy. She was a kind soul – no malice in her at all, unlike Mia. She was… yes, she was weak, and perhaps a little feeble-minded, but it was his challenge to correct her errors, and further, it was his morality-check for not belittling her. She had every right to seek his wisdom, as any normal person might.

He walked through the lounge, drew the curtains and then he pulled the blind in the kitchen, and checked the balance on the electric meter – still seven pounds in credit; plenty for a couple of days. He stood at the cellar door, and took several deep breaths, fingers tingling in anticipation.

After tormenting himself for longer than he thought he could tolerate, he unlocked the door and the smell hit him immediately. It was such a turn off!

He switched on the light. He strode down each stone step not with eagerness any more, not with anticipation, but with dread, and with loathing, and with growing anger. He shouldn't have to deal with this any more. He'd told her time and again to hold it.

As he neared the bottom, his jaw ached from grinding his teeth, and his fingernails dug into the palms of his hands as he screwed them into fists. The lesson for this evening, then, would be altogether more… interactive.

He faced the wall, breathing heavily through his nose, feeling surge after surge of heat in his chest, and listening to her whimper as she squirmed in her chair. Was it time to cut her loose, he wondered? Slowly, Vincent turned, and because he was a reasonable man, smiled at her. "Daisy," he said, "Daisy, Daisy, Daisy. What on earth has happened here?"

She sat naked in a bare wooden dining chair, shivering. The seat had a decent-sized hole cut in it, and beneath it was a tin bucket. There was no facility for dealing with any other bodily waste – he was a thinker, not a practical man, and as such, those bodily functions had to wait until evening. Only she hadn't waited, had she?

"I suppose it's my fault, huh? For cutting the hole in the wrong place? For not making it big enough?" He snorted, then sighed as if upset. "I left as much of that chair intact as I could, Daisy. See, I was considering your comfort." He shook his head, "Pity I didn't consider my own discomfort, eh? I'm too selfless, Daisy, always thinking of others. Never of myself."

She blinked rapidly, staring up at him through eyelashes matted by tears, her face and chest blotched by a red patchwork of fear.

Hands clasped behind his back, he leaned forward, and when he spoke, she jumped. "This is not good enough. We've had this discussion before, and you agreed…You *agreed* not to do this." He straightened, peered down the length of his nose at her. "How hungry are you?"

Daisy writhed on the chair as though she could get free and run away from him. More pungent odour wafted into the room and he almost retched. She was trying to talk to him, her throat was making the noises of speech but the ball gag prevented anything meaningful escaping except a string of drool.

Vincent reached around the back of her head, ready to untie the buckle when there came a loud knocking on the front door. He stared at her, a strange almost accusing look on his face as though she'd conspired with a stranger to interrupt them at this precise moment. She stared right back, a mixture of dread and hope in her eyes. When he stood, she continued to squirm, resumed trying to speak – only now there was an urgency in her whimper.

"Back in a minute," he said, heading for the stairs, "don't go away, now. And you'd better think of a bloody good reason why I don't skin you alive, missy." He turned out the cellar light.

Chapter 25

Vincent was almost sprinting by the time he reached the top step, and fell into the kitchen with rage propelling him, and a growl belching him across the floor. He reached the front door, unlocked it in a tangle of keys, and yanked it open.

And stopped dead.

"Hello, Vincent."

Vincent almost fell over. He held onto the door frame and tried to appear nonchalant, but was still breathing way too hard for that. Anger put on hold, he said, "What brings you to the depths of depravity, Mr Chandler?" The rage had vanished like it was a mist in a heatwave, and he felt vulnerable, defenceless – he felt exposed, strangely.

Mike Chandler smiled heartily. "I erm," he hooked a thumb over his shoulder, "I was in the area, doing a job on a Micra. I scraped your car on my way round the corner. I have a new van, not really used to it yet. Sorry," he said. "I didn't know it was *your* car, if that's what you're thinking. It was an accident, and I thought I should knock and hold my hands up. What a coincidence."

"That's very—"

"Turns out it's your car. Turns out it's your house. Turns out… it's you. Vincent Lightowler."

"I'm sure the scratch will polish out."

Chandler said nothing for a while, only stared, and Vincent swallowed, knowing this wasn't over. He stole a glance over his shoulder at the cellar door, licked his lips. Swallowed again. "It's fine, really."

"You, erm, you alone in there."

"Yup. Just about to start making dinner. Can I… would you like—"

"No. I don't think so." He kicked back off the step, and said, "Look, if you're happy to look after the damage yourself, I'll leave you alone."

"It's fine. Really, it's an old banger, worth about fifty quid."

"Okay, good. Listen, though. Just to make sure everything's on the level, take a look, and once you've seen the damage, if you're still okay with it, I'll be on my way. Okay?"

Vincent bit his lip. It seemed the only way to conclude this and get back to Daisy was to oblige, get it done, and get it out of the way.

"Take two minutes."

Who gave a shit about the fucking car anyway. "Sure. Okay, let's take a look."

Mike Chandler turned and began walking away towards the corner of the street, and Vincent hopped down the steps, clicked the door shut behind him, and followed, hands in pockets, prepared to be back in less than thirty seconds. The street was quiet, the shadows deep, and the van was at angle across the front of Vincent's old Audi A3.

"How's Mia?" It was small talk; something to pass the time, something to reconnect them. Vincent felt isolated out here, and he felt uncomfortable, like there was something going on he should be aware of, something he couldn't quite put his finger on. The small talk was a way of diminishing the fear, of compacting the threat, because once they started talking about Mia, the discomfort would leave, wouldn't it? And they'd be like old buddies again.

Well, maybe not quite old buddies – Mike Chandler was, after all, the father of the girl Vincent used to date. It didn't end especially well because she was another one like Daisy who needed constant encouragement, constant reassurance that she was doing okay, but she needed constant adjustments too – she was awfully time-consuming. And in the end, it had been easier to let her go, and he wondered now as he closed in on the front corner of his car, if Mike held that against him? He couldn't be sure, but he wondered if Mike was a bit pissed off that Vincent had decided to cut her loose. She was, after all, a burden to everyone.

"Let me open the van doors, shed some light on it."

"'Kay." No reply about Mia. Strange. He was taking it as a personal rejection, obviously; I kick Mia out of the relationship and he feels offended – it was to be expected, he supposed.

The rear van doors opened with a squeak, the interior light spilled out, and Vincent stepped forward, peering at the car. He couldn't see any damage. Strange, again. He looked at Mike and Mike was grinning at him. And it made no sense at all to Vincent until he glimpsed the hammer before it all went black.

Daisy was growing colder. The door up there opened and funnelled a cold draft straight down into the cellar. She was uncomfortable, shit between her legs, piss between her legs, hunger in her belly, and no blood circulating her arms and her feet meant a nervous pain that was gradually spreading outwards in something that was rapidly turning to fear. She'd lost the sensation in her hands and feet hours ago, couldn't make them move even if she'd been inclined to. It was as if they were dead.

The ball in her mouth was doing more than stopping her from shouting to Vincent, it was making it hurt to swallow, and the more she was fearful the more her nose blocked and prevented her from breathing.

It was getting colder. She held her breath as a bubble of snot quivered on her top lip. She could hear voices, caught something but it was audibly blurred along with everything else. There was a bang as the front door slammed shut, and the snot bubble popped.

DAY 5

Chapter 26

Charles was on the phone, looking back across the lounge at the empty heap of shit on the table. "I thought it would be easy. I thought that using something I was familiar with would create a surge of story-telling utopia. But when I hit the keys, they weren't there – literally. I've been swindled!" Before the end of the call, Charles added, "And please, don't tell Eddie; he'll just take the mickey out of me. I'm feeling fragile enough as it is."

Charles answered the knock, and ushered Sid in quickly. "Loving the hair, Sid."

"It's Ferrari red – genuine, too."

"Nice. Tea?"

"Got to hurry, I'm afraid; lots to do. But let's get you hooked up so you don't lose the muse, man." He rushed to the table and lifted the Imperial, then slammed it back down, cringing at the pain in his back. "You didn't tell me it weighed two-hundred-weight, Charles. Bloody hell, I've knocked my spine out of kilter."

Charles was running around with a mixture of excitement and shock propelling him. "I never knew story-telling could be so eventful."

"I never knew it could be so painful."

"You sure you wouldn't like some tea?"

"Yes, yes, oh dear God, give me some tea. And some painkillers."

An hour later, Sid had gone, groaning and holding his spine in place as he swivelled into his car seat. The Imperial was in Charles's bedroom, relegated to a corner with a sheet thrown over it. "Shame," he said, "I was hoping for big things from you."

He read the ad again and discovered it said display model only.

"You stupid old fool." Maybe now you'll listen to that voice in your head and put the whole stupid notion of writing out of the window. He sat on the sofa looking at the new laptop that Sid had bought for him. It was in a case, and Sid had already set it up, claiming it was plug and play.

"Hit the Word icon," he'd said, "and you're good to go. Literally."

Hmm, he hadn't registered that 'literally' stuck on the end, and guessed it was Sid's way of taking the piss. He smiled, but he felt no inclination to get up and switch the damned thing on. That's why he'd wanted a proper mechanical typewriter; there was something almost comforting knowing a machine had typed it using an arm with a letter stuck on the end. That letter mashed an ink-soaked ribbon into a sheet of paper and instantly forgot it had done so. It had no memory.

You do that on one of those fancy-nancy laptop things, and it has you to ransom for the rest of your days – nothing is secret any more;

people get access to your work and your errors, read it, judge it, steal it!

Using Word wasn't so bad. Unfortunately, his typing skills didn't come back to him, though, and he attacked the almost flat keyboard of the laptop with far too much vigour using just his two index fingers and the flat of his right thumb on the space bar. And he loved it. *This* was indeed a Magic Machine.

Chapter 27

"You smell like a whore's handbag."

Tom Benson stared at himself in the hallway mirror as Brenda walked past into the kitchen. Whatever happened to stand by your man? Whatever happened to, 'Looking good, Tom, looking sharp!'

"Coffee, Tom? Or might it dampen your pulling power?"

"Pulling power?"

"Come on; not even carbon-14 would date you. You're just too... too cuddly."

"If you don't mind, I'm interviewing the parents of a murdered girl today. I wanted to—"

"Or tea? I could make you tea if you prefer."

Benson closed his hand around his car keys and closed the door on his way out.

He stared at himself again in the mirror that each person entering the building at Major Crime Unit stares into; it was always a good opportunity to find out who was following you so you could adjust your course and get out of their way. Today, it was just the ghost of his youth that followed him, shaking its head and popping its biceps.

The stairs up to the first-floor office seemed steeper than usual, left him more breathless than usual. So was this it, then? Was this the steady decline into old age and death? "Sound like Collins again," he whispered – panted – to himself. Actually, I think I'm already at 'old age'. "Still got it though." Still got that manly attraction. Sure, there were a couple of tyres around his waist, and he'd grown a decent pair of tits over the last few years, but still, he could cut it. Couldn't he?

There, sitting at her desk and looking busy was Regan Parker, the newly appointed sergeant to replace Khan. In fairness, he needed to be replaced – he'd become unreliable; and it wouldn't be beyond credibility to say he'd have done anything to take Benson's crown. "Crown?" he said to himself. He stood in the centre of the office and looked around – sometimes he asked himself if he wanted this at all. Brenda might be a whole lot more welcoming if *she* was my queen instead of this place and the people in it. Not to mention the people who die and those who run away from me and the justice they deserve.

Anyway, Khan needed to be shown the door, and in his place sat someone whom Benson couldn't yet rely on, couldn't yet trust – not in the same way as he couldn't trust Khan; he was just ever so slightly devious – but Khan could always follow orders and got the job done. Could she?

"You okay, Boss?"

Benson blinked and found he was staring at her. "What?"

"You seem a bit distant."

"Stop calling me Boss. Call me Tom or Benson, I already told you this; why must I repeat myself—"

"Sorry, Benson, my bad."

"My bad? I hate that saying."

Regan stood up. "You will let me know if I ever do anything right, won't you. Boss."

Benson watched her go. As she did, he caught a new whiff of his aftershave. It, and the especially shiny shoes he wore today, along with his latest suit – the one that complemented his fuller figure rather than accentuated it – were for her, he realised. And Brenda had realised it, too. How could she know me better than I do myself? "You old fool," he chided. "And don't forget to book out a radio," he shouted.

As he absorbed details of Mia Chandler's family, and of the previous interviews that members of this office had put on the system, he began to build a picture of them, and how Mike Chandler's daughters had come to grow apart from the core of the family, from him. The old alarm bells clanged, and Benson's eyebrows rose as he searched, expecting to find details of child abuse. But there were none. Interviewers had commented on how proud he was of his girls; how fiercely protective he was of them. Benson wondered then, if the girls had drifted away not so much because of lack of love, but because they were drowning in it. Suffocated by it.

He looked up, folded his arms, and tried to reconcile that with his own state. How he'd always just wanted to be loved but always ended up with an Ice Queen as a partner, someone who skipped though life single-handedly while he watched from the side-lines, feeling cold and distant.

What must it be like to actually be in a partnership, he wondered. There were films he'd seen where the husband returned after a hard shift and the wife would be all over him as soon as he walked through the door, almost like a dog, how affectionate they could be. Brenda sometimes grunted when he slammed the door – if he was lucky. But, part of the blame lay at his own feet, he knew.

He remembered talking to Eddie Collins's father, Charles, last year sometime. And he'd said that the other half waits at home wrapped in a protective suit of sorts, something that kept them secure and safe until the worker got home, and then the suit came off and you could be a couple again. Charles added though that sometimes the suit never came off because the worker was always at work, or they brought work home with them and shut themselves away with it, having an affair with it right in front of your eyes!

The essence was this: you learned self-preservation. You looked after yourself, you and your suit, and you literally grew apart while living under the same roof.

"Ready?"

Shocked, Benson stared up at Regan.

"Have you read all you need to read?"

"Well, I don't know, do I? I might have missed something."

"But that's okay. We'll find out when we get there."

Of course they would, Benson thought. That was old-fashioned coppering. He snarled at the computer – that thing that had taken him off the streets and given him a fat arse because he was sitting on it all the time. "We will."

On the way out, Benson held open each door for Regan, and he did the same again when they reached the car.

"What's the special treatment for, love?"

"No reason; I just believe in being a gentleman, that's all."

"Old-fashioned chivalry, eh?"

"Well," Benson smiled across at her as they left the car park, "not sure about the old-fashioned bit, but chivalric, yes indeed."

They travelled in silence for what seemed like an hour to Benson, but which was only about fifteen minutes. "I'm sorry for being a cock," he said at last. "I didn't mean to be so hard on you."

She began laughing, and soon she was howling.

At first Benson thought it rude, and then he caught the bug and joined in but stopped just as abruptly. "What are you laughing at?"

Between snorts, she replied, "Cock. Hard." She snorted again. "Geddit?"

"Oh," was all he said.

Finally she settled down, and said, "It's okay, no probs," and started laughing again.

"I just..."

She looked around at him, but he didn't make any attempt to resume or explain, so she left it, stared forward.

And then they were outside the Chandlers.

"Want me to be quiet?"

"No," Benson said. "Be yourself."

Chapter 28

"You left him in there? Overnight?"

"I got back late, okay? The bastard showed up later than I thought he would, and I had to wait and make sure he was alone."

"I don't get it, why didn't you move him into the garage?"

"At that time of night? A small incendiary device would have been more discreet."

"Alright, alright. So when are you going to move him?"

"This afternoon, late on, just as it gets dark; people will think I'm moving some tools. I won't get a second look."

"But what if he starts kicking and screaming? Mike, I can't believe you—"

"Whoa, whoa. You can't believe I took care of family business? After what we talked about? After the info you gave me? You thought I'd just let it all go? Come on, Sheila, you knew what you were asking when you gave me his address. Don't go all fucking shy on me now. I'll finish him tonight if I get the chance. If not, tomorrow."

"Okay, okay, but what if he—"

"He won't. He's well tied and silenced."

Sheila's eyes widened as she peered through the lounge window. "It's the cops. They're here."

"What?"

"Do they know? Were you followed, Mike?"

Mike almost laughed, "Followed? Last night? Don't be daft; this ain't a James Bond film."

She turned to him, clasped him by the shoulders. "Have you ever lied to me?"

"What? Sheila this isn't the time—"

"Have you?"

"About what?"

"About anything, Mike."

He shrugged, "I suppose. Can't remember what, though."

"You're a good actor, then. And you've got to be a good actor again – he's one of the cops from the mortuary."

Mike felt the blood drain from his face, and he closed his eyes. His shoulders dropped. "I can't fucking handle this."

"You *have* to. Quick, go outside, have a cigarette or something. Pretend the police are bad at their job, that they should have caught Vincent by now. Get angry. Make them believe you."

Sitting on the steps was a young girl, maybe twenty, head down, thumb scrolling on a phone. In her other hand, she held a cigarette. She glanced up as Benson and Regan unlatched the small wooden gate to the side of the driveway. The young girl wore a white polo-neck sweater with sleeves long enough to drape over her hands, and she looked remarkably like Mia, but her eyes were reddened and half closed, like she'd had a rough night.

Reversed on the driveway so its back doors were right up against the garage, was a plain white panel van, a Transit. It had black fingermarks down the edge of the doorway, and through the windscreen, Benson could see the dashboard cluttered with empty McDonald's coffee cups and old newspapers. There was a puddle on the driveway, and Benson saw it shimmer as a breeze floated across its surface.

To the young girl, Regan said, "Hi. We're from—"

"Just knock and go straight in."

"Right," she said. "Thank you."

"They're in the lounge, to your left."

Benson followed Regan inside, and called hello as they closed the door behind them, blocking out Mia's sister in her self-imposed isolation.

They both shuffled into the lounge as Sheila emerged from the kitchen and stopped dead. "Excuse us," Benson said. "The young girl on the doorstep," he hitched a thumb over his shoulder just in case they didn't know which doorstep he was talking about, "said to come straight in. I hope you don't mind."

"Who are you? Oh wait," she said, hand to her mouth. "I recognise you from the mortuary; you were in the crowd of men who tried to stop—"

"That's right, Mrs Chandler. My name's Tom Benson, I'm a detective inspector with the Major Crime Unit. This is my sergeant, Regan Parker."

"Would you pass on my thanks to your CSI? I was very grateful for him letting me be with my Mia one last time." Her red-rimmed eyes filled with tears that just rolled down her face and dripped onto the carpet without Sheila even knowing it had happened.

"I will, of course," he said. "You understand why I couldn't permit—"

"I do. I know what contamination is all about. But I also know what compassion is about, Mr Benson, and he had it in spades. I'll never forget what he did for me. I only hope he didn't get into too much trouble for being so kind."

Regan cleared her throat, and leapt to Benson's aid. "The young girl out there, would that be Mia's sister?"

"Mia was six, almost seven when Clara was born." She took a big breath and let it out through trembling lips, trying, it seemed, to keep the sobbing at bay, and struggling. "My husband… he's… out the back, smoking." She smiled, like a defence mechanism, like a shrug, "taken it up again after quitting almost ten years ago."

"I'm so sorry, Mrs Chandler."

"Thank you. Anyway, do you have any news? We wait to hear from the liaison officer, but more often than not, she hasn't got anything new to tell us."

"We're following all lines of enquiry. We have CSI going over her scene, and—"

From behind them, a voice demanded, "What about Vincent Lightowler?"

Everyone turned to see Mike Chandler, cigarette hanging from his lips, standing in the lounge doorway, face as pale as Marcel Marceau.

Sheila's eyes were so wide they almost rolled out and fell down her face, chasing the tears from before. They almost screamed what the hell are you leading them there for? "Take that outside. I won't have that stinking up the house."

He didn't move, didn't even acknowledge Sheila's disposition. He stared at Benson and Regan. "Well?"

Regan answered. "We're looking into him, one of many lines of enquiry—"

"We can't find him," Benson said. "We're looking, Mr Chandler, but so far we don't know where he might be."

"Check your computers, ask his friends. Someone's bound to know."

"Like I said, we're on with it, I promise you."

"Please, Mike, take that outside."

"I remember her as a baby. Bottle feeding her through the night. I remember her first words, her first steps – she took her first steps right there in front of the sofa." He smiled at those memories. "I remember dropping her, and how she cried. I remember crying because I thought I'd hurt her, but they're made of rubber, aren't they, babies? They bounce. I remember every single part of her life. Right up until *he* got involved with her. And then," he clicked his fingers, "nothing. It was as if she lived in another country or another time, even. It was as if she never existed. I didn't get to see her often, and when I did, she was quiet and somehow withdrawn, you know?

"We found out that bastard had been hitting her. One day she had a black eye from bending down and smacking her face on the sink. Another time she had a scar running down her forehead – looked like something out of a Frankenstein movie. Edge of a door, she said." He grinned at them. "Not so fucking good at bouncing now, Mr Benson." And the tears came, and his voice broke. "If I find him before you do..." He bowed his head and sobbed so hard his whole body shook.

The cigarette fell from his fingers, and Sheila rushed to pick it up before it burnt the carpet. She disappeared with it, and probably threw it into the kitchen sink.

Regan said softly, "I know how upset you are, Mr Chandler."

Chandler looked up. Eyes on fire. Fists ready to do some damage. "Course you do."

"Really, I do. But you have to let us do our job. We will find him; we will get to the bottom of this."

"You have no fucking idea how upset we are!"

"Do not go looking for him." Benson put a hand on Regan's arm, but she didn't stop. "If you see him, let us know, and we will pick him up."

"And do what?"

"Find out if he has any involvement—"

Chandler grinned again, laughed even, but it had the sharp edges of honed cynicism, and it cut on the way out. His voice cracked again, and he shook his head. "Uh-huh, if I find him, he's mine."

"Mike," said Sheila. "Stop it, you're scaring me." To Regan, she said, "He's angry, you'll have to forgive him."

"That's okay—"

"Don't apologise for me, woman."

"Go back outside, Mike. Have another cigarette. Have a glass of whisky, why don't you! Just stop the stupid threats."

Regan was looking between them.

"You sit here in a stranger's house. No concept of what's happened, how it's torn that house apart, how it's affected everyone in it. You sit there, pretending to give a shit, pretending to care, but all you're thinking about is where to buy your lunch today." He nodded. "I know, see. Soon as you climb back into your car, you'll have forgotten about the heartache in here, and the tears, and the shouting; probably glad to be away from it. You'll have forgotten that not only do we not have Mia around today, but we'll never have her around again. Ever. Clara will never get to see her sister again.

"We were a family, see? And now we're just three angry people who've already forgotten what it's like not to grieve."

Regan was nodding.

"Off you go now, love. There's a Subway about half a mile that way," Chandler said to Regan. "And you too," he said to Benson. "You get yourself out now, and thank God you don't have to deal with what we're dealing with. There's a good detective."

"I lost my brother when I was eleven." Regan stood up, held out a hand to help Benson stand. "Some kid on a stolen motorbike knocked him over right in front of me. Took him away from me, forever. I miss him every day, Mr Chandler." At the front door, she turned to them. "I do sympathise with you. But please let us do our jobs."

"Before we go," Benson said, a coldness in his eyes that trampled any sympathy he had when he first entered. "Do you know where Vincent Lightowler is? Do you know where he lives?"

It took Mike Chandler a good fifteen or twenty seconds to respond, but eventually he did. His mouth simply said, "No idea where he is or where he lives." And his eyes gave nothing away.

In the car Benson said, "I'm sorry. I didn't know about your brother."

"Those of us who live with grief don't take out adverts in the papers. We like to suffer alone. It keeps us bitter and twisted. It gives us the right to stay angry, does grief. Angry with life, with people, with everyone who annoys us.

"We get to tread the higher ground that comes with losing someone close. It's a gift, really, where everyone magically feels sorry for you, and puts you centre stage – right in the spotlight as they work out what to say.

"That's great for Mike Chandler; but the only trouble is, it's all null and void if you meet another griever, especially one who's been doing it longer, got some real experience like I have; got stripes and certificates. He was taking full advantage of his new status, lording it over you. Trouble is, he hasn't even begun to feel the pain yet. Wait till her birthday comes around, then Christmas. Wait till he has to make a decision about her belongings, her old socks, even, her notebooks. How much of her can he afford to keep?

"But the worst is years away: the worst is the guilt you feel when you can't even remember their face or their voice. Guilt is a killer, Benson."

Benson stared at the dashboard as she spoke to him, and tried to absorb what she was saying, tried to at least feel the pain she mentioned. "So. Let's play our little game, shall we? If he met Lightowler on a dark night, what would he do?"

Regan contemplated the possibilities for a moment, and eventually said, "Men like Mike Chandler are all talk. He'd turn around and walk the other way. At worst he'd get into a fight with him, and then run away. He loves feeling wounded, and if he killed Lightowler – which he wouldn't dare – he'd have nothing left to fight for."

Benson nodded. "Sound thinking," he said and stared forward. "But *I* think he'd kill him."

In the back of the Transit, Vincent tried to open his eyes but the tape across the eyelids held strong. He'd wet himself, and though he couldn't hear too well because of the cloth around his head, he had the impression it had rolled away from him, probably pooled by the back door. Old nut-job Chandler would get a shock when he opened those doors later and got a puddle of piss splashing onto him.

"You were too forceful, too adamant that *he* was responsible."

"Bollocks. It was perfect, and I'll tell you why it was perfect: because that's exactly how I would react even if I didn't already have that bastard in the back of my van."

Chapter 29

THERE WAS A CERTAIN tension in the air this morning, and it had nothing to do with Eddie's near miss with Beelzebub again. Sid could sense it, how Eddie brooded over his coffee, hunched there like a madman, overly protective of the biscuits on the plate next to him.

"You okay?" Sid smiled at him.

Eddie looked up, nodded, and looked back down again.

"You don't sound your usual spangly self. What's bothering you?"

He sighed, and peered up at Sid. "It's time for Skid's meeting, to sign him off on the probationer thingy."

"It's the end of his probation period?"

"That's what I said, isn't it?"

"But why so grumpy?"

At that moment the door opened, and a young lady strode in with confidence on her face and a smile to go with it. "Hi, Eddie."

"Penny!" Sid shouted and leapt from his chair. "How are you? Not seen you in ages. Can I get you a nice cup of tea, and," he whispered, "we have some delicious Hobnobs."

Eddie groaned.

"Oh my, I love the hair! I brought some brandysnaps."

"Thank you, it's genuine Ferrari red. I'll put the kettle on."

Penny stopped by the desk Eddie was hunched over. "Passed quickly, hasn't it?"

"What has?"

"Six months. Since Mark started with you."

"We need to talk."

Hobnobs and drinks before them, Penny and Eddie tried to spread out in Eddie's office, but it was so small they had to take turns in stretching.

"You're not looking forward to this, are you?"

"You can tell?"

"Subtle body language, Eddie. It's a giveaway, along with you telling me you couldn't be arsed."

"He's…I find it difficult to keep him motivated. I needed someone who would learn quickly and get on with it."

"Not everyone's a natural CSI."

"I know that. I was never expecting him to be, and I was always prepared to invest in him and bring him on. But his confidence is so low it's all I can do to stop him from resigning."

"Resigning? He was full on at his interview, how he wanted a job he could make a difference at."

"And you wonder why I'm not looking forward to this?"

"Scared he'll hand in his notice?"

He looked at her. "Yes, and scared he won't. I really want to give him another shot, but I don't have the energy to push him along constantly – even having two Weetabix doesn't help."

"You think now is a good time for humour?"

"Oh, shut up. Every time is a good time for humour, and I don't need a young whippersnapper from personnel, straight out of fucking school, to tell me when humour is appropriate, okay?"

She stared at him. "I am twenty-one, Eddie, not straight out of school. But you're right about the humour – I apologise."

Eddie blinked, never having won an argument with such ease before. He was buzzing.

"Have you tried a full English?"

He laughed, could see she was a natural – she'd calmed him down without him even knowing she was trying. He nodded at her, a sign of respect. "Twenty-one, my arse; you've got a wise old head on them young shoulders, missy."

"Enough of the pleasantries. Back to Mr Strange."

That took the smile off Eddie's face. He grew solemn again. "He needs a confidence boost, but I can't afford to wait, and if I'm being honest, I don't want to live under the constant threat of him resigning – I can't face going through the selection process again."

"You wouldn't have to, necessarily. You could offer it to one of the previous candidates."

"What? He was the best of a bad bunch, Penny."

Penny was quiet for a moment. "I don't get it; he had such potential; you loved him!"

"And he loved the job."

"So what's changed?"

That took Eddie by surprise. It was a question he ought to have asked but never had. "What's changed indeed," he said.

There was a knock at the door, and Sid peeped his head in. "Sorry to disturb you, but Mark's here. I've brought extra biscuits."

"And a defibrillator?"

"Were you a grandmother in a previous life, Sid?" said Penny.

"Don't be cheeky." Sid winked at Penny, stepped aside and Mark Strange, almost cowering, stepped in. To Eddie, Sid said, "Would you like me to bring a stool?"

"No, we're good."

Sid closed the door, and Eddie cleared the spare chair for Mark.

Mark sat, offered a quick polite smile at Penny, then studied his fidgeting hands.

"How do you feel after your first six months?"

"Good. Yeah, good."

Eddie cleared his throat and took a swig of coffee. "You were buzzing to get this job, you were burning. And now you're here, it's like you took a wrong turn, like you hate it."

Mark glanced up.

"You hate it here? Wait, is it *me*, do you clash with me?"

"No," he said. "That's not the issue."

"Ah, so there *is* an issue." He sat forward in his chair. "Is it the shifts? Is it working with Kenny – I can understand that, he does smell—"

"It's nothing like that."

"What then? Family problems?"

"No."

"What then?"

"Eddie," Penny said. She just looked at Eddie, a faint smile on her face.

Eddie nodded, sat back, folded his hands across his lap.

Eventually, Mark looked up. "I applied for the right job; I was convinced this was the one where I could give my all and get rewarded for it—"

"Ah, the wage is shit. I knew it!"

"Nothing to do with money, either." Mark swallowed and looked at Eddie with eyes that were a little too shimmery for someone who was alright. "I love everything about the job, and I love working here with you and the gang. I really do. But... I thought I'd be able to handle the job itself, but I can't."

"What do you mean, the job?"

Mark traced a finger over the arm of the chair and finally said, "I thought I could handle the number of dead bodies I got to see, but I'm struggling with it. I hate seeing the bodies of women beaten to death, the injuries they have. I hate seeing the bodies of kids thrown out of windows or hit by drugged up parents. Youths stabbed and shot. And suicides; I can't believe how many people are so sick of life that they would rather kill themselves – it's staggering how many people want out." He leaned forward, taking his fidgeting hands with him. "I can't handle seeing what people do to each other. I thought I could... but I can't." He looked at Penny, and across to Eddie. "I wasn't lying to you in my interview; I really did think I'd be good at this job, and I really wanted it, but. Well, it took us both by surprise."

Eddie stared at Penny. His eyes drifted across to Mark and then the floor. He'd never given it any consideration at all – none. That someone could be affected by the death of strangers. Right there and then he realised something quite profound: Mark Strange was normal.

Mark was right to be affected like this, and it made Eddie realise that he was numb to it. His dad always said that seeing so many dead bodies had turned him into a zombie, someone who spent so much time in the company of dead people he'd forgotten all about the living.

How could you surround yourself with the blood of murder victims and yet mingle with people who bought flowers for their partners? How could you photograph the handiwork of some angry druggy who'd taken a craft knife to his girlfriend, and then go home and criticise your father for burning another pan?

Out of the three people in this office – Eddie was the odd one out. Eddie was odd indeed.

He blinked, and brought his attention back to Skid. "This is a bit of a problem."

Mark nodded.

"It's obviously an integral part of the job. I can't remove it, and I can't protect you from it."

"I know."

"Is it why you wrote out your notice?"

Mark nodded. "I didn't want to. It's not a choice I took lightly, Eddie. I like it here, but it's messing with my head. Not in a good way."

"I get it," he said.

"Forgive my ignorance," Penny said, "but is it something you could grow accustomed to? Or, Eddie, is it something we could get him some help for, to reduce the impact?"

"My wife says it's changing me."

Eddie looked at him hopefully. "It can be a grind," he said. "But you do grow a hard skin against it. I'm not saying you ever get used to some of the sights we see, and there *is* counselling available after particularly bad jobs if it's something you think you could benefit from. But you should be aware that in order for you to function, you *will* change." With tight lips, he went on. "If you're not prepared to change – and I completely understand that you, that *anyone*, wouldn't think it worthwhile – then you'll never settle here."

"I don't want to change."

Eddie nodded. "I get it." He sighed, "Okay, stay for a month, to work your notice, and I'll give you peripheral scenes where there are no bodies. Okay?"

"I'm so sorry, Eddie. I didn't mean to mess you about."

"It's okay. You weren't to know. And for the record, I envy how normal you still are." Eddie leaned forward, extended a hand and shook. "Right, go on, piss off now while I find my hand sanitiser."

Mark smiled and closed the door softly behind him.

Penny said, "How do you do it?"

"I had my alcohol gel nearby all along, it was no big deal."

"No, I mean seeing dead bodies. Mangled bodies. Kids. Women. I'd never given it any thought before, but how do you do it?"

Eddie drank more coffee and demolished a brandysnap without taking his eyes off her. Then, as though the spell had broken, he reached up and opened the window, offered Penny a cigarette, and together, shoulder to shoulder, they kneeled on his desk, shared the window, and breathed smoke into the air. "I don't think about them."

"The bodies?"

"Yes, the bodies, that's what we were talking about, wasn't it?"

"Sorry, go on."

"If you wonder how that woman got bite marks all over her breasts and abdomen, if you wonder how her face got so smashed up that her eyes were punctured, that they'd swollen up to the size of tennis balls before he eventually finished her off. If you start to wonder how that kid had so many broken bones, or why that old man's head was practically hanging off… then it starts to mess with you.

"Skid is right; it's not natural to work among these people and come away unaffected. The worst thing you can do is stop thinking about the job and start wondering how painful their last hours were. The worst thing you can do is to start listening to the screaming and the howling, wondering why no one came to their rescue before things got so bad that death was a blessing for them.

"People truly are horrific creatures, Penny. And it's a horrible world."

"So how do you cope?"

"Being mad helps."

She smiled.

He didn't. "You really need self-discipline in massive amounts. You need to look at a body and process it as a forensic exhibit, not a person, not a bundle of suffering and pain. You can't dwell on the circumstances that brought them to be a broken body or a forensic exhibit. These people never dreamed they would end up being a part of a CSI's day; they were looking forward to their fish and chips, or they were dreading school on Monday, or they were worried about their wife, and then life happened to them. Death happened to them. You can't afford to dwell on it.

"We don't all have the good fortune to find the exit and leave this job. For most of us, it grabs you, changes you, and makes you useless at anything else. Until this is all you know; it turns you into something quite different. Mark is unusual in that he recognised what was happening to him and got the hell out before he became a person with no feelings. I admire him for that."

"You do?"

"What's the alternative? Being someone like me, I suppose. And who in their right mind would want that?"

Penny was back in the main CSI office when Eddie walked in to share a last brandysnap with her.

"Will you sponsor me, Penny?" Sid asked. "Sponsored walk."

"You'd make more if you did a sponsored silence," Eddie said. "A shitload more."

Penny laughed. "I'll do it; I'm flush this month."

"Oh yeah, lottery win?"

"Trust fund matured. I'm taking a year off work and just travelling. I can't wait to see the world before I become an old spinster."

Eddie wasn't wearing a smile, but the neutral stance on his face changed slightly and became tense, like his subconscious had latched onto something and was analysing it for all it was worth. "Very nice," he said. "You'll be taking me with you, then?"

"I don't think it'll get two people round the world. Eight grand won't go that far, these days. Interest is a bit poor, too."

Benson was standing in the doorway, listening to the conversation. He looked rigid, almost scared.

Eddie was deep in thought, lost a shade or two of colour, but smiled as he asked, "You just matured into an eight grand trust fund?"

She laughed, "Keep your sticky fingers off, Eddie."

"I'm really happy for you, kid."

"Eddie," Benson waved Eddie over, licked his lips.

"Look at you," Eddie said, "in your suave suit. You making a play for Regan or something?" Eddie was grinning, but it was a façade; far beneath it he was miles away, decades away where families crossed each other, and the futures of kids were swapped for money. He thought about Alex and how she'd been bought by his mum, how she'd been told to fuck off and have an abortion – here's eight grand, have a good time.

Yes, Eddie was smiling, but inside his analysis had stopped and he had hit the pause button before it could reach a conclusion. He daren't press play again, he daren't know for sure, but he was screaming, and his heart was breaking all over again.

"I…" Benson's eyes flicked between Eddie and Penny.

"What's up?"

"Yes, I was making a play for Regan." He swallowed, gave birth to a nervous smile. "I thought I'd rediscover my youth, see if I still had what it takes. Do you like the shoes?"

"Seriously?"

"How ridiculous, right?" Another lizard-like flick of the tongue over dry lips. "Don't be stupid. I have a job for you. An address to examine."

"Okay, I'm on my way." Eddie's eyes were on Benson, but his mind was on Penny. He turned to her as he walked from the office. "When do you leave?"

"Tomorrow," she said. "This is my last stop before I leave."

"How come you didn't tell me?" His voice was tipped with anger, and when he realised that anger had turned heads, he defused it with a grin, and pointed a finger pistol at her. "Safe journey." Once out of the office his face turned to stone.

Chapter 30

Miriam looked up as Benson came into her office. "You look like you've seen a ghost."

Benson hushed her just as Eddie entered.

"What's up?" Eddie looked from one to the other as they exchanged glances – confused on Miriam's behalf, and embarrassed on Benson's. "Something going on I don't know about?"

"No, it's okay, let's get going on these addresses."

Eddie stood there, feeling like the odd one out again. "This is the second time today I've felt like I'm the outsider peering in at someone else's life. Care to share?" He was looking at Miriam.

"I have not the faintest idea what you're talking about."

"Tom?"

Benson stared at Eddie.

Benson's face was blank but his eyes were on fire, burning up with a lie he couldn't escape from, and Eddie could see it a mile off. He folded his arms.

Benson cleared his throat. "I want you to put a good word in for me. With Regan, I mean."

Eddie switched from one foot to the other. Again, he studied both their faces. Something was off here, and he discovered how bad Tom Benson was at telling lies. You'd have thought with all his years in CID he'd be excellent at it. "I think you're both full of shit and if you don't start talking soon, then you can examine your own fucking addresses. Clear?"

"I mean it. I've asked Miriam, and she has agreed to lend a hand."

Miriam's face said otherwise; she didn't have a clue what was going on.

Eddie sighed. "Last chance, you dick. Explain why I feel like I'm being kept in the dark *without* lying to me. As if you're stupid enough to lay your life and your pension on the line for a bit of skirt like Regan. Seriously, you've got more chance of hooking up with Miriam than you have Regan. So cut the shit."

Benson looked at Miriam, and his eyes twitched ever so slightly.

Eddie noticed it, and a small smile grew on his lips. He suddenly knew why Benson was behaving weirdly. He was making a play alright, but it was for Miriam, not Regan. He didn't pretend to understand what shite was curdling Benson's mind, but he understood what he was aiming for, and chose to cut him some slack. "Okay," he said, "enough with the juvenile bollocks. Sort out your own love lives, I'm not stupid and I'm not cupid, okay? But make sure you wear protection, we don't want any little Bensons running around the place, and we don't want Miriam walking sideways." He winked and touched the side of his nose, "Little clue for you there, Miriam."

Miriam blew air through her lips. "I like how everyone here thinks I'm such an easy catch."

"Okay, you two lovebirds, if there's nothing pressing, I'm going for a bikini wax," Eddie almost left before Benson dragged him back.

"Two addresses," he said. "I need them checking over today."

"The first one is in Beeston," Miriam said. "We have a strong connection with the Mia Chandler murder, and his name is Vincent Lightowler; he used to be her boyfriend, and he was known for being abusive. This is his home address, and we want it screening for secondary transfer."

"Okay, I can do that. What else?"

"He's been known to shack up with a young lass called Daisy Wilson. She has an address in Armley, but we suspect she spends most of her time in Beeston, and we need it screening too. Both houses are empty – cops broke in this morning, found nothing of interest. We're wondering if they've both left Leeds altogether."

"If he's a suspect for Mia's death, he's a suspect for Marshall's death, as well."

Benson nodded. "He is."

"Where does he work?"

"He was fired from a supermarket recently."

"Fired? What did he do?"

"Had an argument with one of the assistant managers and shoved his head through a freezer display door."

Eddie gave it some thought. "I like it. It's original, at least." He unfolded his arms and propped himself on Miriam's desk with his fists, looked at them both and said, "Mia has been dead, what, four days? And it's taken you this long to get round to the boyfriends?"

"We've been looking into other boyfriends, and her parents, and work colleagues, so wind your neck in – there's a lot of work to do—"

"But surely, you'd start with the fucking nutjobs first, wouldn't you?"

Benson licked his lips again. "There's a lot of nutjobs out there, Eddie."

"There's more than a few in here, too!"

When Eddie left the office, Miriam said, "Do you want to tell me what the hell all that was about?"

"Oh, the Regan thing?"

"Yes, the bloody Regan thing, and the 'you have more chance with Miriam' thing too."

"There's a young lass called Penelope, Penny, in Eddie's office. I think she works for personnel or something."

Miriam listened.

"She was telling everyone that she's just turned twenty-one and her trust fund has matured. Her trust fund was for eight thousand pounds."

Miriam blinked, and her gaze left Benson and travelled into a daydream that was something like a year old, where she and Benson were sitting at this very desk. Back then she'd discovered that Eddie's estranged girlfriend, a girl called Alex, had given her baby up for adoption, and set up a trust fund for it. She set up the fund with eight grand that Eddie's mum bought her off with. The baby's name was Penny.

Benson checked over his shoulder to make sure they were still alone. "What are we going to do?"

"It was none of our business a year ago, and it's still none of our business, Tom. If I hadn't done some digging back then to find out who Alex was, we would never have known. And I've already smashed data protection by telling you about it."

"I know that. But sometimes data protection laws are protecting nothing but fresh air. Sometimes you have to break these laws to…"

"To what?"

"To do the right thing."

"What gives you the right to determine what is right for Eddie or for this Penny girl?"

"I know that. But what if he makes a move on her, for example?"

"You think that's likely?"

"No, I don't. But still."

"Okay, we'll cross that bridge if 'but still' comes true," Miriam said.

"Could be too late before we're aware of it."

"She's twenty-one. He's in his forties? It's not highly likely, is it?"

Benson shrugged. "Why? Why can't a man flex his muscles once in a while? Why can't he still be attractive to younger women?"

Miriam stared at him, mouth open, eyes half covered by a frown. Calmly, she said, "I get what you're saying, Tom. But have you ever heard the term, just friends? She might not want any romantic involvement."

"But there's always the chance she does. He was a good-looking fellow at one time. Eddie, I mean. He still has a lot to offer a woman."

She took a breath, breathed it out loud through her nose. "I agree entirely."

"You do?"

"Yes. But he has to realise that she might not be looking for that kind of relationship, she might have just come from that kind of relationship. She might not want an older man, even one that dresses younger, that acts younger, or one that behaves like a gentleman, and dresses sharp." She looked at Benson, looked *into* him.

Benson held her gaze for a moment and then glanced away, somehow defeated, cheeks throbbing as he ground his teeth. "We're still talking about Eddie here, aren't we?"

"Who else?"

He shrugged again, his shoulders hadn't worked this hard since he was a youth, and continued watching the carpet. From beneath the gap under Miriam's desk, he could see her legs were crossed, and the foot that was airborne moved. It was her heartbeat that rocked the foot up and down. He stared, and then he closed his eyes.

"You have a wonderful wife, Tom. You have your future planned out, pension, and a good salary right now. You are a very attractive man with a lot going for you. But you don't want to throw away thirty years of wonderful history with Brenda on the chance of some younger woman thinking you're still the dog's bollocks."

He nodded, embarrassed.

"You have nothing to prove – certainly nothing worth risking your history on. Or your future. You're a hell of a catch, Tom. I mean that, I'm not just saying it. But live within your own generation, and be happy with the decisions you've made up to now. You've arrived here at this point after lots of careful deliberating and lots of luck. But think on it now, don't play the lottery with your future; it's so not worth it."

"How would you know?"

She smiled. "I played. I lost, and I had to start over. It's not easy starting from scratch when you're already twenty-odd years down a specific path. You feel like you've got a lot of ground to make up, and try as you might, time goes by too fast and you find yourself lost belonging neither to one generation nor another, swimming like hell to keep up with the younger generation, fearful of floating into the arms of the older one, and all the while there's an undercurrent waiting to drag you to your grave. It's hectic in those waters, Tom. Stick with the things you've got. Be happy in the knowledge that you are a fine man, indeed, with nothing to prove to anyone."

Chapter 31

"How's your back?"

Sid grimaced slightly, leaned forward, "I don't think there's permanent damage, but it clicks when I do the pelvic thrust." He winked, and then laughed with Charles. "How did you get on with the laptop?"

"You can use it without a mains cable – I didn't know that! So I can use it in bed."

"Just don't ever use it in the bath, okay?"

There was a moment's pause before Charles said, "Thank you, Sid. You did me a great favour."

"It was my pleasure. And thanks for the cheque, but you really will have to drag yourself into the modern era sometime soon. Cheques will be obsolete before long, I would think." Sid sipped his tea. "Well, did he take the piss out of you?"

"Haven't told him yet. I'm just too afraid he'll yell something childish at me, and if he does it'll stop me writing. I'm finding it all difficult enough as it is without getting bad reviews before I've started."

Sid nodded, rested a hand on Charles's. "Want me to have a word with him?"

"No," he said, "I want to see his reaction, his genuine reaction. I'll take it from there. I mean, there's nothing to stop me doing all my writing in the library." He took a moment and smiled across at Sid, "The library that holds nothing for our place at all."

Sid sat back and thought about it. "If it's fiction you're working on, being totally accurate doesn't matter."

"I know, I know. I just wanted to find out as much as I could, you know add some real details."

"Have you tried the internet?"

Charles laughed, "No, no internet. Not since my old laptop blew up."

"It blew up?"

There was a silence.

"Charles?"

"When I say it blew up, I mean I was looking at some recipes and I accidentally left it on the stove while the gas was still on. It kind of caught fire a bit."

Sid almost fell off his chair laughing, and Charles laughed too.

"Eddie didn't laugh much," he said. "He had a bugger of a job trying to get the melted plastic off the pan support thingies."

Sid laughed louder. Eventually, he calmed enough to say, "So, tell me what your story is all about?"

Chapter 32

THERE WAS A LOT to be said for the community housing in Beeston. Back in the day, terraces were constructed quickly and cheaply, a whole village to house workers and their families when Leeds was prosperous, thriving, an economic centre of the North booming because of the mills and the mines and metal works. The houses were solid, like the men who lived there, clean because people took pride in them, scrubbing their steps every Monday, and bulling the stove every Tuesday.

But a century later, they looked dated, they were run-down, in need of renovation, and there was no boom to pay for it; the mines were gone, the mills and the metal works were half a world away. Beeston slid into decay, and the modern slum was born.

The house on the Beeston-Holbeck border crumbled and flaked. There was no saving it; it would crumble and flake until it fell down or until it was bulldozed to make way for modern housing. There were weeds growing out of the gutters; badly spelled graffiti adorned each wall and, room permitting, was always topped by a penis or a pair of boobs.

Broken windows, boarded windows, leaking fall-pipes, dead furniture scattered around the streets with litter spinning in the wind, a backdrop for kids playing football with a used nappy, or the little girl crying because her dad hocked her stolen Nintendo for an armful.

These were the natural surroundings of the junkies who lived here; benefit-zombies who would never clean their steps or bull the stove, irrespective of the day of the week. These were people with missing teeth; the lady's tits falling out as she staggered next to her man, a man whose arse was almost all the way out of his tracksuit bottoms. Together they shuffled along piss-covered pavements littered with their own kids who had as much chance of making it to maturity with functioning brain cells as they did of understanding differentiation or calculus. This was a something-for-nothing world where pride was snatched away by white powder or a syringe.

Kenny ignored the surroundings, and instead looked at Mark and said, "So even after all these months you never managed to get him to call you by your name?"

Mark shook his head. "I'll always be Skid to him. A skid mark on the lavatory of life." There was an ironic smile.

"What?"

"Nothing."

"Come on. Out with it. Has he been a dick to you, told you off for snoring in your lunch break? What?"

Mark took a long breath, and eventually said. "I've resigned."

Kenny smiled, nodded. "Yeah, very good. We all like a giggle at Uncle Kenny's expense, don't we. Now, what's really happened?"

Both suited up at the back of Kenny's van, a scene guard hovering nearby, kids stopping to stare at people working for a living, boy-racers with loud exhausts disturbed the peace for ten minutes while they were stuck in traffic.

They gave their details, and the scene guard made a note of their arrival time.

"Seriously, what's happened?"

"I've handed in my notice. I've agreed to work scenes like this till I leave."

Kenny halted on his way to the front door, he turned to Mark and looked into his eyes, searching for the jest which surely lurked there. He saw none. "You are serious, aren't you?"

Mark nodded.

"Why?"

The kids watched them.

"Let's go inside."

They closed the door behind them and stood in a lounge which was not carpeted, where damp and mould had pushed the wallpaper off so it hung in ragged sheets. There was a seventy-inch TV nailed to the chimney breast and a latticework of cobwebs spanned the gap, pulsing in a breeze. A coffee table full of cigarette ash and cannabis grinders and puffer pipes paid homage to the new God, a mind-altering altar. It stank of cannabis in here.

"Go on, then."

Mark blew through loose lips, reluctant to share. "It's my fault, really." He blinked, "I can't deal with dead bodies."

Kenny folded his arms and squinted at the lad. "You are taking the piss. There comes a time when it's polite to have your giggle at the old boys' expense and then admit to your tomfoolery."

"Kenny. I'm serious. I don't like dead bodies."

"Well, I mean, even I couldn't eat a full one." He paused, waiting for the laughing to start, but it never came. "You really *are* serious, aren't you? Can't deal with the gruesome stuff, eh?" Kenny subconsciously took a step away from the lad, distancing himself from a person who pretty soon would be on the outside of their elite little group. "Well," he said as a form of placation, "it's not for everyone, is it? I know it can be quite unpleasant sometimes. One of my worst was slipping on some kid's brains and landing on my arse in the body cavity." He was smiling at the memory.

Mark was not, Mark wore an involuntary sneer.

"So what will you do, how will you earn your daily bread?"

"Probably go back to being a PCSO."

"Never appealed to me, didn't that. Not that or coppering either – you're just a punch bag for the statisticians and your sergeants, and you're a punchbag for the public, too, especially them balaclava-wearing arseholes on stolen motorbikes. I'd get done for murder within a week."

"Can we just get on with this?"

"Sure we can."

"So this house belongs to Vincent Lightowler?"

"You got it." Kenny said.

"So, we're looking for secondary transfer. That is, if he's got their blood on his hands, and he touches something here, yeah? So if we find red stain, we'll need to swab it, and hopefully it'll come back as one or both of his victims, and if it's in his ridge detail, so much the better – a direct and positive link. It'll be good evidence to go with what we already have."

"And what do we already have?"

Kenny shrugged. "You'll need to speak with Eddie or one of the CID lot for that info. I just do as I'm told, mate. I like to keep things simple – they give me instructions and I follow 'em."

"So we just screen door handles and light switches?"

"Yep. And taps, too. Toilet flush lever, I suppose. We've got these and another two floors above us, okay, so we'll be here a couple of hours just screening. Not point in going in the cellar, there's no sinks or anything down there, but I'll do the cellar door handle and the kitchen taps. If we find any blood, it'll probably knock us into overtime, which ain't no bad thing considering my overdraft." Kenny moved to the door. "I'll go grab the KM kit and some brown paper; you start on quartering each room. Back in a jiffy."

And he was gone.

Mark looked at the camera bag and the Nikon camera inside it. "Quarter each room. Right." He assembled the wide-angle lens onto the camera, slid the flash onto the hot shoe, moved the camera bag out of the way in the kitchen, noting how badly it stank of faeces in there, and then took a photograph of the lounge from each corner getting as much detail as he could into each shot. This was quartering.

He did this on the ground floor, the bedroom and bathroom on the first floor, and both attic bedrooms. The higher he climbed the more the place smelled of damp and he wouldn't mind betting this would be a health hazard in winter – cold and damp, mould running rampant, and Daisy would have the electric fire on in the lounge only. Eventually it'd be too uncomfortable to sleep anywhere else but in there, too. The thought of it made him shudder.

Once all the rooms had been quartered, he came back down into the lounge, panting, to see Kenny erecting a small work table, and covering it in a sheet of brown paper. He laid out two pots of chemicals: a plastic bottle of Kastle-Mayer reagent and a bottle of hydrogen peroxide, collectively known as a KM kit. Alongside he threw a box of filter papers. "You done this before?"

Mark shook his head. "Never needed to."

"Fair enough. You take a filter paper, rub it lightly across a door handle or a light switch, whatever it is you're testing – once you're satisfied there's no ridge detail in blood. Bring the paper back here and lay it on a clean part of brown paper. Use the KM first, right, and let a single drop, two at the most, fall onto the filter paper, and add a drop of hydrogen peroxide. If the paper turns pink immediately, you've got blood, see? This is a reagent, and it reacts to proteins in blood. Voila. If it doesn't turn pink straight away, it's negative, move on. Okay?"

Mark nodded.

"Great. You can start at the top seeing as your legs are a few years younger than mine. Take three or four papers with you, write on them the location you're screening, and then bring them back here and test them."

"And if it turns pink?"

"Go and photograph the location. Try to get your exhibit number in the shot. Use a wet swab to mop up the blood from whatever gave you the result. This KM kit is only to detect the presence of blood, the lab can't do anything with it, they need a swab loaded with as much blood as you can, okay?"

Chapter 33

While Mark was taking a lesson on screening from Kenny, Eddie leaned against his van, smoking, and watching some fat man flying a drone with a camera slung under its belly. It reminded him of his agreement to let Fooky Nell follow him around during a murder investigation. Eddie shrugged and put the drone and Fooky out of his mind.

Edinburgh Walk in Armley was once the classic leafy suburb that would have been much sought after when it was built in Victorian times. Now it was a shithole that people ached to leave behind.

Seventeen was a mid-terraced house with a couple of steps leading up to a wooden front door that had been in desperate need of new paint about twenty years ago; now it was powdery and peppered with beetle holes and damp.

The dwelling was typical of most of the terraced houses around here: they were split into flats. The landlords were on a great deal, and they maximised any space in these houses to cram as many people on the Social in there as possible. The Social paid nearly six hundred per calendar month for each tenant. Split these big old houses up and one building could net over fifty grand per year. And they spent next to nothing on their upkeep.

The only way things would ever change is if the local government engaged in slum clearance work, and served compulsory purchase paperwork on the landlord – every landlord's wet dream because the government paid top-dollar for what was essentially a shithole that was going to start costing them money.

It started to rain. Eddie tossed the cigarette end and stepped inside with the camera already set up. He quartered the single room that Daisy lived in. If this was a television drama, he thought, the wall would be covered in occult shit, there'd be candles and pentagrams everywhere. But it wasn't a drama, it was the sad and lonely existence of a woman who succumbed to her demons – whatever they were labelled – and who tried to get through each day. Sometimes, because of those demons, getting through each day meant hurting herself, no doubt. It was sad, no matter which angle you viewed the story from.

One thing was for sure; there would be no winners.

And if it were smellovision, people would swap channels in their droves. It stank of damp and piss in here – not a great combo. "She needs Febreze," Eddie mumbled.

The walls were pretty much bare. The floor was just an ashtray with a filthy single mattress on it, and the rest of that wall was taken up by four pairs of trainers arranged just so, half an inch gap between each pair, laces tucked away neatly inside. There were two large screws sticking out of the wall with something like a washing line strung between them; this was Daisy's wardrobe, it's where her leggings were hung, and her t-shirts draped.

In the corner was a tiny fridge. There was one bottle of Stella in it, and a bottle of something that used to be milk, but which now had separated into layers of curds and whey. And that was pretty much a metaphor for humanity: how it was made up of constituent parts that are bound together, but under the wrong conditions those binds break and the ugliness surfaces. It's what had happened to Vincent Lightowler and probably to Daisy as well.

It was a room you could pluck from any one of three thousand homes across Leeds, hundreds of thousands of homes across England.

"I like to see a man deep in thought."

Eddie jumped and the camera smacked him in the face.

"Ooops."

He rubbed his face, and sighed. "I didn't know you were coming here. What the hell do you want? I nearly knocked my teeth out, then."

"Well, it's lovely to see you too, darling."

"I have work to do."

"Me too." She smiled. "Were you busy doing your 'seeing' thing?"

Eddie set up his table, draped brown paper across it. He opened two bottles of chemicals and Regan stood at its side, arms folded, the brown leather jacket she wore creaking. He closed his eyes for a moment, and exactly ten seconds later he opened them again.

"I'm annoying you, aren't I?"

"See, this is why you're a detective."

"I heard that one of your CSIs doesn't like dead bodies."

"It seems you are infectious – he was fine with them until you joined. I only have two CSIs; it's not exactly an ensemble cast. In fact, I might move my office into the main CSI office, and Kenny – he's the one remaining CSI I have, can have the poky little broom cupboard they gave me as an office."

"Why don't you just move into the main office, anyway?"

"Because I'd have to listen to Sid moaning about the cost of nail polish, and Kenny grumbling that there was no decent totty on *Strictly Come Dancing* any more. *And* he has a problem with wind."

"So you're soon to be in charge of a department with only one CSI."

"And an admin assistant. Yes. Luckily, I like small teams."

Regan fidgeted with her fingers. "How will you manage, just you and the old guy."

"Kenny. He's very competent. We'll manage until I can get someone else. Preferably two someone elses."

Her arms dropped to her sides, and she said, "I wanted to apologise about the briefing. I didn't mean to put you on the spot like that. Well, I did, but I didn't know you'd be uncomfortable about it. If that makes sense."

"It seems these days the human condition is experiencing serious health issues. In days gone by, no one would have given a shit whether you or Skid hated dead bodies – you'd be forced to get on with it and endure them. Same for me and my… for my dislike of the spotlight. I'd have been made to give that presentation."

"Not now, eh?"

"No. Not now. Now I just walk out."

"In the olden days you'd have been flogged for that!"

Eddie laughed. "I would. People are very understanding. Doesn't stop me disliking them, though."

"Me included in that."

Eddie paused and tried to study her. She was complicated, and the lack of light in this room did little to help reveal her true self or her thoughts. That said, even if he had a couple of spotlights in here, he wouldn't be able to fathom her – or anyone for that matter. Reading people was not one of Eddie's strong points. "I don't know you, Regan. My bravado hasn't had a chance to develop with you yet. Once I'm used to you, I'll abuse you like I do everyone else. But for now, because you're new, I'll just keep my distance and mock you from afar."

"If you keep your distance, you'll never get to know me." Her eyes glistened.

Eddie suddenly felt uncomfortable. Perhaps he *could* read her. "Look, I have seen that look before and I'm not up for it, okay?"

"What look?"

"The puppy-dog-eyes look."

"I see. Are you... are you gay?"

"Just because I don't want to leap into bed with you? I'm just sensible, that's all. My old man used to say if it's got wheels or tits, it's nothing but trouble." He paused, "Actually, he didn't say that at all – I did. Women are trouble, people are trouble, relationships are nothing but trouble. I prefer to be with the one person I know won't fuck me over: me."

"No one mentioned a relationship, Eddie."

"Really? Well that includes sharing bodily fluids, okay. Leave me the hell alone, woman."

She held out her hands. "You are fucking prickly."

"Listen, Regan; if you're after a fella, I know one who'll lay flowers at your feet and be really good company. But it's not me, okay?"

She squinted at him. "Really? Who?"

Eddie grinned, "You not worked it out yet?"

"You're not talking about Tom Benson, are you?"

Eddie winked and shrugged.

"Seriously? Come on. He's old enough to be my granddad."

On Benson's behalf, Eddie felt a little hurt. "He still has a lot to offer."

"Like a wife, you mean? Or a will, maybe?"

"Anyway, it's none of my business. I know that he's put in a lot of effort recently, to smarten himself up. And I figure he's doing it for you."

"Nonsense. He's been awful to work with, always having a pop at me – don't chew gum, don't call me boss."

Eddie smiled. "For a detective, you have a lot to learn. Don't you remember in the school yard, how the kid who fancied you the most hit you on the arm the hardest?"

Regan looked away, thinking about it. "He's a sweet man. But..." She shook her head. "I have work to do while I'm here, too."

"Good."

She was about to leave but turned to face him. "You know, it really pisses me off that men see a single woman and jump to conclusions that she must be longing for a man, any man, just so long as he has a pulse and a dick. Well I have news for you, darling, you're fucking wrong. I'm more than happy being alone." She cleared her throat, stepped closer, and gently smiled. "But thank you."

"Hang about," he said, "*you* were chatting *me* up, remember? *That* was jumping to conclusions. And now you're pissed off because you're not used to being rejected... by a straight man." He felt like applauding her, and resisted the temptation to laugh at her – and he only did that because it would have been cruel, laughing when someone puts their soul out there for examination. He just stood there with a wonky smile zigzagging across his face.

"Could I borrow a pen?"

Eddie stared at her. It had been a thoroughly shit day, and all he wanted to do was piss off home and sink a beer. He puckered a sigh out the side of his mouth and glared at the sky through the shit on Vincent's lounge window. "This has been the worst summer I've ever experienced."

"Say what?"

"We had three hot days. Before then, and since, the house has been full of wet clothes hanging off the radiators and the curtain poles. The windows are always steamed up because of wet fucking clothing."

He waited for the typical nod that comes with commenting on the unpleasantness of persistently bad English weather.

Instead she blinked at him like a confused pigeon and asked again, "Could I borrow your pen?" She swallowed and Eddie noted the confusion on her face. "I promise it's not a trick question. I can go and ask someone else if you like?"

"Where's *your* pen?"

She shrugged. "If I knew that, I wouldn't be asking to use yours. Now," she stepped forward, "all I want to know is if I can borrow a pen. It's not that complicated. Is it? Really?"

Eddie said, "Go on, then."

"See, it wasn't that difficult, was it?" She held out her hand. "Well?"

"No, I mean go on and borrow someone else's pen."

"What? Seriously?"

Eddie bent slightly. "You've already displayed an inability to look after your own pen; what chance would mine stand? Anyway, I'm using my pen."

She turned and walked off, "You're fucking crazy, you know that?"

"Hey."

She stopped and turned, hands on hips. "What?"

"I have a spare pen that you can use." He produced a shiny black Bic from a clip on the spine of his folder. "Never been used." He smiled.

She clicked her fingers, "Tell you what, fuck you!" and she walked away.

Eddie stared after her, slightly perturbed but buoyed by the fact she'd finally left him in peace. "Not crazy," he said. "For the most part."

It didn't take him long to forget all about Regan and to screen the place – a couple of door handles, the window latch, and the taps in the tiny sink against the back wall.

This was Vincent Lightowler's house, this is where his crazy mind had its crazy thoughts, and it's where he planned his crazy deeds, and Eddie hoped that, now the screening was out of the way – with negative result – there might be something else around here that could point to that craziness, something like a plan, preferably written down and signed.

The so-called kitchen had one drawer with cutlery inside. One fork, a knife, and a spoon. And just for those special occasions, there was a steak knife with the top three-quarters of an inch missing. There were a couple of wooden spoons and a spatula. There were three pans, one of them a frying pan, and there was a single plate. He stared at them all – this man's possessions, and thought how sad it was. Genuinely sad.

Vincent had once been fairly high up in electrical retail, verging on area manager-status, even, and staying sharp thanks to energy drinks and focussed thanks to the odd hit of amphet. But then, along came the modern-day equivalent of the old lady with an apple, the witch in *Sleeping Beauty*, no less. So many people ate that bastard apple, and so many good people turned bad because of it, had to find money for more of that apple every single day of their short lives. Vincent had been one of them, graduating to heroin with crack as a treat on Sundays, and it was like he'd thrown the dice and landed on a snake's head, sliding all the way to the bottom of the board and this shithole without a pot to piss in was his prize.

When he'd just about given up searching, Eddie sat down on the arm of Vincent's tip-rescued chair and thought about it. He'd been tasked with screening two addresses because Benson thought Vincent was guilty of murdering his ex-girlfriend, Mia Chandler, and a kid called Marshall Forbes. Now Vincent and his current girlfriend, Daisy whatserface were nowhere to be found.

On the surface, everything pointed to Vincent being guilty – especially his absence. But what if he wasn't guilty? Everyone loved jumping to conclusions because it was a fucking sport, it was easy and it was what made most jobs like this come to a speedy conclusion – and usually, he hoped, the correct one.

But what if it wasn't the right conclusion this time – like Regan's hadn't been: assuming all men would lie at her feet and give her a hard-on upon request. What if Vincent's absence was just a coincidence. "Hate that word," he said. But what if it *was*, and we're all walking right over the truth because it blends in with the carpet. What if he had nothing to do with Marshall and Mia at all?

If that were the case, where should he start looking? Without that supposition, they were nowhere; the entire investigation had nothing to go on, no direction to take. And that was the saddest of conclusions. Eddie knew that when people signed up to the police these days, they were taught how to disregard bias and that everything they'd ever known about bias should be discarded and one should approach life with an open mind; that was the idea.

One approached a person and a scene open to all possibilities, and to have bias cloud one's thoughts only increased the possibility of being wrong, or of being discriminatory towards any person involved in your investigation. And that, in theory, would work wonderfully well except when someone is approaching you with a knife. He might be smiling at you, but he's going to stab you to death – and what good is an impartiality theory then? That's when you really needed bias.

Eddie Collins didn't practice bias eradication. He believed it saved lives – his in particular, and it served as the hunch that everyone talked about when it came to crime scenes and victims and suspects. Eddie worked by the values he always had: treat everyone as a victim until they proved themselves a suspect. Mostly. Everything had its exceptions.

But, if there was one, what was the exception here?

Chapter 34

Piggybacking on the West Yorkshire Police CSI system was a Major Crime Unit piece of software imaginatively called CSImages that allowed the transfer of scene images directly from the scene. They landed on a local server and so were instantly available to all members of the police community who had legitimate access.

Eddie had blown off the Armley job pretty quickly, and got back to the office in time to steal another spoonful of Kenny's coffee long before he and Skid walked back in. He'd exchanged pleasantries with Sid – altogether surreal in its own right, Sid was behaving very strangely, even more strangely than usual, shutting down some computer document or another as Eddie approached him – and buried himself in his own office, and fired up the pre-historic computer.

He scrolled through CSImages until he found the house that Skid and Kenny had screened, and thumbed through the images telling himself that it was too late to offer guidance on over-exposure here and camera movement there, and his pet hate, direct flash in all shots. It was while he was going through them all for the second time that he realised there must be some images missing.

He opened his office door and strode out into the main office just as Kenny walked in.

"Eddie," he said.

Eddie nodded at Kenny, and the coolness in Kenny's greeting wasn't lost on him. He supposed it was to be expected – Skid had a captive audience, and Kenny was fiercely protective of his colleagues, and so would have taken the kid's side. Fair enough, he thought, think what the fuck you like. Eddie walked to Sid and Sid hurriedly minimised something on his computer again. "What's that?"

"What's what?"

"Sid. I'm not stupid—"

Kenny laughed.

"—I know you're hiding something from me."

"I am not hiding anything from anyone."

Just then, Skid walked in, banging the camera bag against the door, and puffing out a big sigh. "We should have a lift in this building."

Eddie looked at him, then at Sid, and then at Kenny. "Six months he's been here. How come none of you have shown this dipshit where the fucking lift is?"

"I thought he knew," said Kenny.

"I thought he liked the stairs," said Sid.

"And I thought you had a phobia," Eddie said and then grinned.

"Very funny," said Skid to Eddie. "Phobia about lifts, phobia about dead bodies, yeah, that's just hilarious."

Eddie was confused. He pointed a finger at Skid, ready to explain himself, that it was an innocent turn of phrase, when Skid just grabbed his coat and walked past him, back out of the office, letting the door slam behind him. He looked at Sid and Kenny, and could not help laughing so hard that he got cramp in his ribs.

When the laughter died down, which didn't take too long because only Eddie had found it funny, he rubbed his ribs and turned to Kenny. "Just been looking at the images from the Beeston house you and Skid went to. Why didn't he make a mess of any shots in the cellar?"

Kenny shrugged, "Why would he?"

"I asked for all rooms to be covered."

"The cellar's not a room."

"Then what the fuck is it, Bamber?"

"Bamber?" asked Sid.

"Really? Bamber Gascoigne. *University Challenge* host."

"Never heard of him."

"Freak." He turned back to Kenny.

"I've never heard of him, either. I've never heard of *University Challenge*, come to think of it."

Eddie slapped his hands over his face. "I don't fucking care. I was trying to illustrate that the cellar is a room."

"Well it's not a room you live in, is it?"

"Noooo," Eddie said, "but nevertheless, it has four walls and floor, ergo, it's a fucking room!"

"I'm not arguing with you," Kenny switched on his computer. "Bamber Gascoigne my arse. Jesus."

"Ergo," said Sid. "What a wonderful word."

Eddie paused. He spun on his heels and pointed a finger at Sid, mouth open, ready to tear into him, when he realised he couldn't understand why. There was something strange going on here. Back to Kenny, he said, "Irrespective of whether a cellar is a room or not, and it most definitely *is*, and yes you could live in it, why did Skid not photograph it?"

"Well since you insulted him and he left, you can't actually ask him, can you?"

"I'm working with a bunch of morons, I swear, your IQ is smaller than your shoe size, both of you."

"I'd go back," said Kenny, "but it'd push me into overtime, and the missus wants servicing tonight, so we have a meal and foreplay planned. And you insulted me, too. No can obligio, amigo, as they say in Spain."

"You speak Spanish, Kenny?" asked Sid. "That's amazing—"

"It is considering he hasn't yet mastered fucking English," shouted Eddie. "I'll go and do it myself." He marched down the office, chuntering, "If you want a job doing right, do it yourself, Eddie. Bunch of fucking morons!"

Sid said, "I always fancied speaking Italian. It's such a romantic language."

Eddie stormed back up the office for his own camera kit. Sid and Kenny watched him. "Morons."

When he slammed the office door, Sid said, "Never fancied German much; it's very aggressive."

Chapter 35

Three and a half hours after Skid and Kenny had left this very spot, it was drawing dark when Eddie parked the van outside Vincent's address on Dalton Road in Beeston. He climbed out of the van, slammed the door, and was met by the scene guard. Eddie's heart sank; he recognised him from Mia's scene.

"Name."

Eddie blinked at him. "You'll have to remind me; my memory is shite."

The scene guard nodded slowly as if to say, here we go again, another joker who isn't funny.

It came to him, and Eddie clicked his fingers. "Hali. Halitosis! Colin. Am I right, am I right?"

"Very good. Now, what's your name?"

"The last time I saw you I was hoping it was the last time I saw you."

He shook his head. "Name. Please."

"Drew Peacock."

Hali squinted. "Drew Peacock?"

Eddie nodded.

Hali stared and began writing it down. "I'm sure it was... I know you."

"I have a very common face." Eddie grabbed the camera, and let himself into the house, laughing as he did.

"Wait a minute. Drew Peacock. As in droopy cock?"

Eddie closed the door to Vincent Lightowler's house.

"'Ere, I know you, you prick."

He'd studied the photographs so he knew what the other rooms looked like and despite what he thought were poor quality images, he had no intention of re-photographing the whole house. He set the camera bag down on a chair and hit the light switch at the side of the door. Nothing. It was dark in here, and even after hitting the switch a few more times, it remained dark. He put his lit torch down on the floor and assembled the camera, checking the settings before he picked up the torch and headed into the kitchen and the cellar head door.

The smell of shit hit him, and he wondered if the plumbing was a bit on the dodgy side. "Fucking landlords need flogging." He photographed the cellar head door; it had carrier bags hooked over the door knob, and was partially obscured by a shit-coloured fridge-freezer with cannabis leaf magnets on it.

Ammonia stung his nostrils as he swung the creaking door open. He understood why Skid hadn't bothered coming down here, but it angered him that he should have so little concern for a forensic strategy just because someone had emptied buckets of piss down here, or because the soil pipe was leaking. He hadn't even tried to do his job properly. It was time to stop being so lenient with him, so understanding. If there was one thing Eddie detested, it was people who cut corners.

Speaking of corners, Eddie hit the bottom step and turned a corner, the torch light illuminating the source of the smell.

Eddie stood there motionless, mouth open, eyes wide in disbelief. His heart chugged and his head grew heavy, like it was about to throw up and fall off.

He approached her. She was a young girl sitting naked on a wooden chair, tied there with bright yellow cable ties. Her hands were white, and her fingertips and toes had turned black. The poor girl was sitting in mounds of excrement, flies climbing all over it, piss leaking into the gaps between the flagstones beneath her purple feet. In her mouth was some kind of gag, and from her nostrils clear mucus had run and then solidified, crusted against her cheek as her head had lolled to one side.

As he reached for her head a spider crawled over her cheek and Eddie squealed and dropped the torch. "Fucking thing! Fucking spiders." He retrieved the torch and the spider had gone. Where the hell had the spider gone? Suddenly he itched everywhere, and when he looked closely at the girl, she opened her eyes and Eddie screamed again.

If this had happened to Skid, it would make his fear of bodies much more understandable.

"Daisy?"

She blinked, but it must have been painful; you could almost hear her eyelids grating over dry eyeballs. With gloved hands, Eddie pulled out the gag ball, and it was almost stuck solid, her saliva had turned to cement and glued it in place.

The first thing she did was scream. "My hands... my hands are killing me, pleeease."

Eddie shone the light on them and marvelled at how shiny and black her fingers were. Dead. "I can't untie you; I'll go get an ambulance."

"Why? Untie me, please, I can't feel my hands!"

"Stay there," and then he tutted at his choice of words, "I'll get help."

"Don't leave me," she slurred. "Where're you going? Stay! Help."

Eddie bounded up the stairs and ran outside. "Get a paramedic here now."

The scene guard turned to him. "What's up, Drew Peacock? Very funny, you almost had me there. Now, what's—"

"Get a fucking paramedic!"

"What's happened?"

"There's a girl down there, tied in a chair. Her hands and feet are dead."

"Quick, untie her."

"No, no, you can't do that. Just get a paramedic here and do it now."

"Why can't you untie her?"

Eddie grabbed his coat from the van. It was an excellent question, and at any other time he would have reached for his Gerber and sliced those cable ties and got that poor girl out of there – spiders or no spiders. But something he'd learned years ago, clambered to the front of his mind and waved furiously at him. "Potassium poisoning," he said. "If you cut the ties, she'll have a heart attack because of the potassium build-up pumping out of her hands and feet."

The scene guard looked at him like he'd just shit on a kitten.

"Fucking do it, now!" Eddie watched him get on his radio and then ran back inside, searching for a glass by torchlight, and filling it with tap water. He returned to Daisy, draped his coat around her shoulders, and made her drink the water. "You have to drink lots of water." He knew the worry on his face scared her.

"What's... what's the matter with me?"

He smiled but it was obviously fake. "We've got paramedics on the way for you, sweet. No need to worry." The smile again.

"Why, why can't you untie me? Why? What's happening to me?"

"They're on the way," Eddie turned to see Hali standing by the corner, his hand to his mouth, gagging at the smell. He held a small torch in his hand and shone it around, disturbed and disgusted by what he saw. "We need to get her out of here."

"She's been down here for days," Eddie rationalised. "A few more minutes won't hurt her. We wait for the paramedics. Okay?" Eddie stared at him to make sure the message got home. "Okay?"

"Fine." He nodded at the empty glass. "Why don't you go get her some more water?"

"Why don't you go back outside and guard the scene?"

"You said that to me once before, remember?" He put a hand on his hip. "Said you'd call me back in. You never did."

"You need dipping in Femfresh, you annoying, smelly c—"

"You said you'd call me!"

"This isn't the time." Eddie eyed him, and it clicked – Hali didn't just want to be in on something big, he wanted to be the hero – hence the stance.

"She needs water, man."

Eddie held out the glass to him. "Off you go."

"What's happening?" she whispered.

"I just don't get it, why you can't get blood back into her feet at least."

"Who else is there?" she asked. "Vince? Is that you?"

"I'm not arguing about it now in front of her, so go and get her some water."

Hali licked his lips, shone his light on the cable ties at her feet and looked up into Eddie's eyes.

"I don't believe you're contemplating what I think you're contemplating. It will kill her, now go and get her some fucking water."

Hali took a step forward, slowly reached out for the glass.

In the background, a siren split the night wide open, and Eddie had never been so relieved to hear it crack like that in his life. He breathed out, and relaxed a little. Hali ignored the glass and ran back up the steps, the grit under his boots scraping against stone. Eddie was more than happy for Hali to be the one leading them down here, pretending to be the one who found her. None of that shit mattered to Eddie, so long as the girl was okay; that's all that mattered.

Moments later there were voices, hurried voices, and more boots on the steps.

Eddie brought them some lighting from the van, and then went and waited outside, but before he left them to it, he leaned forward and whispered in Daisy's ear, "Who did this to you?"

Her drooping eyes widened a fraction, and she whispered back, "Vincent Lightowler."

"Where is he?"

She shrugged. "There was a knock at the door. He never came back."

The night was growing cold, and a small crowd had gathered outside the house and Eddie's van. He found it strange that they had thought Vincent and Daisy had run off together, and now this. Vince had left with someone, but he didn't think he'd meant to leave Daisy there for this long. Vincent had popped out, back in a minute, kind of thing. Instead he'd left for good. "Snatched." He closed his eyes and his sympathy lay with the poor girl in the fucking cellar. Who ties up a young girl naked and lets her soil herself, and then just leaves her? What is this world coming to?

He hoped the murder victims were getting their own back on him. But seriously, who would snatch him? Perhaps it had nothing to do with Mia's family or Marshall's family; perhaps Vincent Lightowler was in deep over his head in other business – drugs business – messing about in someone else's playground instead of sticking to what he knew.

Eddie opened his van door and perched on the seat, lit a cigarette and waited for the people to come to him and complain not that there was a dying girl in the cellar, not that the place was rife with drugs dealers and prostitutes, but that he was brazen enough to light a fucking cigarette in public and while there were kids around. Screw them.

"Can you spare one?"

He looked up to see a young woman standing before him, she was maybe eighteen, nineteen. She was so skinny you could put your fingers around her biceps and still have your fingertips touch each other. Her lips were cracked, and her hair was thin and ragged, long and black, clinging to her shoulders, greasy and yet frazzled too. Her fingernails once had red nail varnish on them, but it had chipped away so much there were only fragments of it left.

He reached inside the van for the packet and the lighter, and handed them both over to her. "Keep them," he whispered.

Her eyes lit up, and she had a superstar's smile. He wondered, for a fleeting moment, why she was living rough around here, why wasn't she a TV celebrity, or an actress, or a bishop, or a prime minister. Luck sometimes dealt the good a shitty hand.

She took one and lit it, savouring the flavour, letting the drug soak into her tired mind and ease the aches in her body. After a while, she opened her eyes. "Will she be alright? Daisy?"

He clamped his lips together, looked past her to the house where men shouted instructions, and from where a lone copper, the scene guard, stepped. He didn't look good, he pincered the bridge of his nose between a finger and thumb that trembled every bit as much as this young lady's had. "I'm not sure. I think we got here too late."

Her lips trembled. "Oh," she croaked. "That's bad. She was a lovely lass."

Eddie smiled at her, and almost reached out to her. But he didn't.

"I wish I'd known she was still in there when he left." She took a drag. "I would have—"

"When he left? Vincent? You saw him leave?"

She nodded.

"Was he alone?"

"No. Some fella called round. They were looking at Vincent's car."

"Vincent's... Which is his car?"

She nodded to an Audi. "That one. They were touching the front end."

"And then what?"

She bit her lip. "I dunno. I passed out."

"What did this other man look like? What was he driving?"

She shook her head. "I'm not good with details." The tears ran down her cheeks and she shivered out a sob. "I liked her, Daisy; she looked out for me."

"What's your name, sweet?"

The waif shook her head.

"You're not in bother, and no one's going to come knocking at your door."

"Just as well," she said, "I ain't got a door." She turned and began walking away.

"Hey."

She stopped, and looked back.

"Thank you. And what's your name?"

"You can call me Libby."

"You going to be alright?"

She nodded.

Eddie reached into his pocket and pulled out his wallet, but when he looked up again, she was gone.

Regan's face was washed with blue strobe lights. She blinked against it, but they were powerful, and eventually she turned away, forcing Eddie to spin around too.

"The number plates are stolen," she said. "The VIN comes back as an Audi that was stolen with keys last year in Adel, North Leeds."

"Can we get it lifted, get it under cover quick before it rains?"

"Already organised. Who's this kid you got your info from."

"She didn't give any details, just legged it." He stepped closer, "Do you smoke?"

"Why?"

"Because I could really use one right now."

"I'm supposed to have stopped." She handed him one.

"Got a light?"

"Got a pen?"

"Ah, touché," he smiled.

"It's lucky *you* found her."

"Me? Why's that?"

"If I'd found her, or your CSI had, or just about anyone else I can think of, she'd have died instantly, soon as they cut those cable ties."

"Her hands and feet were dead and were decaying. If you introduce a blood supply into them, it'll bring all that decay back into your body. It'll attack your kidneys and the shock will stop your heart."

"Well, at least she has a slim chance of living. Better than no chance at all."

"That's all some people have."

"Now's not the time to be so philosophical."

"Yeah, well, keep a guard on this place now and I'll get Kenny to do the cellar. He can have the fucking pleasure of the stench for not doing a proper job in the first place. I'll get on with the car first thing."

As he was walking away, she touched his arm. She looked up at him and said, almost as an afterthought it seemed, "Do you think this thing is finally going somewhere?"

"It feels like there's movement, yeah?"

She smiled, dropped her arm away. "Hope so."

Chapter 36

Sheila Chandler parked on the drive behind her husband's van. She wrestled with a bag of shopping. As she closed and locked her car door, the wind hit her square in the face, and then the despair followed it; just as hard, twice as cold. She looked up, squinting against the flecks of rain stinging her skin, and saw the silhouette of her house just as the security light blinked on and blinded her. She didn't need to see it to know that – no matter how cold it might be out here – inside would be colder.

She flicked the keys in her hand, and the one for the house presented itself just as she, and the wind, sighed against it all. She let herself in and closed the door behind her, eyes squeezed shut as she leaned back against it. She would not cry tonight. She had promised herself.

Thoughts of preparing a light meal skittered into her mind. Just the act of preparing something helped, and she knew Mike wouldn't have eaten. "Mike?"

The house was quiet, and it was empty; Clara would be at work. There was just that feeling of isolation and coldness here. "Mike!" she called again, not even expecting an answer. The kitchen light was on, the keys dangling from the lock in the back door. Shelia swallowed, "Oh God, no."

Once outside and shielded from the wind by the hedges and by the fence at the foot of the garden, she could hear what sounded like a kid sobbing. The light in the garage was on, and Shelia rushed across the wet grass and took hold of the door knob, knowing exactly what she'd find on the other side of it.

She hesitated; this would be the last moment in her life where she was an innocent party. She could choose to turn around now, and go stay at her mother's house, distancing herself from the hell that was inside here. She could remain outside looking in, watching the world eat the rest of her family, watching everything disappear into a black hole, leaving her sharing mother's table, her towels, and her opinions, waiting to die alone.

She opened the door, and the tears came.

Exhaustion had killed the anger.

It was unfair that it should peter out like that, stolen away by his fat unhealthy body, rather than the retribution he'd dreamed of for days. The anger had been pure, it was refined as though it had been through a still and was dripping into a bottle – a pure red hatred.

He panted, totally out of breath, lungs and heart labouring, face red, sweat dripping, hands shaking. The man's face was unrecognisable, but still Mike Chandler felt robbed of what was his by right: a life for a life. This man's life was small change, and the life it was matched against was a treasure trove, a lottery win in the millions – it didn't fit, it wasn't recompense enough, not by a long way.

The motivation anger had given him in the beginning had waned and keeled over the same time that exhaustion had stolen its way onto the stage and kicked anger off it.

It was so unfair.

And once he'd brought his breathing back under control, and his heart boomed at a rate more sustainable than the 150/170 it had been raging at for the last hour or more, he stared at his handiwork.

Mike had on a pair of his oldest and oiliest overalls, and he'd found an old respirator mask that was covered in blue spray paint from when he repaired that old Fiesta's door. He thought that and a pair of dusty goggles would suffice, that they would keep him clean.

They didn't, not by a long way. And even if they'd presented a physical barrier to this horror, his psyche was swimming in blood.

The man on the plastic sheet, still tied to eyelets in the concrete floor of his garage, didn't look much like a man any more. To begin with, he'd stripped him naked. And he'd taken out the Black and Decker hammer drill with the wire brush attachment. He'd taken out a half-pound hammer, too. And over the course of an hour, he'd turned a thirty-year-old male into a pretty well tenderised six-foot steak. Of course, it was still crunchy on account of the all the bones sticking out, but he'd given it all a damned good go.

"I have no sympathy. You brought it on yourself."

Mike had kept him conscious for as long as possible, and he'd suffered some fantastic injuries before his heart had eventually given out. It had been a revelation to witness blood pouring from all those open wounds, and for it to suddenly cease flowing as the heart stopped pumping – strange. Fascinating.

"I didn't ask for any of this," he said.

Mike's hands trembled. The Black and Decker was covered in blood and meat, and it had started smoking as blood had found its way inside and shorted out the stator and rotor. The smell was horrific, like barbecuing gone-off meat, and Mike had to throw the drill across the garage to keep from retching. The hammer and the chisels were mounds of red shininess scattered across the floor.

He perched the blood-speckled goggles on top of his head, unclipped the respirator and let it fall. He took off the Marigold rubber gloves he'd stolen from under the kitchen sink and sat back against his bench, noting how his overall shone with blood now, not oil. His fingers were white and crinkly like they'd been immersed in sweat for too long.

His eyes settled on the barbecue against the far-right wall, a spare gas cannister next to it, and all the accoutrements on shelves above it: the pincers, the spatulas, the wire brushes, the skewers. He found himself smiling as he had in Mia's bedroom not so long back. Everything in this place had memories attached to them just as the barbecue had; wonderful family times where all he could clearly remember was laughter – great bellows of haughty laughter all afternoon long. It had cobwebs on it now, the barbecue. Not used since Mia moved out. And the memories, they had cobwebs on them too, were slowly fading away no matter how hard he grabbed at them. It wouldn't be long before even seeing these things didn't conjure up the memories attached to them any more. They'd just be things. Cold. Isolated.

Just like Mia.

And there, by the double up-and-over doors was her bike in among several – one each, a small trailer and a set of wardrobes. There was a couch and a dining suite, all things he'd got for her, but all things she didn't want. He smiled; what the hell should I do with them now? He was saving them for Clara now – if she ever decided to bloody move out.

Over his harsh breathing, Mike could hear the wind outside, and the windows – blacked-out with bin bags – rattled. Overhead the corrugated asbestos roof rattled too as the rain began to fall like an omen. Despite being hot and sweaty, he shivered, and scurried even further away from his handiwork. No amount of backing away could take the thing that once was Vincent Lightowler out of focus. It was there, sharp, steaming a little, but always in line of sight.

"It's your fucking fault!"

A slice of light arced under the garage door then, and he heard a motor, heard it stop. A car door opened and slammed shut; the light went out and the security light came on. Mike closed his eyes and tears ran down his face. His bottom lip curled out and his shoulders heaved. He sobbed like a kid, and he scooted back further, under his bench, pushing aside his big toolbox and finding comfort in the darkness and cobwebs, the discarded rags, bits of wood, sawdust.

But still the body was there, and what had been a road to salvation, a cure for his hatred, and a way to avenge her death had instead become a blood red mountain of a problem. It hadn't been a cure, after all; it hadn't put right his daughter's death. All the promises made by anger and retribution as they huddled in a corner with their backs to him, snatching glances over their shoulders and nodding as he looked on hopefully for them to provide a way out. They had come to him with open arms, smiling, promising to put an end to the pain, promising to make things right again, just the way they were. They promised. They promised.

"They promised me!"

Once he was dead, once he had gone and left a pile of red meat, it would all be over. Mike wanted to reach Vincent's mind through his body, but when his body died, the mind did too; there was just no way to reach it. It seemed like such a bad deal, like the bastard had escaped before the sentence had been carried out it. He cheated.

Footsteps outside the door.

Mike held his breath and grimaced. The door handle turned.

I didn't lock the door. Why didn't I lock the damned door?
The door squeaked open, and Mike screamed.

He was curled up under his wooden work bench, the handle of the vice bolted to it dangled in front of his face. He was crying, sobbing loudly, almost out of control, hysterical, like a kid who'd found his new puppy run over by a speeding car. His bottom lip hung out in an almost comedic fashion, and it would have been funny if he'd had a few pints and was performing like Mike always did down The Foundry on a Friday evening.

Sheila stood in the doorway letting the wind whip her hair around her head, letting the rain soak into it, mat it, and she stared with equal amounts of horror and pity – horror at the lump of meat on the garage floor, and pity for the big man who cowered under the bench afraid of the wrong he'd tried to right. He looked at her, he saw her, and he reached out to her.

Around his eyes in a goggles shape was a spray of blood just above the mask shape over his mouth and nose – like a sunburn shadow but formed by speckles of blood. Through the speckles, tears had cleared a track like a snowplough and left a clean, shiny trail that gradually spread out across his face, and each time he rubbed away a tear, he smeared blood all over the place. He peered up at her, his sunken eyes drowning in tears pleaded with her to do something about this situation.

"It still hurts," he croaked. "It didn't work. It didn't stop."

Sheila rushed to him and crouched, holding his shaking hand. "What hurts?"

"I do. Me. It won't stop."

She gently pulled him forward, coaxing him out from under the workbench.

"This... this was supposed to stop the pain. You said killing her murderer would make things better; that Mia would be... that she'd be better. Avenged."

Sheila looked at the mound of lumpy blood on the garage floor. Mike had gone the whole nine yards – he'd turned that man to mush. On the floor, by a small rivulet of blood that had snaked across the plastic sheet, was the bottle of smelling salts, and it was empty. Yesterday it had been full. Mike had done his best to keep him awake, to make him suffer as long as possible. "I wish I could have been here."

"Hmph," he said. "I thought you'd try to talk me out of it. I waited till you went out."

"If I hadn't wanted this, Mike, I wouldn't have given you his address."

He was shaking still. "I was so... I was so angry. I was furious." He swallowed, and took a gasp of air. "Look what he made me do. Look what he's done to me. Look what he's done to us; all of us."

"Sssshhh, it's okay," she soothed. "We'll get rid of him tonight, and then we never have to—"

"I'll never rest again." His eyes were drawn to the blood. "How can I?"

"Listen, don't you go folding on us now. We've done half a job, we need to finish it tonight, okay?" She clasped his face in both hands, made him look at her. "Okay?"

He nodded, and she tried to smile at him, the way a doting teacher might smile at a stupid kid. The only thing missing from the ensemble was her patting him on the head and whispering, 'There, there.' "Get in the shower, clean yourself up. Scrub yourself. I'll get changed, and start wrapping him up."

He nodded, slid out from under the bench and stood, avoiding the dead man on the floor. He towered over Sheila by a good eight inches, but she had a personality, an abundance of common sense, and a way of manipulating him that towered above any intellectual capability he had tucked away. She was the graduate, he was the monkey. Both knew their roles.

Chapter 37

The light was dazzling, and the heat was almost unbearable. There were crowds, there were hurrying people; blue lights flashed through the double doors, sirens in the distance. But most of all, the smell of antiseptic. Eddie spun his thumbs, played solitaire on his phone, tapped his feet, kept a distance from other people, and eventually approached the desk again and asked the young lady, "Hi, any news yet of Daisy Wilson."

"Are you family?"

"No, I explained to the other young lady—"

"I can't give out any information—"

"It's okay, Coreen," said another woman behind the reception desk. She nodded to Eddie, and he went to the end of the desk, leaned in towards her. "They think she's going to live, but…" she looked at him, "she's lost a hand. Going to lose a foot, too. He'd tied the cable ties very tight, lots of tissue damage."

"Oh no."

"But her heart seems fine, kidneys are working okay too. We have high hopes."

"So she'll live but she might not thank me. Not that I want her thanks, you understand, I—"

She smiled again at him. "If it's any consolation, *I* thank you. You did an awesome job; you saved someone's life, and that's something to be very proud of."

"Just doing my job, ma'am," he grinned, nodded his thanks at her and walked away feeling lower than a snake's balls. All he had to look forward to was nailing the cretin who took Vincent and then – if he was still alive – nailing Vincent too. The wanker.

Chapter 38

HE FELT ROBBED OF his enjoyment and felt disinclined to become a writer, and at that moment, a Land Rover Discovery squealed to a halt on the gravel at the side of the house, and Charles closed his eyes and prepared himself to be mocked to death.

The door burst open, and Eddie marched in with a large paper bag. "Didn't fancy food poisoning tonight, so I got us a KFC."

Charles sat there dreading the evening.

In the kitchen, Eddie threw chicken and fries on Charles's plate and flicked on the kettle. "Good day?"

"Not really."

"Why, incontinence pads leaked again?"

"Very funny, Eddie."

Eddie stopped chewing and stared at his dad. "What's up?"

Charles took a deep breath, and said, "I thought I'd quite like a go at writing a book. They say everyone's got a book in them. But I messed up."

"Spelled 'book' wrong?" The kettled clicked off. Eddie made the drinks, and herded Charles through into the lounge. "Wow," he said, "you have been busy. New lapdog?"

"It's to replace my old typewriter."

"I didn't even know you *had* a typewriter, let alone an old one. Did it blow up on you?"

"I lied," he said. "Connor wasn't wrong; he delivered a typewriter to me not an iron. It was the same model I used fifty years ago, but I couldn't get it to work. I'd bought a model that was for display purposes only, apparently. Who knew there was such a thing?"

Eddie stopped chewing, looked at his dad with confusion on his face. "Let me get this straight, you hoped to write a book on a typewriter that was for display purposes only?"

"I didn't know it was—"

Eddie spat chicken across the floor, and was too busy choking to see Charles get up and leave the room. After a few minutes, he opened Charles's bedroom door. "Hope you're not playing with yourself," he said as he entered.

Charles was sitting on his chair staring off into space. "I make a mess of everything I do."

"That's what tissues were invented for. Oh, I see what you mean."

He didn't even look up.

"Nah," he said, "you don't. Not everything. Mostly." He was smiling, but Charles wasn't playing, obviously not in the mood. "Look," Eddie said, "so the typewriter wasn't a success, but you've got a nice shiny lapdog out there and you can make a start on it, tell your story. You're right, Dad, everyone's got a story in them." He looked at his dad until his dad looked back. "What's yours?"

Eddie closed the bedroom door, and the shadows took over again. Charles listened to the silence punctuated every second by the Westclox on his bedside table.

Nothing changed. And nothing *would* change unless he made it so. Each second would follow the previous one and it would go on like that for a very long time. "Until the old clock wound down, at least," he whispered. "So, are you just going to sit here and feel sorry for yourself? Or are you going to tell this little story?"

Like a frightened mouse, Charles came back into the lounge silently, head down, peering at the world through the tops of his eyes, hands holding each other as though they needed the reassurance of something familiar. He stopped, and watched Eddie reading the laptop screen. Eventually he couldn't take it any more, and cleared his throat.

Eddie looked up, and Charles might have expected to see some embarrassment on Eddie's face at having being caught reading someone else's material, a bit like being caught reading a private diary. It wasn't the done thing.

But Eddie wasn't at all embarrassed, it seemed. He tapped the screen. "This is bloody good, Dad."

The hands let go of each other, and the smile was buoyant enough to lift Charles's face. "You think so?"

"Yeah. Hey, if you put your mind to this, you could be an author, reach out to a publisher and see what they have to say about it."

"Nah, it's really not that good." Another pause. "Is it? Do you think it is, Eddie? Really?"

"So tell me what it's about."

"Shall I get us a drink first?"

"No. I want to hear this, it sounds great."

Charles, feeling twenty-one again sat in the seat next to his son, and said, "Mankind has some strange stories to tell, and most of them are just really good ways of us learning lessons and passing those lessons along."

"Yep, familiar with story-telling."

"Okay, okay. But I think the best genre for doing that is psychological horror."

"Stephen King?"

"And Thomas Harris's *Silence of the Lambs*, and *Psycho* by Robert Bloch. Anyway, yes, the lessons are stark and terrifying, but they can be thrilling too. So my own story is a mix of all of them, really. Well, I like to think so—"

"Come on, then."

"Greed. Those who are greedy have the greatest need to hide."

Eddie stared at him. "That it? Is that your pearl of wisdom?"

"Well, I mean it's what this story is based on: greedy people hiding so as not to get killed by those who they swindled."

"Ah, I see! It's about you catching up with a certain typewriter seller." Eddie laughed, and the remark caught Charles off guard sufficiently to have him laughing too. He was feeling better about things at last.

"I thought you'd take the piss out of me."

"Give it time. I'm sure when you start complaining about writer's cramp I'll be able to think of something." Eddie patted Charles on the shoulder and whispered, "Proud of you, old man."

"Thanks, Eddie."

"Ah, now I understand the hard-on every time I said ergo. And Sid, too! The little git; he's been reading your stuff, hasn't he?"

"I wanted his opinion. And he got me the laptop." Charles shrugged, obviously embarrassed. "I didn't trust myself not to mess up again."

"And you didn't trust me, either, eh? I don't blame you – you did the right thing. But I still want to read your story. That okay?"

Charles nodded.

DAY 6

Chapter 39

Eddie had driven to work after only four hours sleep, and even labelling it sleep was probably being a bit optimistic. He parked the Discovery, had a biscuit and half a cup of coffee with Sid while telling him what had happened to an innocent young girl at a scene that Kenny had been in charge of. Sid's mouth formed a perfect O, which he then covered with blue-nailed fingers. "Do you think… No, surely not."

"What, Sid?"

"If Mark and Kenny had… Would she…"

"Let me get this straight. If Mark and Kenny had found the girl when they should have done a thorough job as I asked them to do, several hours before I went and did that job for them, would that girl have lost so many fucking appendages? Would she have a greater chance of survival?"

Sid only nodded.

"I don't think it would have made a big difference. But that's between you and me, okay? I might need leverage for something in future and this will do very nicely."

"You are a bad man, Eddie Collins."

"And tell Kenny he's doing that scene – there's a strategy for it in his email."

"You attached a forensic strategy to an email? My, you are getting tech-savvy."

Eddie rubbed his nails on his jacket, and blew them, "Seems I'm not the only one, eh."

"What does that mean?"

"What does that mean?" he mocked. "I finally found out why you keep closing pages down on your computer when I get close."

"I'm sure I don't know what you mean."

"Really?"

Sid blushed and looked away.

"I think it's awesome. Thank you."

Sid looked up, smiled, and blushed even more.

Eddie waved with two fingers and left the office. He didn't speak with anyone else, just gave Beelzebub the finger as he walked past with his head down, climbed into his van and pointed it towards a police-designated recovery garage.

Once there, he found Vincent Lightowler's white Audi, parked himself and his gear next to it, and then pulled the shutter down, enclosing the two of them in peace and quiet away from engines and airguns and hammer drills, from mechanics shouting shit jokes, radios playing shit adverts with an occasional shit song thrown in, and telephones ringing so loudly they made your ears bleed.

He mounted the Nikon on a tripod to begin his record-keeping, that meant photography, when the one thing he hadn't counted on let himself in.

"Morning."

His arms dropped to his sides, and he closed his eyes. "You're fucking kidding."

"Pleased to see you, too."

"Knew I should have locked that *fucking* door."

Benson sidled up next to him. "They tell me you're a hero."

"They tell me you're a knobhead."

"No, seriously. You're a hero."

"I've been trying to tell you that for years. Would you listen? No."

"Seriously, Eddie. Well done. You saved a young girl's life."

"Seriously, was it worth saving, though?"

"Sorry?"

"Look where she lives, look what she does, look who she shacks up with. We're fighting a losing battle, mate. Frankly, I don't know if I can be arsed any more.

"The problem is just too big; it's massive and I've been fighting all these years against it, and it's just getting worse, it's just getting bigger and infecting more and more people, and there's nothing I can do about it.

"It doesn't matter how hard we fight; we're sinking; there's literally no hope; it's an epidemic. What we do makes no fucking difference at all."

Staggered, Benson's mouth fell open. He didn't know how to respond, so grinned, and said, "You need a new vial of Valium."

"There's the door." Eddie clicked the shutter release and the flash popped.

"Don't be a cock."

"Please, I want to find out who Vincent left with, so if you don't mind."

"I do mind. Eddie, I get it that you're pissed off at the state of the world, really I do. And I don't have any answers, but don't get yourself all depressed about it. You really are a hero; you did what no one else would have thought to do."

Eddie stared at him. "It's pointless."

"Then why are you doing this?" He nudged the Audi with a foot. "You might as well go home."

"And spend the day with Linwood Barclay?"

"Who?"

"Never mind."

"Anyway, your efforts are not wasted. And you want to find out who Vincent Lightowler left Beeston with – there, that's you wanting to do some good."

"It's only so I can go and kill the fucker."

"And there you go, doing more good!" Benson stopped smiling, tucked his hands in his pockets. "Libby said thank you for the offer of money."

Eddie blinked. "How do you know Libby?"

"I've been keeping her fed for years. She gives me a bit of info every now and then, I make sure she's not starving to death. And before you ask, she won't take anything else; she's not interested in a house or flat, she's not into designer clothes or posh phones, and she hates the thought of not being on the streets."

It was Eddie's turn to be surprised.

"All you can do is what you're doing. If we all do our bit like that, then eventually we'll win."

"Ha. You actually think that?"

"Yes, I do. Might take a while. But one thing's for sure: if we all do nothing, the world will burn."

When Benson looked up again, Eddie was already getting to grips with his examination, so he slipped out unnoticed.

The door closed quietly behind Benson, and Eddie punched the air, delighted to be on his own again, able to concentrate at last. He finished photographing the car, including outstanding marks and damage in case they proved useful linking it with possible CCTV images. He photographed each quadrant of the interior, including anything that might yield DNA – bottles and cigarette ends, and then sampled them or seized them.

Although the car was needed just for the potential fingerprint ridge detail on the front somewhere, he didn't know how valuable the vehicle might be in the investigation when it came to other aspects of this crime or another crime, linked or not. And as such, there was a minimum standard he worked to – a 'just in case' scenario.

And then it was time for the fingerprinting. His heart kicked a little; this could be the crux of the exam, the piece of evidence that shattered the case. It was a white car, and he chose a black globular powder that floated in the air like soot, but provided maximum contrast when photographing any latent ridge detail he developed. The whole car took him forty minutes, and he paid particular attention to the front wings and the bonnet, and was rewarded with a set of four and one single fingertip. There were other marks around the doors and handles and the boot lip, but these two sets at the front were what made his mouth water.

Eddie wrote out two labels with his report number, the vehicle details, and a gravity mark so the bureau could orient the image Eddie would send later, stuck them next to the marks and took location photographs before getting the important close-up high-resolution shots.

On the screen on the back of the camera, he zoomed in and could clearly see the sweat pores on both marks, so was happy he'd got what he came for.

While he was sending the marks on his tablet via CSImages, he contacted Leo in the bureau and asked him to check the fingerprint images as soon as he was able, labelling them as urgent, possibly lifesaving. He didn't say the life they might be saving was utterly worthless anyway, just a scumbag.

When he hung up, he finished sorting out his exhibits and tidied up the report on the tablet, and stepped out for a smoke. Sometimes, and it was becoming rarer, these times of satisfaction were what kept him in this job – well it wasn't the fucking wages that was for sure – and he couldn't think of another job he'd rather have that paid as much in the satisfaction stakes – though, he remembered, the jobs where you got sod-all or the jobs where your efforts were just CIDs ticky-box policing in action were increasing in number.

"Better enjoy these while I can, then."

Eddie's phone rang halfway through his third cigarette. He was sitting on an old tyre with his legs outstretched, feet crossed, enjoying the clouds and a fresh cup of coffee brought to him by a mechanic who didn't look thrilled at reaching the dizzy heights of tea-boy. Eddie wondered if he'd spat in it, and asked him so. The mechanic looked offended, and told Eddie to, "Fuck off you cheeky twat." That was good enough for Eddie who quite happily drank it.

The phone call was from Leo Brightman at the fingerprint bureau in Wakefield. "The group of four," he said after securing another imaginary bottle of whisky for his sterling efforts, "belong to Vincent Lightowler."

Eddie closed his eyes. "And the single digit?"

"It's a right index."

"Belonging to whom?"

"A Mike Chandler, born 17 April 75."

Eddie thanked him and hung up. He guessed this Mike Chandler was Mia's father, or uncle. Whichever it was, it dragged Eddie to his feet and got him back in the van, engine on, ready to rock. First, he rang Benson for the simple reason that Benson would know where Mike Chandler lived.

"The fingerprint on the Audi came back to Mike Chandler."

Benson woo-hoo'd in Eddie's ear, and Eddie selected a gear.

"I knew he had something to do with this, the sneaky bastard."

"So where's he live? I'll meet you there."

"What? No, no, no, we need an arrest strategy. Come in, and we can travel down in convoy."

"What? Convoy? This isn't *Heat*, Tom. Did you ever think that Lightowler might still be alive, and if we wait to form this convoy and wait to create this wonderful arrest strategy, he might not be by the time we actually get there – which sounds like a week *next fucking Tuesday*!"

"Don't be flippant."

Eddie took the van back out of gear. "It sounds like you'd rather he *was* dead. It sounds like you're giving Chandler every opportunity to kill him."

"Eddie, there are procedures to follow, precautions to put in place."

"I'll give you an arrest strategy – go in and put some cuffs on him. Tra la!"

"Come in. We'll get sorted quick, and then head out together."

Eddie hung up. He looked through the phone book he kept in the back of his notepad, found Regan, and rang her. "Regan, it's me, Eddie."

Benson answered. "I can read you like a copy of the *Beano*."

"Well, it's about right for your IQ."

"Eddie, don't—"

Too late, Eddie hung up. Next was Sid, and he was about to press 'call', when his phone rang. The display said 'Miriam', and he toyed with declining the call, with just letting it ring until it stopped, or answering it. Eventually, he answered.

"Of the three choices available to you, you picked wisely."

Eddie shook his head.

"We're setting off now. We will be there in forty-five minutes. I'm going to give you his address, but we arrive together; you must not arrive before us. Forty-five minutes, got it?"

Eddie nodded. "Fair enough. Thank you."

"Play by the rules, Eddie."

Chapter 40

Eddie wondered what you did with yourself when your daughter was taken from you. How do you get from one morning to the next?

He had a daughter, Becca, who lived in Ireland with her mother. They had an arrangement – between the three of them – that Eddie wouldn't play a significant role in Becca's life as a teenager, into womanhood. Unless Becca wanted it. So far, she hadn't. They exchanged birthday and Christmas cards, and that was about all; no one likes to think they're crowding someone out, eh? Especially a daughter, for whom you would be there if and when requested.

And he knew it was a strange setup that got a lot of sideways glances whenever he shared that story. But it worked for them all.

The Chandlers were a different kettle of fish altogether. Their daughter had left home, just like Eddie's had, but they were still very much in contact, he'd like to bet. He could see her parking up for Sunday lunch at least a couple of times a month, phone calls to her mum a couple of times a week. Despite living apart, they were still a tight-knit family.

And Mia's death would absolutely gut the parents.

He wondered again, what you did with yourself when your daughter was taken from you, when she was killed. When you got up in the morning, did you grab a coffee and some toast just as you always did, and maybe sit and watch the television news for half an hour. And that's when it would hit you – that Mia was never coming home again for Sunday lunch, and she wasn't just the other end of a phone if you felt lonely and wanted to chat.

Or did you not wake up because you didn't go to sleep. Was she on your mind all the time? And if so, what were you thinking of: her childhood, the good memories? Or the bad times, like when she met up with the freak of a boyfriend? That's when the badness crept in, wasn't it? That's when it all started going black, and her life was getting away from you.

He was there a full ten minutes early, but he stayed in his van a hundred yards away from the Chandlers' house, smoking, thinking, dreaming, and wondering what stories those walls could tell. Whatever stories they did tell, Eddie would find out; and he'd feel sorry for them, no matter what they had done or had not done because of Mia's death. Theirs was a position he didn't envy. He'd seen the state of Sheila in the mortuary, and it was horrific to witness – an image of her with her arm outstretched, face contorted into a picture of agony. The pain must have been horrific to bear.

Benson waved to him, and Eddie drove the van to a nondescript semi-detached house that could have been on any one of a thousand Leeds streets – just plain, ordinary, sad… not exploited to any potential at all. It's like this was the place that people came to lick their wounds after a day of being mundane. This was the ultimate beige street – so forgettable he had to remind himself of the street name for his report.

Both Mr and Mrs Chandler were sitting in the lounge when Eddie entered. They were sitting either side of a young girl, very obviously

Mia's sister, and all three were sitting opposite Benson and Regan. Benson went to stand by the front door with a uniformed officer, and Regan sat in a chair as she gently questioned them. There was another uniformed officer at the rear door.

"I have to inform you that you're both under arrest for conspiracy to murder Vincent Lightowler. You do not have to say anything, but it may harm your defence if you do not mention when questioned something which you later rely on in court. Anything you do say might be used against you in a court of law. Is that understood, Mrs Chandler?"

She was stoic, sitting with her back straight, her hair up in a tight bun on the top of her head, hands clasped in her lap. She nodded, "I understand."

"Mr Chandler?"

He was the opposite. His chin was made of jelly, his top lip looked like it had a life of its own, both eyes were leaking taps, his face constantly wet, snot hanging from the tip of his nose. He was rounded, almost folded in two, quivering on the sofa. He could barely see Regan because of the water in his eyes. He nodded, too. "Yes."

In the middle was their daughter, trying to be brave but crumbling.

"Can't you let the young lass go?" Eddie asked Benson. "Does she have to see this?"

"What do we do with her?"

"Let her go to her room at the very least. Get a female from CID down here, and take her to a Starbucks; something, Tom. Anything. Look at her."

"Regan," Benson said. "Clara doesn't need to stay unless you need her. She's free to go."

"No, she stays with me," Mike Chandler blubbed.

"Let her go, Mike. She doesn't need to see any more tears – she's seen enough for a lifetime."

"Mum, stop being so dramatic." Clara stood. "Can I go to my room?"

"Yes, of course," Regan said.

Eddie watched the girl leave – she was tall, lanky, skinny, long greasy hair, pimples, and a disposition that said she was so depressed living here, that perhaps it would be preferable to leave and die somewhere else. Maybe she envied her sister, who knew. But being here was suffocating her.

"We've brought our CSI in here today, because we'd like him to conduct a quick search of your house and vehicles."

Both just blinked, but Eddie detected a softening towards him from Sheila, and had circumstances been different, she might have stood, shaken hands, and thanked him again for what he did for her at the mortuary. Mike eventually looked away.

"We'll be taking you both to Elland Road Police Station for questioning in a few minutes, but I'd like to grant you this chance to tell us anything you might know of Vincent Lightowler's disappearance."

Mike cleared his throat. All eyes swivelled to him. "Nothing," he said. "Had a frog in my throat."

"If you're arrested on conspiracy to murder, shouldn't we be granted legal counsel before you begin questioning us?"

Regan nodded, "Indeed, you're entitled to counsel, and as I already said, you need not say anything to us. I was merely being courteous."

"We thank you for your courtesy, but we'll take the offer of counsel, please."

"We had nothing to do with his death. You're barking up the wrong tree."

Everyone was silent for a moment, and then Regan said, "Who said he was dead?"

Mike became flustered, hands writhing about in his lap, words falling over themselves in their eagerness to get out, "I was... I was just saying *if* he was dead, we had nothing to do with it. Let's get that quite clear. Is he... is he missing?"

"Do you know where he lives, Mr Chandler?"

"No. Nope, never really had much to do with him, even when he was knocking about with Mia."

"Did you like him?"

"Despised him!" He smiled awkwardly as if suddenly remembering who was asking. "No, I wasn't keen."

"Did he beat Mia?"

"Detective," said Sheila Chandler, "this has developed into formal questioning, I believe."

"My apologies. I was just chatting. In fact we were chatting to one of our IT men back at the station about audits trails on our computer systems. I'm useless with computers, but some people are really clever, they can trace who did what and when. Amazing. We asked him if the NHS IT department could do likewise, and apparently they can. And they do. Lots of sensitive information on those computers. Addresses, partners and *their* addresses, that kind of thing.

"We know you're friends with a Christine McFarland who works in the mortuary. It's how you managed to get to the mortuary so quickly after Mia was brought there. And guess what, someone with Christine's login details searched Vincent Lightowler's address that very afternoon, and that same person searched partner's addresses, too."

Eddie saw Mike turn to Sheila, and he saw his fists clench even tighter that they already were.

"I have nothing to say about that."

"Would you have anything to say, Mike?"

"No, he wouldn't like to add anything, either."

Regan nodded.

Benson said, "Strange. See we found your fingerprint on Vincent's car outside his girlfriend's address in Beeston."

Mike's eyes widened so much they were in danger of falling out onto the carpet. He bowed his head, played with his fingers.

"We'll be putting you both into dry cells because we'll need to take samples from you later. Wouldn't want you washing yourselves, would we?"

"You were seen, Mike, you know that, don't you?"

"Rubbish!"

Eddie glanced at Benson and there was the faintest of smiles growing in the corner of his mouth. This was going to be easy.

"Shall we go now?"

Regan stepped forward and offered her hand to Mike Chandler; Benson did the same for Sheila. And Benson said, "Off the record, Mike. You'll never guess what I found out only this morning. I went back to the address in Beeston, and a young woman told me that Vincent Lightowler was at that address the day Mia was killed. He was there all day long. And she knows that because she was one of the two women he beat up that day while in a ketamine hole – while being under the influence of drugs." Benson stared hard into Mike's eyes. "Vincent Lightowler didn't kill your daughter."

Mike looked confused, first at Benson, and then across to Sheila. "You said the cops thought Vincent did it."

"Shut up, Mike. Just keep your stupid mouth shut."

"But you said they thought he'd done it."

"We discuss many theories, Mike," Regan said, "but we do a lot of fact-checking before we act. You killed him because of your history with him, and because of his history with Mia."

"I don't get it," he said, "who the hell killed her, then?"

Regan slid cuffs on Mike's outstretched hands, and that's when he went ballistic demanding to know who killed Mia.

Eddie stood aside, letting the uniformed officers and Regan deal with him. Benson cuffed Sheila too, and she marched out with an officer, completely docile; neither of them even glancing back. "You know what to do, Eddie," shouted Benson as he went upstairs to arrest Clara.

Chapter 41

AND HE DID INDEED know what to do. He basically had to find bits of Vincent Lightowler at this address. But not every piece of evidence he could find would prove Mike and Sheila Chandler had killed him. Fingerprints, for example, in the ground floor toilet, would not suffice because he had been a member of the family at one point back in the distant past, granting him legitimate access.

Eddie chewed this over, and decided the first place to begin looking was the van. There was nothing to suggest Mike wouldn't be stupid enough to bring Vincent back here once he'd abducted him from Daisy's house in Beeston.

He found the keys, opened the van's side door, and peered inside, torch throwing the shadows into oblivion. The van had racking up the right-side walls alongside a couple of tall Snap-On toolboxes. Against the bulkhead was a trolley jack, an air jack, and several large crowbars. It was a mechanic's van, not especially clean but quite tidy – a place for everything-kind of tidy. The only thing of note were the drag marks on the oil-stained wooden floor, but nothing to suggest what might have caused those drag marks.

The most disappointing thing was the lack of blood, and he began hoping that Mike Chandler was not cleverer than he made out to be – there was nothing worse than doing battle with an idiot who was blessed with luck. No matter how hard you looked for evidence, luck would always ensure there was none to be found, or it had been damaged, or it had been inadvertently destroyed. You could not win against luck.

Okay, so there was nothing visible using white light, but he could use the Crimelite, and he would too, but only after he'd had the van recovered, so he could do a proper examination like he'd done with Vincent's car. As he was walking around the back of the van, he noticed the same old stickers on the back doors that a million other vans bore: *No Tools Left in This Vehicle Overnight*, and *This Vehicle has a Tracker Fitted*.

"Tracker fitted." Eddie smiled. He'd soon see how clever Mike Chandler really was.

The garage was big, a double garage, but it was a dark and dismal thing. The door banged Eddie in the back as the wind picked up. With a gloved knuckle, he turned on the lights, but 'dismal' hung in the air like the cobwebs in the steel rafters and across the bicycles and old wardrobes in the far corner. There was a workbench with a vice bolted to it, and yet more tool boxes. Along the left wall was a barbecue and tools, gardening tools, hand tools and power tools, watering cans, pressure sprayers, and a roll of plastic sheeting with a frayed end.

The floor was bare, powdery, concrete, and the walls were brick. It smelled damp, but there was another smell, an undercurrent that had no immediate identity, but seemed to go hand in hand with the word dismal.

The blood was easy enough to see if you stood and paid attention, if you'd done this kind of thing a thousand times before. There were broken arcs of blood up the walls where Mike Chandler hadn't been careful enough to tie up the plastic sheeting. And there was more across the ceiling. The ceiling was corrugated asbestos sheeting, but despite it being dark, the blood was darker, and it had a certain property of reflecting direct light, whereas the surrounding asbestos absorbed it. There were more definite arcs.

Even the floor had a story to tell. Eight feet apart were two pairs of holes in the concrete, and Eddie shone his torch in each to reveal a threaded inside – a wall anchor. The threads had blood in them, and the powdery concrete surface did too; it was a place you couldn't clean easily, couldn't access, maybe didn't even notice. This was where someone had been tied down.

This garage was nothing short of a torture chamber.

Eddie wondered if he should feel sorry for Vincent, after all, ten miles away he had his very own torture chamber, didn't he, where a young girl had almost died, where she'd suffered life-changing injuries. He decided Vincent Lightowler deserved no sympathy, and so he blotted him out, and concentrated on the search.

Hanging up on a wire next to one of the toolboxes was an electrical extension reel, and that thing was literally covered in blood, slick with it. Seems Mike Chandler was in such a state he didn't have the first clue about making sure the torture chamber was cleaned down after use.

His gaze fell on the floor under the bench. He squatted to see two full hand prints in blood. They were so perfect they looked like a kid's hand-painting. The fingertips were pointing out into the garage, so his back would have been against the wall underneath the bench. Eddie thought about it, about why someone would want to be in that position, and his only conclusion was the despair he was in; how he'd crawled under there, and sat staring at his work.

Of course, Eddie admitted, he could be wrong – perhaps Mike put his can of beer under there so it would be shielded from spraying blood, and he went under there for a breather, for a cigarette and quick swig of John Smith's, laughing at the screaming man. But he didn't think so.

From here, squatting in front of the bench, he saw the torn-open pack of smelling salts. Still three bottles left of the five originally in the pack.

He stood, confident he could put Vincent Lightowler here in this garage, confident he could prove that Lightowler was encountering a process of severe injury, and possibly torture – probable torture. And he was equally confident he could nail Mike Chandler as the torturer. The handprints under the bench were glove marks – he could see a faint hexagon pattern on the fingertips – but the coiled-up extension reel would give him ridge detail in Lightowler's blood.

When they downloaded the journey history from the van's tracker, it would not only complete the picture of how Lightowler died and where and who did the killing, but it would also show where the Chandlers had dumped Lightowler's remains.

So there would be another scene for Kenny to deal with.

The only thing that disappointed Eddie so far was proving that Sheila Chandler had a hand in all this. There were two things for sure: Sheila would plead innocent and happily throw her grieving husband under any and all buses the police would drive at her, and secondly Eddie regretted breaking the rules so she could have a moment with her dead daughter – that kindness should have been reserved for someone who was genuinely lost, genuinely eaten up by a grief so strong that it would not listen to reason.

That was Eddie's mission now, to put Sheila Chandler here.

The door banged closed and open again as the wind got stronger. He went to jam it open with a brick, and looked up at that moment to see a light on in an upstairs room. It was Clara's room, he thought, and she'd left with Benson, forgetting to turn out the light. From here he could make out a motivational poster on the wall that said, *Opportunities don't happen, you create them.* From what Eddie had seen of her, young Clara wouldn't know an opportunity if it smacked her in the face.

Poor lass, she's the one who's going to suffer the most, she's the one who's probably suffering the most right now. How old was she? Eighteen, nineteen; just the right age to roll off the tracks and into something bigger and more disturbing that the death of her sister and the new label that just dropped through the letterbox – a label for her parents: murderers. How does someone so young deal with that for the rest of her life?

Was it any of Eddie's concern?

Should he go on and get all the evidence, no matter whom it pointed to, and allow that girl to sink into a short and painful life with no parent around to guide her?

This was the part of the job he hated. Sometimes he hated knowing more than was necessary, but he chose to let the evidence he found be the judge and jury as to whether he was doing the right thing. If Sheila was directly involved, then so be it.

Eddie went and collected everything he'd need from the van, including a scene suit, and it wasn't until he got back into the garage ready to begin photography before collecting evidence and searching for more, that the final question occurred to him: if Vincent Lightowler didn't kill Marshall Forbes and Mia Chandler, then who the fuck did?

Eddie's phone danced in his pocket, and he almost dislocated his shoulder trying to pull the stupid thing out. By the time he got to answer it, he was so angry that he shouted, "What?"

It turned out to be Kenny with news of another death, and he wanted to know if Eddie would be, "Dicking around in some garage all day, so shall I just go and deal with it?"

Chapter 42

STAN COULD NOT STOP crying, and it was getting on Regan's tits.

"Mr Forbes, I need you to calm down; we're not making any headway, and we won't while you're out of control."

"I'm so sorry," he sobbed. His face looked like it was being operated by someone else, someone who was totally pissed or totally wasted. "I can't... She was my wife."

"Mr Forbes, I know she was your wife. But I want to know why she's dead. In fact I want to know how long she's been dead for."

His chin took a break from wobbling only long enough for him to say, "Look, Sergeant, would you like a nice cup of tea, and we can settle down here and talk it over."

"Sit down, Mr Forbes."

His chin resumed breakdancing on his face. "But I—"

"I said sit down."

He did and stared up at her, tears dangling from a jawline that looked like a wonky shelf, then running down the creases in his neck to settle among the whiskers there. From this angle with the long white eyebrows and big eyes he looked like Owl from Winnie the Pooh, and Regan had to blink to get rid of the image. "What's your phone number?"

"I beg your pardon?"

"Your mobile phone number. Does it end in 4086?"

"Well, yes it does. I've had it years. I don't change things often, unlike most people who like—"

Regan held a finger to her lips, "Sssshhh," she said. "I don't intend dying of old age in this house, okay? It's great to talk, but please, keep it relevant, love, okay?"

"Sorry. I... It's been a very stressful..." She was staring at him. "Sorry."

"We have a special department that can analyse computers and mobile phones. And they pulled out your number – from four years ago, actually." She turned to a page in her notebook. "It says here that—"

"I know what it'll say, Sergeant. Yes, I was infatuated with Mia Chandler." He swallowed, looked away, fingers playing chase with each other. "I'm over it now."

"I should hope so; she's dead."

He looked up. "I had nothing to do with that!"

"Ah, getting to the point now, eh?"

"Sergeant," he said, "it was years ago. I found her attractive; she left a window of opportunity for me to pursue her romantically."

"And you climbed through this imaginary window?"

"I'm not proud of my actions, but in fairness, she was encouraging – well, she was not discouraging, if you see what I mean. And it went nowhere very quickly indeed."

"Mrs Forbes found out?"

"About Mia? No, not at all. Never. Like I said, it was very short-lived, never even got physical, never even earned the title: affair. Seems I had misread the open invitation, slightly. It was an invitation to help Marshall with his schooling, not help me with my love life. I regret my naivety, Sergeant. I looked very foolish."

"You might have looked foolish back then, but you look guilty of killing her about now."

"What! No, no, I could never. I certainly did *not* kill her, Sergeant. You have to believe me. It was a few ill-conceived text messages, nothing more."

Regan made notes – many officers didn't bother, either relied on their memory or chose to record everything on bodycam, but she liked to read her notes later, go over things, formulate actions and strategies based on them. She looked at him, his fingers were gradually wearing themselves out. "How long has she been dead?"

The chin wobbled again.

"Mr Forbes, concentrate. How long?"

"Four days. Maybe three." He almost pleaded with her. "I've lost all track of time; I have barely slept. I don't really know what I'm doing." The tears fell silently, and Regan felt sorry for him. He was the kind of man who would not cope well without his wife by his side.

Kenny kept the doors and window shut; sealed like the room had been when he came in here. The door was tight-fitting, one of those that dragged across the carpet when opened. The smell was intense; it was pungent, and it made his eyes water a tad. He stood and took several deep breaths, took a moment to get used to the... aroma. For a brief moment, he thought of Skid, and couldn't help smiling. He'd be in a corner now throwing up into his hands.

The body was on its side, staring at the window, a reflection of the curtains in her cloudy eyes. Her skin was marbled, green with rot, and her fingertips were black, nails long witch's nails, brittle, sharp. There was vomit down her cheek and it had formed a pool on the bed, and was now black and shiny, a string of it attached to her nostrils. Her face had swollen, and her abdomen was stretched tight, ready to blow.

It could have been a lot worse – especially if the flies had got in here. They tended to help decomposition, and they turned bodies into maggot farms in hours. Kenny shuddered.

She had, of course, soiled herself and the smell of neat piss wasn't lost on Kenny. "I hate you, Eddie," he whispered, as he took up position and began photographing the bedroom and the body. On the bedside table was a box of Valium – enough for 30 days it said, empty. Next to it an empty glass. He photographed it all.

He photographed her face and head, hands, and her arms where he could to show there were no defensive injuries. He pulled up her t-shirt as far as he could and photographed her front and rear to make sure there were no puncture wounds. There were none. More marbling, more swollen green, mouldy, skin.

He swallowed, changed his gloves, and took hold of her shoulder and hip and tried to roll her but she was stuck to the sheet by dried fluids, dragging it with her. She farted and Kenny almost hurled his lunch across the floor. After a few minutes, he tried again and failed again, and then stood back and reappraised the scene. The window was secure, no one had broken in through it. She had no injuries. A five-day-old box of Valium was empty.

"Executive decision," Kenny muttered and took off his gloves. "Suicide. Pending tox reports from the PM."

"We've had reports of the smell. And now, since we found the old text messages… It made a compelling case to call on you."

"Yes, I can imagine."

"She was dead when me and DI Benson called on you, wasn't she?"

He nodded. "I know what you're thinking, that you heard her snoring."

"It had crossed my mind."

"I took a recording, played it on my phone in her room." He swallowed, fidgeted.

"Why?"

"Why? Why did I play a recording of someone snoring."

"Yes, Mr Forbes. Why?"

"Well... I mean..." The tears came again, and Regan sighed. "I know this all looks straight-forward to you, Sergeant, I can see that, I can feel it in your demeanour, how you're fed up with this stupid old man, and wish you were out of his smelly house. But to me," he thrust a finger into his chest, "to *me* this is all very new. I lost my only son five days ago, and everything me and Mrs Forbes had built up over the last eighteen years was suddenly gone. It was quiet around here. It was eerily quiet, actually. If you stopped breathing, you could literally hear a pin drop. Actually," he smiled, "you could hear it landing, perhaps. You couldn't hear it falling. That would be silly."

"Silly?"

"Like I said, this is all new to me. I lost my son, and the house suddenly expanded. Or I got smaller, I don't know which. There was so much room suddenly, and I was missing him much more than I imagined I would. We weren't the kind of partnership where we went camping, you see, or fishing, hunting. We didn't even like the same TV programs. He was growing up and we were growing apart, Sergeant. He spent much of his time in his room, alone, playing games, and whatnot. Our paths didn't cross often. Except when he was kicking my laptop around the lounge." He smiled. Mouthed, "Sorry."

"And Mrs Forbes?"

"Ah yes, I tend to drift off course, these days. I think it's old age."

"Mrs Forbes."

"She was much closer to Marshall than I ever was. He wasn't a mummy's boy – I don't want to give you that impression; he was his own man, or was heading that way. But he and his mother were especially close. She, it seemed, felt the same as I did, but perhaps magnified, amplified."

"She missed him, then?"

The smile left Stan's face. "Are you being funny, Sergeant?"

"No. No, I'm not. I'm sorry if it came across like that."

He looked away briefly, fingers still as he contemplated the bloated body of his wife in a room above his head. The floor was creaking as the CSI did his thing in there. "I never gave it a second thought. I put the box of Valium on her bedside table, and I never thought she'd take the whole... you wouldn't think it of her. She's such a strong woman. She keeps this house alive. She keeps it afloat; she makes the decisions, looks after the money, cooks – except for curry – and she makes sure everyone is alright before tending to herself. She is... Sergeant, she is everything."

"It doesn't explain the recording of her snoring."

"No, I suppose it doesn't." He sank into a shallow well of thought for a moment or two and then surfaced. "I needed time after Marshall's death to come to terms with the new way of living, and that was denied me when my wife took her own life, too. Don't you see, she would rather just kill herself than talk to me about it; she would rather *die* than live with me."

He smiled again, but it was the saddest smile Regan had ever seen.

"She would rather not be alive than be alive without him but with me, like we used to be before he was born. It left me in a place I'd never been before, a place I didn't know existed – true abandonment.

"Part of me recorded that snoring from the internet so I could rebuild things, pretending she was just asleep upstairs, while I came to terms with Marshall dying. I could cope with him dying – just, I'm not trying to say it was easy, because it wasn't – but pretending my wife was still up there asleep helped me process it and move on. I didn't think I could do that with both of them gone, Sergeant; I might have sunk.

"I didn't do it as a way to deceive you – I didn't even know you were visiting that day, did I? That recording was strictly for my benefit."

She stared at him, and he matched her stare. "But there's more," she whispered.

"There is. But it's not your concern."

"Everything is my concern, love." She folded her arms, said nothing, and waited.

"I was taking a few days making up my own mind whether I really wanted to be here all alone, or whether it might be good form to follow my family. If there was anywhere to follow them to."

Kenny opened the door to the lounge and a waft of dead air came into the room with him that made Regan blink. She hated dead bodies, but the smell of them could set her off retching. She held a perfume bottle under her nose, and glared at Kenny as though it was all his fault.

Kenny just nodded at her, and then headed for the front door.

"I must say, your CSIs are jolly good."

She watched Kenny leave, staring at him. "Yes. They are. I'm going to arrange for the undertakers now, Mr Forbes. Are you okay with that?"

Stan Forbes began crying then.

"Before I leave you, Stan…"

He peered at her through the tears. She could tell he was wondering why she'd suddenly called him by his forename.

"We checked into rock concerts in London that Marshall had booked to see. We couldn't find any. Nor could we find any hotels he'd booked, or trains."

He squinted at her. "But I don't understand. He told me he needed that money for the trip."

"There was no trip."

"Then why was he so upset I'd taken his money? He said he needed it, and I was convinced."

"He obviously needed it for something else."

"But what?" Stan asked.

"I was about to ask that very question."

Chapter 43

Eddie watched Sally leaving, and felt the familiar tug as his eyes yearned to watch her arse as she walked away to her car. He wasn't sure if the strings behind his eyes were connected to his heart or his dick; he felt the tug in both regions, and an involuntary sigh fell out of his drooling mouth. He relented, and allowed them to watch, and was so glad he had – and so were both regions. He was very tempted to walk to the gate between the garage and the house, just so he could watch her climb out of her scene suit by the back of her car.

"Sigh," he said. Better get back to it, though; there was lots to do, and it was already getting dark.

He retreated into the rear garden, along the garage wall to where the side door was, and fished out his cigarettes and lighter from his kit box on the floor. He allowed himself ten minutes to think of a strategy to work to, something that would allow him to get it all done much quicker than bouncing around from one thing to another like a fucking pinball.

It was cool, but no rain was forecast just yet, and Eddie felt he could take his time and work the scene without having any pressure put on him – it was a rarity and something he was determined to exploit, to enjoy at least. The first thing he'd like was a coffee, but that was out of the question so he'd have to make do with the bottle of water he'd stuffed in his bag before he set off here.

The phone ringing in his pocket was not in the script, but he knew something would come along to spoil his thinking time – he wasn't surprised, but he was annoyed. It was Benson. Eddie pressed the green phone icon, and said, "What the hell do you want now?"

"We've finished the first interview with Mike, and it didn't take long for him to fold. He killed Vincent Lightowler."

"Ah, good, we do like to wrap up a case with a good old-fashioned confession. Did you have to beat it out of him?"

"Nope. All above board. He also went on to say that Sheila helped him dispose of what was left of the body. It's in woodland near a place called Hope Pastures. It's where all the old horses and donkeys go to retire."

Eddie's eyebrows rose.

"Don't say it."

"Would I?"

"We'll still need the tracking info from the van – would be good to verify it. We'll throw a scene guard on it tonight, and get it searched tomorrow. You okay to be on standby if we have a find?"

"Of course. I'd be interested to see how much of the body is still intact."

There was a pause and then Benson asked, "How was it with the biologist? She still there?"

A subliminal image of Sally escaping from her scene suit wafted across Eddie's field of vision. "Just left. It won't take too long to process this thing. There are a dozen blood swabs to take, some ridge detail to photo and swab, and that's about all. If I see anything else of value, I'll take that too."

"Good result for Vincent's murder considering we haven't even got a body yet. Just got to find out who did Mia and Marshall now. Listen, I can't hang about, but I wanted to let you know that we've finished with Clara, and she's going to stay with a friend tonight, so you'll have plenty of time to get through it all, okay? Give the house a very quick walk-through and see if anything pops up. We'll have OSU do a Section 18 search tomorrow."

"Righto, I'll see you for the morning briefing."

"This evening, however, I'm turning my phone off."

"Why?"

"I'm taking Mrs Benson for a meal in town and we're going to see a late movie."

Eddie opened his mouth to abuse Benson, but after all he'd been through with his recent struggle with self-appearance and low esteem, he thought it better to cut him some slack. "Hey that's good to hear. Hope you have a great evening."

"You can say what you wanted to say, you know. I won't be offended."

"I did say what I wanted to say, except the part where I wanted to remind you about the dangers of spreading syphilis to your good lady wife."

Disappointingly, Benson said nothing, just hung up.

Eddie rested his head against the garage wall and carried on smoking as dusk grew thicker around him, and Sally's tail lights briefly lit up the house wall up to his right before fading away, leaving only dark brickwork behind. Of course, the morning briefing would be a private affair – him, Regan and Benson, and Miriam. It was the new way of doing things, and Eddie felt much better for it too. Maybe being a diagnosed nutjob had its plusses. Speaking of Regan, his mind began, I wonder—

He put the phone away, and flicked the dead cigarette over the fence at the foot of the garden. He got back inside the garage, and picked up the camera. Sally had marked a dozen spots of blood she was interested in. They were important to her; she'd compile her report based on the results of the DNA work on them, and could conclude with certainty that the blood stains were there because of cast-off from a weapon, or from arterial bleeding, or from contact, whatever. And it would be her testimony, along with whatever the prosecution put forward that would prove Vincent's murder had taken place in this garage. And if the ridge detail on tools left at the scene belonged to Mike, and possibly Sheila, and were, again, in Vincent's blood, it would make compelling evidence for any jury.

Add that to all the other evidence, the tracker evidence, the body, and whatever it had been wrapped in for transportation purposes, and it was a wriggle-free case. Despite Mike confessing to the killing, it still had to be processed correctly to satisfy the courts that it had happened at all, that it had happened here, and that Mike Chandler was the killer – nothing was taken for granted.

Once he'd photographed all the blood spots alongside a hanging scale – the same scale he'd measured Mia's body and ligature against – showing how high from the floor it and the group of stains were, he then re-photographed them in detail alongside a much smaller right-angled scale with the case details and exhibit number on.

Next came the swabbing, and Eddie labelled all twelve swabs first, dampened them with sterile water, and prepared twelve exhibit bags.

He was on number eleven, and his heart practically fell out of his anus when someone said, "Hello."

He jumped and the swabs went everywhere. Next came the cursing and the shouting.

"Sorry," she whispered. "I didn't mean to make you jump."

A very small and a very fragile Clara stood in the garage doorway shivering, pulling a silk scarf tight around her.

The anger on Eddie's face took its time leaving not just because she'd scared the shit out of him, but because the fucking scene guard up there at the front of the house should have stopped anyone from coming down here. "What the fuck—"

"I'll go. I'm sorry, I didn't mean…"

She looked so heartbroken, so alone and so scared, that Eddie let the rest of his anger dissipate through a well-disguised and discreet sigh. He took a long blink, and when he smiled and opened his eyes, she was crying.

"What are you doing here?" he asked. "You were staying at a friend's house, weren't you?"

"I… That was a bit of a lie, I'm afraid." Her eyes filled with tears again, and Eddie's anger needle moved up a notch. "I don't really have any friends. I thought it would be okay if I sneaked back in and went straight to bed."

Eddie imagined him having a quick walk-through of the house as requested by Benson, only to have a heart attack in Clara's room when she sat up and screamed. He asked, "How did you sneak past the scene guard?"

She looked confused. "There wasn't one. I came over the back fence, and there was no one there. There's a guard at the front, he's sitting in his car, but not back here."

He shook his head. "I'm sorry, Clara, but you can't stay here while I'm in the middle of an examination."

"I won't interfere, I promise. You won't even know I'm here."

"I won't know you're here because you won't be here."

She held out her hand, pleading, "Please, don't send me away. I have nowhere to go, and no one to be with. I'll be out of your way, mister.

I won't disturb you." She swallowed, and looked away, demure, frail. "They finished asking me questions, said I could go. They're keeping my parents in custody. Said I could go, but I have to stay close. They gave me a lift."

Eddie picked up the swabs, and felt a little guilty about shouting at her. "How old are you?"

"Twenty-two."

"And what do you do for a living?"

"I work at a local newsagents."

He looked at her. "Okay, what do you aspire to be?"

"I don't have any aspirations. I've reached my ceiling, which considering how young I am, is a pretty good effort." There was something pretending to be a smile loitering on her lips. Maybe it was a secret trying to break out, or a lie crimping her lips shut.

"I would agree, except that particular ceiling is fairly low, wouldn't you say, eh? Wear thick socks and you'd bang your head on it." She didn't smile this time, and Eddie thought maybe the comment went over her head. "I'm sorry… about your sister. It must be very difficult for you."

"Thank you. It seems everyone is leaving en masse. First my sister, now my parents. They won't be able to keep up mortgage payments, so the house'll be repossessed." That non-smile again. "I don't really know what I'll do. Do I go to the council, apply for a house? I don't know. How do I live? My wage won't cover bills and food."

Eddie stared at her, felt sorry for her.

"This has kind of mucked up my life. A bit."

There was a huge amount of sympathy for her blocking Eddie's throat, and he wanted to reach out to her, but of course he was working a forensic scene, and she was a part of the case. It made Eddie feel very uncomfortable, her being here, and he was about to walk out and go and get the scene guard, make him take this kid away, but he wondered about her. "It kind of mucked Mia's life up, too."

Clara nodded. "She's free now, though. She doesn't have to struggle any more. I have a whole life of struggling in front of me."

"Can I be honest with you?"

She shrugged, held her arms around her shoulders.

"It sounds to me as though you're not too bothered your sister's dead."

"What's your name?"

"Eddie.

"I've cried myself dry, Eddie." She shuffled her feet, then said, "Anyway, she probably got the better deal. She always got the better deal in life," she smiled, "why not in death, too?"

"Do you think she was killed, or she took her own life?"

A long stare right into Eddie's eyes, and it was long enough to make him feel even more uncomfortable.

"They say you have to be selfish to kill yourself. And that more or less sits squarely with Mia. She was always a selfish cow. And not only that, mum and dad are too stupid to realise their golden child could ever fucking kill herself – oh no," she mocked, "it's something Clara might do, but Mia? No, never in a million years! Someone must've killed her!" In anger, she wiped a trail of snot across her face. "Fucking Golden Girl – I used to call her Blanche!"

Were there any tears there? Eddie stared at her, shocked by her choice of words, and shocked at how she could express herself like this, unless she was just upset that she'd been left all alone – but there was no upset in her eyes, only anger.

"Everyone has the capacity for suicide. All it takes is the right trigger, the right ingredients."

Eddie swivelled and thought on those words for a moment. Her mind was way older than a twenty-two-year-old's mind. Staggeringly insightful, shockingly true.

"And now look what's happened because of it. Dad got cross, picked on her ex and killed him, and now the whole family's gone to shit. All because of her. She was always his favourite – always everyone's fucking favourite. I grew up as the runt of the litter while she got the jewels and the praise, she was always the princess, and I was always the pauper." Her eyes sparkled. "She was always the doctor, and I was always the disease."

She sobbed, and Eddie thought the floodgates would open now, and sadness for her lost sister would spill all over the floor and all over his crime scene, but the sparkle stayed a sparkle and the anger seemed spent already, like she had genuinely come to terms with it, like it was over for her, just the bruising left to heal.

"Do you have any idea how debilitating it is to live in the shadow of an angel? How cold and lonely it is? How everyone smiled when she walked in the room and how those smiles disappeared when I followed her in. It's like everyone hated me. At least now I'll be allowed out into the sunshine." Her eyes slipped out of focus; the sparkle became a tear and the tear fell. She pulled her shoulders tighter, tried to get smaller, tried to hide. She looked up at Eddie, and said, "I'm glad she's dead, Eddie. There, I said it." Her lips quivered as she took a long breath in, and snot hung from her top lip. She wiped an arm under her nose again. "I'm sorry – it's not what a grieving sister is supposed to say, is it?"

"I don't think there's anything you're *supposed* to say. You can only say what you feel."

She nodded, "Thank you."

"Do you know who killed her?"

She shook her head.

"Do you know who killed Marshall Forbes?"

She didn't look up for a long time. "How could I know that?"

"Do you know who Marshall Forbes is?"

"He's the lad found in that alley off Flintlock Yard. Stabbed, they say. Are you telling me they're linked; him and Mia?"

"He was about your age; did you know him in school? Did you know him after you both finished school?"

She switched leaning on one foot to the other. "Yeah, I knew him. Mia knew him too."

"She did?"

Clara nodded, buried her head in her hands.

"What's the matter? Do you have something to tell me, Clara?"

"Marshall's dad had a thing for Mia. It was a few years ago, when we were both still in sixth form. Mia worked there as a junior member of staff. He sent her text messages, wanted to get together with her. It was gross."

Eddie was shocked, that there should be more connections between the main players in this case than he was aware of. "Does Inspector Benson know about them, the text messages?"

She nodded. "I told him, but he already seemed to know. Either someone else already told him, or he wasn't particularly bothered by the news. Makes you wonder if he had anything to do with it. Doesn't it?"

He finished swabbing the blood from the walls and the ceiling, put them in individual bags and sealed them, and noted the time he seized them. "Can I be honest with you, Clara?"

There appeared a kind of panic in her eyes then, one almost fully concealed, one that could have been easily missed, just a slight widening of the eyes, a bloom of the iris and a blushing of the face. She countered quickly, "You're the guy who let Mum get close to Mia in the morgue, aren't you? She mentioned you, how kind you were."

"That was me, yes."

"You're a kind man, Eddie. And I wonder what kindness you could do the remainder of this family now. There's a lot of honesty floating around here tonight."

"I can tell you that your sister didn't kill herself." Eddie watched carefully.

"How do you know that?" She was quick to ask; and if she'd been a dog, her hackles would be up, ready to fight or run. Her eyes were fixed on him as his had been on hers.

"I just do." And if you'd just been told your sister didn't kill herself, wouldn't your first question be who killed her? Eddie thought it rather strange that hers wasn't.

"Ah," she smiled. "The penny dropped; you think *I* killed her?"

"I'm open to suggestions."

Clara shrugged, "I have none."

"Why do you think the killer wanted Mia's death to look like suicide?"

Clara's eyebrows rose up her head. "You're assuming that Mia was incapable of killing herself. Just like my parents. I already said everyone's capable."

"And I know when someone has killed themselves and when someone was killed. Trust me, I've done this kind of shit before."

"Ever been wrong?"

Eddie smiled. "Of course. It's how we learn. But I'm not wrong about Mia."

Clara didn't carry on the conversation, merely looked away.

"So why would the killer want your sister's death to look like suicide?"

"Isn't it obvious? They'd want it to look like a suicide so the police wouldn't start looking for a killer. They wouldn't want that, would they?"

Eddie folded his arms, leaned against the doorframe on the inside of the garage, staring at her leaning against the opposite doorframe on the outside of the garage. "So how did I spot Mia's death was murder?"

Clara shrugged again. "Isn't it time for a cigarette?"

"Didn't know you smoked?"

"A bad habit, but everyone is allowed at least one. Besides, I don't smoke in front of Mum. She hates it." She stared off into the distance as though those words had just sunk in. "Guess I don't answer to her any more."

"They're in the camera bag, pass them up."

Once they both had a cigarette, Eddie asked the question again, "What gave away Mia's death as murder?"

"I have no idea; you're asking me as though I was there."

"Were you?"

"No!" No humour in her face now. "I was not, and I don't take kindly to being accused of her murder, either." She puffed furiously, hand on her hip. "Detective Benson already went through all this with me, and he practically accused me of killing her, too. That's twice in one fucking day, and I don't care what a nice man you are for letting Mum see Mia, that's out of order, mister."

Eddie held up his hands, "I sincerely apologise."

Chapter 44

Regan stared at Stan Forbes and could barely conceal her dislike of the man. Yes, of course she felt sorry for him – who wouldn't? But if it hadn't been for the phone call where he declared his wife dead, she would still be at MCU now, earning Brownie points from Benson as they continued to interview the Chandlers. So, she settled for the dislike, and didn't really bother to hide it – especially considering he'd landed her here at the site of yet another fucking dead body. For someone who hates dead bodies, she thought, I spend an awful lot of my time with them.

She blew through slack lips, and said, "There's just one more thing."

Stan raised his eyebrows. "A Columbo moment."

"Really?"

He nodded and rubbed his hands together, as though up for the challenge, rather than trying to keep warm.

"I wonder if I might use your toilet before I go?"

"Is that all?" He laughed a kind of 'phew' laugh, shot through with relief. "Of course, of course. Listen, I erm, I feel awkward about this whole thing; won't you allow me to make it up to you, somehow? Just something simple, a cup of tea, perhaps? A cinnamon swirl?"

Regan considered this in two distinct ways. One: he was fucking creepy, but wanted to improve things with the police before she left his house, and considering he played a recording of someone snoring when he knew his wife was dead, no wonder relations needed improving. Two: he was fucking creepy and... No, she was stuck at fucking creepy. "I don't know. I think I'll just be on my way."

"Please. I've been through such a lot lately, and..." He sighed, and dropped his head. "I could use a little company until the mortuary people arrive for my wife. When they do, and she's in the back of their van, you can leave too – no obligation, as the saying goes. It'll be the first time I've been in this house on my own since... well, for ever. Going to take some getting used to."

She stood still and bit the inside of her cheek. On the face of it, it wasn't an unreasonable request, and the body removers would be here in twenty minutes or so. Yet... "Okay. Just one quick cup of tea, and then I must be going. I have paperwork, Mr Forbes."

"Please," he said, "call me Stan again. And the toilet is just along the hall." Like an air steward, he chaperoned her along. "I'll put the kettle on."

And then he was gone.

Regan stood in the darkness at the end of the hall and contemplated just walking out of the house and getting in the car. But, come on, she thought, how would it look if she just abandoned him? And more importantly, how would it sound as a complaint the next morning to DCS Miriam Kowalski and Inspector Benson? The people she was trying to impress. Or at the very least, the people she was trying not to piss off.

Along the other end of the hallway, off into the kitchen, she could hear Stan filling the kettle. She also thought she heard him whistling.

At this end of the corridor, the darkest end, were two doors – both open. One was the lavatory and the other was a small office. There was a window behind the desk and through it shone orange light that, if one stared long enough, could convince you that the desk was painted a grey shade of magnolia. Peculiar.

The office was a place she found interesting. He was a copywriter, whatever the hell that was, and that explained the cheap shelves – just white melamine-faced chipboard – nailed to the walls and stacked with magazines and books, and journals, of loose paper, files, boxes of notebooks, a printer, even an old fax machine buried under an inch of dust and a pile of old photos.

She heard the water shut off, a bang through the house pipes, plumbing from before the war.

There was a shitty little chair with the foam poking out of the seat base at the front, and the black plastic armrests were worn shiny, one of them wound with black tape as a makeshift repair that had become permanent. Copywriting didn't seem to be a lucrative business. On the desk were two things that caught her eye.

In the kitchen, the kettle began to whistle, and if Stan had also been whistling, it was drowned out now.

Regan licked her lips, took a last look down the hall, and stepped inside Stan's office.

On the desk towards the back was a pen holder made of wood, intricately inlaid with different colours of wood, and inside it was a pair of scissors and a half a dozen pens. One of the pens was green. It had a green cap. The other thing to make her sit up and take notice was a jotter of sorts to the side of the main desk blotter. Its paper was yellow.

"I brought sugar too."

Regan jumped. She turned and Stan was right behind her wearing his customary smile.

"Tea's ready. And the cinnamon rolls are fresh today. Please, you must have one – they're just exquisite."

Regan looked back at the green pen, her mouth suddenly dry, her heart heaving in her chest and the beginnings of a headache right behind her eyes. She tried to stay cool. "I always wanted my own office at home," she said. "Somewhere just for me, where I could read—"

"Kitchen. Now."

Chapter 45

"I'VE BEEN DEAD MOST of my life. Just treading water until I could leave home and start being my own person. The economy is flat at the moment."

Eddie smiled inside, that a twenty-two-year-old girl whose idea of stretching her intellect was stacking shelves in a shop, should think the economy was flat. And what the hell did it have to do with this?

"It's expected to grow less than two-per-cent this year, that's after a fairly dismal final quarter last year and an equally shit first quarter this."

Eddie blinked at her.

"My investment is worth less than it should be and it's this as much as my family suddenly not being there for me, that causes me... I'm in a tailspin, Eddie." She swallowed, and said, "I've kept my whole life a secret from my parents because they never liked me. Tell you what, my life with them reminds me of Cinderella – how they used me and treated me like rubbish while Mia was the ugly sister, and she got everything handed to her.

"Everyone feels so sorry for poor old Mia, but she was a lazy-arsed cow who was given everything on a fucking plate." She nodded to the cigarettes, and Eddie responded with a nod of his own, and a tiny ironic smile. As she lit them, she continued, "So I've been digging my way out. The money I get from the newsagents goes to mum as board and lodgings, and the money I make from investments goes into a tax-free savings account. So far, I have twenty-eight thousand quid in there." Her scarf gaped.

Eddie's eyes sprang wide.

"I was waiting to hit thirty-k, and then I was going to bail."

"Not far to go."

"No, but I'm not ready. I need another year before I'm prepared to make the leap – this has all come at the wrong time."

"I'm sure Mia didn't mean to get murdered."

"I know, I know, of course not, but," she looked up at the black sky, the veins in her neck throbbing, and growled. "Just another year, Mia, you selfish cow; that's all I needed."

Eddie envied her. He envied her youth – echoes of Benson there, he thought – but he envied how organised her life was. At her age, he'd bummed around from job to job and just managed to strike it lucky getting into the police force. But the truth was, he was aimless for most of his adolescence – totally aimless. This young lass in front of him had her head screwed on right, and no matter how bad this year was, Eddie knew it would be the springboard to wonderful things. "I've been dead most of my life too."

"Really? You strike me as a man who's got his priorities in order, a man who's sure of his direction in life and has found his niche."

"How old are you again?"

She smiled, shrugged. "Just stating the obvious facts."

He nodded, flicked ash. "You're given one life, and you should exploit it; you should be daring and dashing with it; you should push your own boundaries and feel afraid but still do it. You know what I mean? All those motivational posters that they used to have in Athena back in the nineties, they all meant something to me.

"But I am a coward – always have been and always will be. I settle for security, and I hate change, refuse to push myself for fear of failure, no, no, that's not right; I don't mind failing. I refuse to push myself because I don't see the fucking point, and I can't be arsed anyway. I'm happy doing this shit." He looked at her, realised what he'd said, "I'm sorry, I didn't mean—"

"It's okay, don't be sorry. It's good to get things out – and there's no one better to talk to than a stranger." She puffed some more, head turned but eyes always on Eddie. "Can I tell you something?"

He shrugged, and would happily kill her for a hot cup of Starbucks about now, with one of those Lotus biscuits to go with it. "Of course."

"Marshall?"

"What about him?"

"We'd formed a kind of friendship."

Eddie flicked away his cigarette. "Earlier, you made it sound like you hardly knew him."

"Another bad habit. I've been hiding him from mum and dad for ages. It's been killing me." She stepped forward, lowered her voice. "The night he was killed he was going to give me five hundred quid to add to my portfolio. I was going to invest it for him, and he should have earned at least five percent on it in less than three months."

"Wait, wait, wait. Back up a bit here. You were going to meet a lad who was stabbed to death, and you didn't think the police might need to know?"

"I didn't know he was dead."

"What?"

Clara bit her lip, sighed, and said, "What I mean is I went into Rothwell as arranged, and it was crowded with cops, and so I left again. Then my sister was found… I…I wasn't thinking straight. It was all a shock to me, and I still didn't know that Marshall was dead."

Eddie stared at her, suddenly unsure of everything. He soaked up her words, mind a blank, waiting for the punch line. And when it came, you could have pushed him over with a blade of grass.

She licked her lips, glanced away as she said, "Even though I wanted to wait another year, we were going to leave together."

God, it was hot in here. Regan shrugged out of her leather jacket, and draped it across her arm. Green pen, she thought. Yellow paper. Was it just a coincidence?

"Cheers," Stan nudged her cup with his. "Help yourself to a cinnamon swirl, they really are adorable – I have no idea how I've kept my hands off them. Want me to take your jacket?" He reached for it, but she pulled back.

"No. I'm okay, thanks." No intention of stopping. Considering the two most important people in his life were dead, his cheeriness – fake or otherwise – freaked Regan out slightly.

That cheeriness shrivelled, and then it was an aeroplane about to crash. Hurriedly he put down his own cup of tea and covered his mouth. His shoulders shuddered, and his whine sounded like an injured animal. He looked up to Regan, and the tears brimming on his lids, tumbled down his face onto his shaking hands. Embarrassment made him turn around, reach for a piece of kitchen roll, and shield his eyes with it. "I'm so sorry," he said, "I can't hold it together. I thought I could, but it's too much. What can I do?"

Regan, her misgivings about him dismissed – at least temporarily – put down her own cup and rubbed his arm. It was about all she could do – anything more would be asking for trouble, and anything less would be seen as cold and aloof.

Regan, the green pen!

And she'd had misgivings because he was still fucking creepy, and yes, she supposed half of him being creepy was because he'd appeared at her side in the office like a puff of smoke solidifying, and then ordered her out. But was that anything she wouldn't have done if someone needing the toilet was lurking in her bedroom? Probably not.

Run, Regan, run!

"There are some excellent organisations out there waiting to help you, Stan. I know this because I've used them myself. Well, some of them. I'm not saying I've grieved like you have, not even close, but I've had a lot to deal with and these people got me on my feet again, got me to see the way forward. There really *is* a way forward; I know it all looks so bleak right now, I get that, really I do, but there are things you can do to help."

He was nodding in all the right places, but Regan sensed his listening face was just a facade, and instead of taking in her comments, he was thinking of something else – he was absent.

"Are you alright? Stan?"

He blinked, looked at her, and the smile on his face was one she didn't recognise. It wasn't the friendly smile she'd seen all evening; it was a smile one might wear if inflicting pain on someone on purpose. It was the kind of smile someone who is evil might wear, and he had the eyes to go with it.

Before she could take a step backward, she felt a tug on her arm, like a stinging pain, the kind you'd get after an injection by the doctor. She looked down and protruding from his hand was indeed a syringe.

"I'm sorry, Regan," he said. "But this has gone quite far enough."

Chapter 46

ALMOST IMMEDIATELY, SHE BEGAN to feel different. If she took the time to abstract herself from the fear now plundering her thoughts, to actually sit and listen to her body, she would have said she could feel the poison spreading throughout her body, vein by vein. With this sensation came an additional heat that was not at all uncomfortable, but reminiscent of warm holidays on a sandy beach, sun on your back, soaking it up.

But these feelings didn't reign for long, and then the fear that had always been an undercurrent grew and ousted anything in its way, until she was shaking slightly, until her legs felt too weak to hold her up.

She looked into Stan's eyes, questioning him. Surely, she thought, this was too big a punishment for loitering in his office? She couldn't bring to mind any words, though; she couldn't bring to mouth any of them either. Her eyes threw the question at him, and he only stared at her, the evil stepping aside for a moment to let wonder and amazement have a look.

Regan sank to the floor, and Stan had her round the arms, clasping her in front just beneath her breasts, and he laid her out gently, pushed the jacket out of the way.

Her eyes were still open, still blinking, but slowly, like the effort was too extreme. She could see across the floor, the crumbs around the table legs, the hairs congregated by the kickboard in front of the sink. About six inches away from her hair, if she looked up as high as her eyeballs would go, she could see a spider staring at her, hunkered down like it was sizing her up, ready to attack. Now would be a good time to be able to scream, she thought.

"I've given you a medicine not unlike Valium, Regan," he said. His voice had changed too; it wasn't the creepy, smooth voice of a meek man any more but the sharp, commanding voice of someone in authority who knows exactly what he wants and who has already set in motion the apparatus to make it happen. "It will debilitate you. At first, anyway. If I administer too much, it will eventually put you into a coma, and any more after that could easily kill you. But for the time being," he said, kneeling beside her, peering into her eyes, checking the pupils were still working, "I'm keeping you relaxed, catatonic, if you will. After the men arrive to take away my wife, we'll be taking a journey, you and me. I'm afraid only one of us will wake up tomorrow. I hope you enjoyed your final day on earth; was it everything you'd hoped it would be?" He laughed and Regan's eyes watered all by themselves. Tears spilled across the bridge of her nose and dripped onto the kitchen floor.

She could still see the spider. Her mouth moved.

"What? What did you say?"

She spoke again, and when he lowered his head to her, she tried once more.

"Why?" He sat back on the floor, one knee in the air, arm draped over it. "It's a bit of a sad story, I'm afraid, but we have another few minutes before the men arrive in their black van. "Where to begin?" He gave it some consideration for a while and then said, "My son had always been a little bastard, and I detested him. He didn't fit into this family at all – he was like the odd one out, you see. He was selfish and spoilt, a brat from generation z, or whatever they call themselves. Anyway, he was different from us, stayed in his room, refused to socialise with us – his own parents! She adored him still, did Coreen, but I just could never get along with the lad.

"When he was at school, three or four years ago, his teacher was… can you guess?" He laughed again, enjoying the game, enjoying the reveal. "You got it, it was Mia Chandler. She was utterly stunning, and she had an equally stunning personality. I really liked her, and as I told you and Inspector Benson, I tried and failed to hitch a lift on her – forgive me, I know how crude that sounds.

"Anyway, two or three months ago, Marshall declared he was friends with a girl called Clara – out of the blue, not so much as a by-your-leave; probably someone he met online. As far as I was concerned, he was an introvert who played with himself in his room all day and would amount to absolutely nothing. He got a part-time job in a veterinary clinic, and was going for some minimum qualification so he could get a small wage rise. Incidentally, he's how I laid my hands on the stuff that's currently rendering you cabbage-like – sometimes he can be so gullible. Anyway, that's a story for another time, maybe on our final journey, eh? I'll save it for then.

"I saw him in town one lunch time. He was with this Clara girl, and she was the spitting image of Mia. She stopped me in my tracks. They were sisters. And I got thinking, I got wondering how she was doing these days.

"Long story short, I 'bumped' into Mia one day after school. I invited her out for drinks, she declined again. I nearly threw up. I'd pinned all my hopes on her again, you see," he smiled bravely, remembering. "Turns out she'd just come out of a really bad relationship with someone called Vincent. I was the last thing she wanted, she said. She also had the temerity to call me too old." He drifted away into thoughts all by himself, and returned to Regan with a snap. "Too fucking old! I ask you…The bitch. This went on for some time; I was determined to show her what a nice chap I was – am!

"You're probably thinking to yourself – I understand you can't speak, so I'll put the words in your mouth, okay? *'Stan, but you're happily married. Why would you want to go after someone like Mia?'* That's a fair question, and you're right, I am happily married. Well, I *was* happily married. Not so much now. Now it's like being in prison, now it's like being under surveillance by a person you hate the look of, someone whose mind does not ignite one's desires or… I can't explain. Suffice to say I found that I was not in a happy marriage any longer; I was stuck in a house with someone I didn't like. Two someone's, actually.

"Mia was the woman I deserved, the one I'd promised myself. We would be good together; we could enjoy each other's company, each other's bodies, each other's minds. It would be ecstasy. Oh, and my old mobile ended in 4086, new one isn't registered in my name," he winked. Stan was looking up at the ceiling, delight on his face, but it suddenly clouded over and turned sour. He looked back to Regan, and Regan's heart boomed. "And then they turn on me. Those I've cared for all these years, those I've supported and fed and clothed, turned on me as though I were the enemy. *They* were the fucking enemy!

"Oh. Excuse my language, Regan." He turned a gentle shade of red and sniffled as though rebuked, "Marshall confronted me. *Give me five-hundred pounds, Dad*, he said, *or I'll tell Mum you're pestering a teacher from my old school*. I could not believe what I was hearing. It took what little faith I had in my son and pulverised it. We weren't two people from the same family any more, we were enemies. He wanted the three hundred I'd taken from him when he smashed my laptop, plus another two!"

Stan grabbed Regan by the throat, and his bony hands started to squeeze. His eyes bulged, and he drew his lips back in a snarl. "I wanted to slash his face. I wanted to cut him a new smile, Sergeant! I wanted to gut the little bastard." He licked his lips, and he withdrew his hands as he recalled his feelings, "But I didn't. I played it cool; I was smart. I told him I'd need to get to a cash machine in Rothwell, and I'd see him up by Flintlock Yard at eight o'clock. Of course, I made all the noises about making sure he kept his word, and that he wasn't allowed to threaten me again, blah blah."

Stan leaned in close, closed his eyes and breathed Regan's aroma from just a couple of inches away. He licked his lips, and Regan managed to close her own eyes and seemed able to shrivel up a little tighter. "We had a little tussle. I stabbed the little bastard. Just once, right through the heart." He was smiling, but he was thinking too, back there reliving the whole thing. "Should have seen his face. It was the ultimate face of regret; it was ten out of ten, couldn't have done better. How he wished he hadn't crossed me. How he wished he could have gone back and turned a blind eye, or even encouraged his old man. *Go on, Dad, you deserve a bit of happiness.*" He grunted. "No. That is not today's way. Today's way is to grab money at every opportunity; no need to work for it, just put a claim in, or just extort your father!"

There was a knock at the front door. "Oooh," he said, climbing to his feet, "that'll be the body removers." He looked down at her, grinning, "I don't envy them their task, do you? Back in a moment. Don't go away now." He winked, and left the room.

Regan could barely move. It was as though the connections to her muscles had been severed or were constricted somehow. The only thing she could do without much of a struggle was blink, everything else needed some real thought, some real effort.

One of the things she put some real effort into was pulling her phone out of her pocket. If she could have screamed because of the effort that little task required, she'd have been hoarse. It was as though her arm weighed a ton or was bound to something immovable by a hefty bungee cord. She heard Stan answer the front door, heard the dull tones of his widower's voice and comforting replies of those dressed in black suits.

The phone hit the deck in front of her eyes, the spider didn't skitter away. It crawled closer, and Regan tried to push out her bottom lip and blow as though she were blowing hair out of her eyes. But she couldn't manage it, ended up shushing dust across the floor. Exhausted, she took a breather before she flipped it over, screen side up. The keys appears and she dragged a finger up the screen to get to the text icon – no point in ringing because she couldn't speak. She selected the recipient and began typing, almost passing out because of the exertion.

She could hear Inspector Benson right now, shouting at her for not having a radio. She could see him pointing his finger, growing redder in the face, spittle flying out of his mouth as he berated her. And fuck, he was right. If she had one on her right hip now, all she'd do was press a recessed orange button on top of the radio for a couple of seconds. It would broadcast an automated distress signal, and relay it to everyone on that channel. Dispatch would coordinate an immediate response in the form of coppers – lots of them.

She stared at the spider.

Chapter 47

THE PHONE IN EDDIE's pocket buzzed, and he ripped through the side of the scene suit to fish it out. He opened it, typed the PIN, and read something that caused his brow to furrow somewhat.

"What is it?" Clara asked. "You look like an elderly person faced with a password question."

"Not in the slightest funny," he said, eyes never leaving the screen of his phone. "Computers are sent to give people anxiety attacks and coronaries. And they're bloody good at it." The consternation grew as he typed something, biting his lip in the process.

"Something the matter?"

He looked up from the screen, contemplating his decision. His decision reached, Eddie swivelled the phone around to show her.

It was a text message from Regan. "The detective?"

He nodded.

It read: *Help stans nw*

His reply was: *What? Grammar was invented for a reason, you know.*

For a moment, Clara's confusion matched Eddie's.

"Stans?"

"Stan's!" Eddie said. "Stan needs help!"

"But why is she asking you to go and help him?"

"I have no idea; she knows I'm busy doing this."

"Unless..."

"Unless," he said, "*She's* at Stan's—"

"And *she* needs the help? But what does nw mean?"

"That's youth-speak, you should know that, not me."

"I have no idea. Unless it was supposed to say 'now'."

"Why don't you ring her?"

He looked across at her, almost startled by her logic. Under normal circumstances, the thought of using a phone to ring someone was utterly absurd – he hated speaking to people on phones – that's why he used text, exclusively. But this could be an emergency.

But if it was an emergency, she would have called. Instead, she sent him a text. "Unless *she* doesn't like phones, either," he whispered. Nope, he decided not to ring her.

Eddie began tearing at the suit and eventually wriggled his way out of it like a lizard shedding skin. He grabbed the swabs, grabbed his camera and the van keys. And then halted. "I have no idea where Stan lives."

"I do," Clara said. "Me and Marshall were going to run away together, remember?"

"Get in the van." He could feel another bollocking coming his way from Miriam, but he shoved thoughts of it aside – he'd deal with that bullshit later. "You used to date him? It's gone from not knowing him, to having a thing with him, to eloping with him."

Stan closed the kitchen door, rubbed his eyes hard, and opened the front door. Two men wearing smart black suits stood there looking forlorn. "Mr Forbes?"

"Have you come for my Coreen? Come in, gentlemen. You'll forgive me, I'm not myself these days."

"That's perfectly understandable, Mr Forbes. May we offer our condolences."

"Thank you, that's very kind."

"And can I also thank you for choosing Mercer and Biggin to take care of your wife and manage the procedure from here on." They came in and closed the door behind them, the smaller of the two stood behind a board that had carrying handles and large Velcro straps on it, peering around it like someone wishing he was on a surfing holiday. To one side, he placed a folded trolley, and stood next to his colleague who was still rambling to Stan.

Stan had momentarily zoned out as he imagined the stretcher, burdened with Coreen's bloated body, sliding down the stairs, imagined her being wheeled out to the van, and then imagined her being behind the van door, trundling down the street. True freedom. Half an hour away. He could already feel his blood pressure dropping.

"…but don't let it intrude on your thoughts tonight. I'll leave you a leaflet with the details, but don't forget the ten percent offer, okay? And we'll get cracking if that's okay?"

Stan nodded, took a couple of steps back to allow the men past, head bowed in abject misery all the time.

"I presume the police have finished? CSI done what they needed to do?"

Stan nodded again. "Yes, there's a release form somewhere. They couldn't hang about, a job to go to apparently. My Coreen obviously isn't important enough for them to stay behind for."

"No. Quite. They're very busy, though. And they wouldn't have left if this had been anything other than a straightforward passing. If you get my drift, Mr Forbes."

"Yes, yes, I do, thank you. It's straightforward. Well, gentlemen, if you'll forgive me, I'll er, let you get on with it." Stan rubbed his eyes again until they were good and red. "First floor, front bedroom."

Regan heard the front door close and indeed, the cold draft blowing against her face ceased and things grew quiet. She peered up at the top of her vision; the spider was even closer. She also noticed something else: the phone was still there. It buzzed and the screen lit up. She heard Stan giving the men instructions, and she dragged her arm towards the phone, praying the kitchen door wouldn't open yet. *Another minute, please, another thirty seconds. Come on!*

"I wonder what kind of help she needs?"

Clara looked at him as he opened the van door. "Password type help?"

"Well, yes. I mean, it doesn't exactly scream 'urgent', does it?"

"Depends. Hard to tell with texts. They're often ambiguous."

Eddie nodded at the scene guard and decided not to offer an explanation as to where a strange female had arrived from inside a controlled scene. "Sign me out, I'll most likely be back in an hour. Nah, fuck it, I'll be back tomorrow." And to Clara he said, "Get in."

Seat belts on, he looked at her, not sure how to play it. Regan could look after herself, for sure, so just how urgent was this? Should he summon help and then apologise when it turned out Regan had forgotten how to unlock her tablet?

"Just drive quickly. You can get backup or whatever you call it once you get there, if needed."

Eddie set off; having a debate with himself about it all but eventually arriving at the conclusion Clara had reached minutes previously. "Where'm I going?"

Stan closed the kitchen door and was about to get on the floor next to her again, when he noticed it. "So, this is how you treat me while I'm away, is it, Regan? I can't trust you." He knelt beside her, reached over her shoulder and was about to shoo the spider away, when he saw how it affected her, how much she disliked it. He withdrew his hand, smiling, and settled down to watch. "Two-timing me. You're a hussy," he whispered. He got close to her ear, and whispered, "This is how I killed my darling wife. It's painless, don't worry. It was strange to watch, though. It's like you're trapped inside a cage – you, I mean, not me, obviously. Anyway, it's like you're trapped inside a cage, can't move, can't scream, and me – the observer – just sees the lights growing dimmer and dimmer, until, like a candle flame getting smaller until… poof. It just goes out. Fascinating."

Chapter 48

EDDIE WAS THANKFUL TRAFFIC was light, and now he was heading from Horsforth to Rothwell, a journey of some fifteen miles, he was heading back into familiar territory. Indeed, this used to be his old patch when he worked divisional CSI, and recently it felt like he'd never left.

The job at Daisy's house was in Beeston, only four miles away, and more recently, the job at Mia's was just a couple of miles away in Hunslet, near the river Aire.

"Left here," Clara pointed as though speech wasn't quite enough.

Eddie saw the road sign. "Knightsbridge," he said, noting how it was a dead-end road with only a narrow path at its head, probably leading away to the park and the tennis courts. It was years since he'd been around here, but he put the brakes on his wistful thoughts as soon as he saw the black VW van with the tailgate wide open and bright white LED lights coldly peeling the darkness back a few layers.

"There," she said, "thirty-eight."

He pulled up just opposite the private ambulance, and just behind a plain police car. The road and the beginning of the path was bathed in orange streetlight, but beyond its glare was blackness. It was like being in a microcosm, a secret place well hidden from the wider world beyond Knightsbridge.

And this place, this secret place, seemed to be the perfect place from which to get a message asking for help. It was cryptic; it might have been just playful trickery, and Eddie wore the kindling of a smile, ready for Regan to leap out and scare the shit out of him. But even someone of Regan's childishness, embellished with a low IQ, too – he must remember to tell her that! – wouldn't drag him away from a scene exam just to jump out on him.

That realisation killed the smile, and he took the keys out of the ignition.

"What do you want me to do?"

Eddie looked across at her, licked his lips, unsure of what to say. "You'd better stay here," he said at last, "can't have you in there while they're messing about with the body." And then the penny dropped. He knew what was wrong, why Regan needed help. They'd begun moving Mrs Forbes and found something unexpected. Maybe the lividity suggested she'd moved, or they found a recent injury that they couldn't explain.

But what was fogging Eddie's thoughts right now was Kenny. Kenny had attended the scene of a sudden death, and he'd taken the required photos, and conducted a visual examination that obviously showed no signs of foul play, and left that scene, happy as a pig in shit. If that was the case, either Regan called him here for things not relating to the body of dead Mrs Forbes, or Kenny had fucked up again. Again! First there was the Daisy girl, how Kenny and Skid hadn't bothered to check the entire house when they'd been asked to because they'd 'forgotten', and now this: he imaged a sixteen-inch bread knife protruding from her back, and Kenny chose not to notice it. If that was the case, he'd have words. And maybe he'd boot Kenny out the door, hot on Skid's tail.

"Yeah," he opened the door, ever more unsure of what he was heading into, "just... just stay here."

Eddie closed the van door and sank into a chill he hadn't noticed when in Horsforth only half an hour ago. This place was like a bowl hollowed out of a hillside and then hit with a vacuum; it was deserted, it was as though the whole village was holding its breath, too nervous to make a sound.

This in turn made Eddie feel nervous, and he thought about calling for some police backup before he'd even found out what the problem was. 'So, why do you need the officers, Eddie? We have P1s coming out of our ears'. There was no satisfactory answer to that question.

He gritted his teeth and was about to cross the road and head up the short path to the red-painted door of number thirty-eight. *Do I knock, or just go straight in?*

This thought was made redundant as soon as it fired the question synapse somewhere in the arse of his brain. The red-painted front door opened and a man wearing a black suit and a pair of shiny shoes stepped backward out of the house, down the single step and onto the garden path. He pulled a gurney with a body wobbling under a cheap and cheerful body bag as though trying to break free. His mate, the chap pushing the gurney and facing Eddie wore a similar suit, only much slimmer, and he wore a grimace too and a face full of sweat. It looked as though he was trying to hold his breath. The whole scene reminded Eddie of a Laurel and Hardy sketch.

The duo, and the body on a creaking gurney, dropped down off the garden path and onto the pavement. "Evening," Eddie said, and then understood the grimace and why the guy was holding his breath. Mrs

Forbes was… ripe, eye-wateringly so. The van door was open, spilling illumination across the road, and Eddie hoped they had some good air fresheners for the journey and some Febreze for after they off-loaded her.

Both men just nodded, neither opened their mouth to speak.

Well, Eddie thought, Regan's plea for help seemingly had nothing to do with a sixteen-inch bread knife sticking out of the body. Kenny was off the hook.

So what could it be? And if it wasn't urgent, why hadn't she the decency to reply to him?

He didn't need to knock because the door was still open. He popped his head inside and got another whiff of the death farts that made his throat close up, so he never managed to shout, 'Hello'.

Directly ahead of him, along a short hall with the stairs to the right – still bearing gurney skid marks in the carpet pile of each stair - was what he assumed to be the kitchen. He walked towards it, soon to encounter Regan or Mr Forbes, surely. It would be quite nice to see Stan Forbes again; he always came across as a decent kind of man who was polite and endearing. Before the door, he stopped. To his right was a long hall, two doors at the far end, and Eddie was about to turn right and head down there to see where those doors led and to see if he could meet anyone.

But a noise coming from the kitchen stopped him.

Chapter 49

STAN WATCHED THE SPIDER crawl closer to Regan, and despite her facial muscles being as useless as all her other muscles, he could see her flinch. That confused him. He'd given her enough drugs to render her a blob of meat with eyeballs – immobile.

And then he saw it, the unmistakable bulge of a mobile phone in her jeans pocket.

He pulled it out, swiped the screen, but it was locked. However, there was a summary on the lock-screen. It said, 'Eddie Collins – *What? Grammar was invented for...*' It was sent twenty-eight minutes ago. Stan looked at Regan's eyes. They hid behind half closed eyelids, but there was no mistaking the guilt hiding along with them.

"Regan," he said. "What the hell have you done?" He stood and went to a cupboard. He took out another vial of drugs, filled a syringe. "Stupid woman."

Chapter 50

EDDIE SWALLOWED AND THEN just opened the door.

He couldn't quite believe what he saw. Regan was lying on the ground on her side and Stan Forbes, meek and mild Stan Forbes, was kneeling next to her ready to inject something into her arm. Regan didn't even move at the sudden intrusion, but Forbes's neck almost snapped as he flipped his head around and found Eddie standing there.

He smiled. "Shut the door."

Eddie's mouth fell open.

Regan squealed something almost incoherent. It sounded like 'Trap', but her lips seemed incapable of forming the 't', and instead she squealed, 'Crap'.

"What the fuck are you doing to her?"

"Eddie, listen to me. I want you to close the door. Now."

"I said what the fuck are you *doing*?"

"I gave her a mild sedative to help her relax."

"Noooo," squealed Regan – almost inaudibly. "Crap."

Eddie charged into the room, but Stan didn't move from Regan's side. He looked up at him, no friendliness there any longer, no fear either, it seemed. He licked his lips, and pressed the syringe against her arm hard enough to depress the skin. "This is a second dose," he said.

"It's likely to put her in a coma or it'll kill her. Not sure which. Now please close the door."

Eddie pushed the door, and it latched. "Come on, Stan. This isn't like you; you're a nice guy. There's no need to do this." Eddie approached slowly, both hands in the air as though someone had a gun to his head.

"Here's your choice: I can give this dose to her, and you get me. Or I can give it to you, and I walk out of here."

"What? Are you for real?"

Stan shrugged. "Your call."

"Why are you doing this? Have you lost your fucking marbles?"

"I'll give you to the count of three. Then I'll give it to her, okay?"

"Okay, okay, give it to me. Christ's sake, man."

"Take off your belt. Pull your trousers down around your ankles and then fasten the belt around your ankles."

"What? Seriously."

"If you question me again, I'll give her the dose. Okay? Just do as I ask."

Eddie fumbled with his belt, pulled it out of the loops, then dropped his trousers and secured the belt in place and pulled it tight.

"Lie down on your back, but put your left arm under your body, leave your right arm outstretched."

Eddie shook his head in disbelief. "You've really thought about—"

"Just do it. Don't have me ask again. It makes no difference to me who gets this dose, so think the next time you open your mouth."

Eddie complied, and Stan stood on Eddie's right hand and bent to administer the drug. The syringe didn't even touch Eddie's skin before Eddie spun, released his left hand and punched Stan square in the side of the face, managed to drag his right hand free and would have grabbed Stan by the leg, but he staggered backwards, out of reach.

Stan gathered his senses quickly, and ran out of the kitchen, holding his reddening cheek. Eddie had knocked the syringe clear, and he could see it over by the sink unit. He untied his ankles and crawled across to Regan. She blinked at him.

This left Eddie in a bad situation: chase after Stan or tend to Regan and get some help on the way.

Regan won; they'd catch up with Stan soon enough.

He knelt beside her and watched her breathe; it was very slow, and she was cold too, her forehead clammy. "Regan, can you hear me? It's Eddie Collins."

There might have been a slight flicker of the eyelids, but it was difficult to tell. He took out his phone, hit three nines and called for help.

From the warmth of the van, Clara watched the two men struggle to get the gurney off the pavement and into the road behind their van. It was like watching a Laurel and Hardy sketch. The front wheels dipped into the gutter and for a moment she thought the whole thing was going to tip over, but they caught it in time and the big guy tried to lift it and steady at as the thin guy swung the rear end around so that it approached the precipice of the kerb edge straight on.

At that moment, a blur took the form of a running man whose momentum, as he sped away from the house with the red-painted door, could not prevent him from running into the thin man who was steadying the rear of the gurney with fifteen stone of jelly strapped to it.

Consequently, the gurney began to tip and the thin man lost his grip, then shot his hand out to grab the frame, mis-calculated and instead added to the problem by pushing the gurney over. The running man, who it turned out was Stan Forbes, leapt off the kerb in slow motion with the grace of an Olympic hurdler and the wide eyes of a cow in the company of a man wearing long rubber gloves. Thin man overreached himself and began to fall after the gurney, and fat man let go of his end and began to corkscrew himself into the ground, his own grimace mirrored that of the thin man.

Clara, stunned by the event, opened her van door, and climbed out. She began running after Stan, just as the tipping gurney hit the road and the body bag burst like a water balloon. Thin man followed, less gracefully. There was a small tidal wave of clear liquid with flecks of red and green in it, like someone hurling a bucket of slops across their yard; it was a mini tsunami splashing right across the road.

Thin man fell into the soup, immediately stood and vomited down his trousers and shoes. The wave brought a stench that caused her to retch as she gathered speed, following Stan Forbes as he headed towards the dark and overgrown path at the head of the dead-end road.

Chapter 51

Clara gave chase and Stan ran through the weak orange cone of the streetlamp directly outside the entrance to the secluded path, and was then swallowed by shadows so thick they felt solid. "Stan! Stan, it's me, Clara."

Stan pulled up, and was panting, hands on knees, rasping as Clara stopped next to him.

"What the hell are you doing here?" he asked. "We're not supposed to meet until tomorrow. That was the arrangement."

"We don't have time for chit-chat. This has all gone to shit, the whole fucking plan."

"Stop swearing."

"Shut the fuck up!"

"He'll be along soon—"

"Where are the keys?"

He said nothing for a few seconds, bit down on his lip and tried to breathe through a nose that whistled. "Did you tell him you and Marshall were planning—"

"Yes! But she sent a text. Regan sent him a text asking for help at your house. What the hell happened? She was supposed to see your wife get shipped off and then leave you alone."

"Something happened."

"No shit. What?"

In the near darkness, he eyed her. "I got the feeling Regan thought I'd killed your sister. Hell, I got the feeling she thought I'd killed everyone!"

Clara licked her lips and checked over her shoulder. All she could hear were Laurel and Hardy shouting and grunting and hurling. "Why would she think that?"

"I don't know, but she was stringing me along; I could just tell."

She peered down at him as he still tried to catch his breath, and as her eyes grew used to the darkness, she could see he was being honest with her, there appeared to be no malice there, only a keen interest in what was happening over her shoulder. "Keys?"

"Where I said they'd be. Look, Clara, nothing's changed, okay? This is a hiccup, but we're still good to go. Tomorrow at noon, get the keys and we'll get sorted." He stood up and held her face gently in his hands. He leaned forward and kissed her. "I love you," he whispered.

Behind them, they could hear hurried footfalls. They could hear Eddie Collins chasing Stan.

"You want to know what gave the game away for her?"

"What do you mean? Hurry, Clara."

"I left a suicide note for the police to find in her handbag. It was on yellow paper and written in green pen."

"So?"

"The note suggested Mia and Marshall were having an affair, but your ugly little fantasy about Mia didn't sit well with the police. I'm guessing, but I think I'm right. You became a suspect in something that should have been wrapped up and filed away as a murder-suicide. They began looking for a murderer, Stan. So I put the yellow paper and the green pen in your office. I gave them a murderer." She smiled.

"What? Why would you—"

"You're the murderer they're looking for and I gave them you."

Stan's eyes widened as his mind gradually absorbed her words and their meaning. "I killed my son for you! For us!"

"You killed your son because you were stalking my sister, you fucking pervert, and he found out and blackmailed you. And that was good for me – both parts were good for me because when she rejected you, I used a bit of thigh and a lot of cleavage, and took my chance with you. You thought you chose me, didn't you? Wrong, I chose you, and you doubled my portfolio. And now Marshall is out of the way, I don't have to share your money with him."

"You'll not get one fucking penny."

"Really?" Clara screamed.

Stan screamed too. He was frightened, and she'd shocked him. It took him several more seconds fumbling around the darkness inside his head to realise what she was fumbling around in the darkness in the alley for. Her eyes: they were feral, they were foreign to him; they scared him. Stan suddenly felt quite alone, as though Clara had played him and was watching him die swinging on the gallows. Smiling, clapping in time with his twitching feet.

He didn't understand what was happening. He could hear Collins puffing as he entered this weird tunnel of bushes they found themselves in. The lack of light, just a streetlight that flickered like sunlight through the trees on a windy day. It was all wrong, somehow.

The pain came not long after he realised she'd cleverly found herself a way out of it all, and left him to bleed out on a rough pavement with empty beer bottles, condoms, and a cigarette ends scattered at the edges like fat in an artery – like father like son, he absently thought.

He would never have guessed he was to end his days in a place like this, having forsaken his past, eliminated his present, and having given over his future to someone who thought nothing of it, just wanted his money. A whole life wasted for a few thousand pounds. He felt so sad, so regretful.

He watched her and was mesmerised by her beauty, still. Her eyes twitched as they watched him. There was pain in his chest, yet it was weird, like a heat, and then it felt like a barb was tugging at something. The last thing he saw was Clara's eyes as he fell forwards to the ground. The last thing he heard was her laughing. He didn't feel his face smash into the pavement.

Clara was crying hysterically when Eddie reached her. Screaming might have been a better term. She had blood streaming down her hand, dripping almost constantly from her fingertips, and as he guided her back towards the light, he lifted it, tried to keep the blood flow to a minimum. "What the fuck just happened?"

"I saw him run out and push the trolley over. He ran down here, so I chased him."

"You daft girl, it could have been you lying there!"

"I knew he'd done something bad, or else he wouldn't have run out of the house like that."

Eddie shone his torch onto Stan and noticed something like a ring-pull sticking out of his chest.

"What is that?"

He got closer and realised what it was. "It's a skewer, like you'd find in a kebab shop."

"Is that what he tried to stab me with?"

She held her hand out, and despite the blood pooling in her palm, it was easy to see a ragged little hole in its centre.

He shone the torch again onto Stan, just a quick glance top to bottom, and that's when he noticed the buttons on Stan's cardigan, or hoodie top, whatever it was called. They had black centres, but around their periphery were shiny blue rings, like earrings, he supposed. He closed his eyes for a moment and remembered the horrible little alley where Marshall was killed; Flintlock Yard, Clara had called it. He looked across at her and wasn't wholly surprised to find her looking directly at him – studying him. Eddie didn't even know it was called Flintlock Yard. Hell, even the police system didn't know it was called Flintlock Yard. Clara did.

"You okay?" she asked.

He nodded. So far from 'okay' that it was on a different continent. "He's drugged Regan; she's barely responsive. Come on, let's get back to her. The paramedics will be here soon."

On the way back up the hill towards Stan's house, he had an arm around Clara, supporting her. He could feel her shivering. "Try to keep it elevated."

"He tried to fucking stab me."

"I know, I know. You're alright, okay?"

"He fell, though, somehow. It was dark, I don't know—"

"Don't worry about that now; we can sort it all out later."

The two undertakers had collected most of Mrs Forbes, leaving behind a stain on the road the size of a cowhide. It wasn't a pleasant thought that all her life amounted to now was a pungent stain on the road. Anyway, they'd gone now, and in the near distance he could make out the distinctive flicker of blue lights.

Chapter 52

The Beginning

The look of relief on Mia's face was something to behold: how she looked like she'd just run a 10k and was looking forward to a refreshing drink – only to discover someone had handed her a bottle of fresh cat piss; kind of a relief but not really. "You?" she asked. She was about to slam the door when Clara shoulder barged it and Mia fell backwards, jolting her spine as she hit the floor on her coccyx. It hurt enough to bring a yelp to her throat and tears to her eyes. "What the fuck do you want, Clara?"

Mia scuttled away a few feet.

Clara had been in Flintlock Yard only half an hour ago, and watched how Marshall Forbes got on his knees and pleaded with his old man to forgive him. His face was earnest, his tears genuine and the sobbing, the snot bubbles, and the pleading was straight from the heart, and was delivered with truth, with such passion, that *she* might have been inclined to believe him, and so not plunge the steak knife into his own son's heart.

She had watched Stan put on a pair of latex gloves, and deliver the fatal blow with precision minus emotion, and she'd watched as

Stan helped his dying son sink to the ground like a deflating balloon. Perhaps he did that to preserve the boy's dignity, or to prevent unnecessary suffering or pain; she didn't know, but it touched her how benevolent this father was in his son's final moments.

And if she'd expected Stan to be covered in Marshall's pumping blood, she was mistaken. The heart stopped pumping immediately, and the knife was plugging the hole. There was but a seep, and Stan didn't have a drop on him.

When Marshall was laid down, when the look of fear and the look of misunderstanding and regret had faded from his eyes and from the cramped muscles of his face, smoothed out by the passing of life, she felt a certain sorrow of course, but she felt a release too. He was gone, and so too were the problems he had created: blackmailing his father, for one. Wanting to be a part of Clara's investment portfolio another. Marshall was a good kid, a good man, actually, but he had nothing to contribute to Clara's future, and certainly little in the way of money to add to her investments. The money he owned had been confiscated, and no amount of blackmail would get it back for him.

The silly thing was he was trying to blackmail his father to a mother who already knew Stan was being unfaithful. She was content to ignore it so long as Stan was a good father to their boy, and was a reasonable husband to her. She had her head screwed on right, thought Clara; why spoil a good thing? And the woman with whom Stan was being unfaithful, actually wasn't being unfaithful at all. Mia had rejected him for the millionth time, and so rebounded right into Clara's open hands – easy as that.

Stan was in his forties, and Clara barely glided into her twenties – she had a lot to offer, and it wasn't difficult getting him to switch sisters. But the best bit was the package he came with. Research into Stan Forbes showed he was not short of a few quid, and it was the kind of money that Clara could use to further her career. Stan was on board with it all, but then he would be, seeing as his sexual needs were being well catered for. She found it more than a little amusing to see his cock cloud his judgment, to see him rendered ridiculously open to manipulation. There had been hoops to jump through first, of course, as there always were in any successful business venture.

They'd talked, and this was the best course of action – this thing lying on the shitty cobbles in front of them as the rain began to fall – was the best course of action. Stan turned to her, not a single tear in his eye, not an ounce of regret in his voice. "You sure you don't want a hand with Mia?"

She didn't hesitate, "Nope. I'm good." She was looking forward to it, had even planned to make her think Mad Vince was out to get her again – nothing like a bit of low-level terror to get someone fired up. "Just gimme the knife and I'll go get it sorted."

The plan was simple: eradicate both of the thorns in their lives, be happy. Simple. But when thinking about things in finer detail, they got creative – to the point of rinsing out a screw-cap Budweiser bottle and using that to transport the knife to Mia's address without any of Marshall's blood being smeared from the blade. They'd tried it and the neck held the knife handle pretty well and prevented the edges of the blade touching the sides of the bottle. Beautifully simple.

Stan pulled out the knife, and because Marshall was semi-sitting, the blood spewed out like toothpaste from a split tube, and he doused the blade in it until it began to coagulate and still with his gloves on, dropped the knife into the bottle. He smiled all the while.

Clara's heart jerked when he handed the knife over. Now it was down to her; he'd passed the baton along, and the game rested on her ability to kill and make it look like a suicide. "The only way the police will come looking for a killer," Stan had said, "is if they don't believe Mia's death is a suicide." It made sense. Of course it did.

And now standing here panting, smiling down at Mia as she screamed at her for scaring the shit out of her, Clara just wanted to plunge the knife in and piss off – who cared what the police thought; Mia'd had this coming for the last twenty fucking years, and Clara just wanted it finished with. Her heart pummelled, and beneath the latex gloves, her hands were sweaty.

"I'll tell dad about this, Clara." She struggled to stand, but made it to her designer feet eventually. "This is going too far. And another thing," she said, before she'd even managed to straighten herself up a bit, "What's this I hear about you and Stan Forbes getting together?"

If Clara's heart had pummelled before, it positively back-fired now and Clara almost fell over. "Who says anything about me and Stan Forbes?"

"Marshall says, that's who."

Clara closed her eyes for a moment, and pictured him lying on his back with a blood puddle growing in his Queen t-shirt, getting rained on, growing cold and not regretting anything in life – including spilling the beans to Mia – not regretting anything any more. And that would become the basis of the note she'd leave. "My life has nothing to do—"

"Clara, he's a fucking letch! He's twice your age, for one thing, and for another, he has a family! He has a wife and a son. He's just an old pervert. He just wants a bit of young p—"

"You're not going to say the p-word, are you? That is so below even you, Mia."

"It's true! He's been after me for years!"

"Well, you should be glad he's switched his attention then, eh? Or perhaps… that's it! You're fucking jealous! He's chasing me and all you have are memories of Mad Vincent scaring the shit out of you. Is that it? Can't cope with living alone, not being the focus of a man's affection, eh? Your fingers are a poor replacement, aren't they? But at least you don't get beaten any more." She smiled, knowing full well that one had hurt, it had gone deep and it had wounded her. Victory was close, and she had to remind herself how detached Stan had been when the time came to despatch his own son. She'd need that resolve over the next few minutes – she simply had to consider only her future, and not entertain thoughts of their past as sisters. Mia was nothing more than an obstacle.

"What are you doing here, anyway?"

Clara swallowed, puffed out her breath and stared at Mia trying her hardest to develop a meaningful smile, one that didn't look like she hated her sister and was trying to distract her. "I… I er, I wanted to try and make up with you."

Mia laughed. "Are you fucking serious? We've gone twenty-two years rubbing each other up the wrong way, not caring if we don't see each other from one dismal family Christmas to the next, and here you are trying to make up?" She folded her arms. "Try again, dear sister."

"Okay, okay… I've come to kill you."

Mia laughed even harder, and that made Clara smile – genuinely – and then it made her laugh too. The more they both laughed, the harder it was to stop. Clara took a step forward, and made to embrace Mia, only her hands never made it round her back. They aimed for her throat and once there they clamped tight, suddenly the laughter died, the good feeling left town, and fear climbed on board with a front row seat.

Mia's eyes widened, and her fingers clawed at Clara's wrists, as she realised that this wasn't a jolly jape after all. This was serious. Deadly serious.

Clara's face was devoid of expression, determined, much as Stan's had been when Marshall slumped to the ground. Android murderers. Clara stepped forward pushing Mia backwards, her legs cycling frantically trying to stay upright. Her hands tightened and Clara almost lost her grip, but she pushed harder and smacked the back of Mia's head into the corner of the hall wall. It knocked a good percentage of power from Mia's escape attempt, and it was like she'd given up, as though fighting back was useless.

And in that moment, the very moment when she sensed Mia had given up, she hated her more than she ever had in their entire miserable lives as siblings. How spineless she was, how she relied on mummy and daddy to get her through life's bad patches. Well, this was one fucking bad patch daddy dear couldn't help with.

She folded! She just fucking folded, and bailed out, like the pathetic piece of shit she was.

As Clara took a slim coil of rope from her backpack, she put her mouth to Mia's ear, and whispered, "Enjoy death, you fucking waste of life."

Half an hour later, Clara turned off the light and closed the door behind her.

Before leaving she'd searched the house for some cotton buds, and had spent a good ten minutes making sure that any skin cells beneath Mia's nails were cleaned out. No point in taking chances just in case the police didn't believe this was a suicide. There were some welts on the back of her wrists; looked like she'd be wearing sweaters for a while.

Walking away from the address and leaving the door slightly ajar so the postman would find her, Clara congratulated herself on performing like a machine, just as Stan had. But the very edges of her proud smile looked downcast, sad almost, as if a little bit of her had died with Mia.

Chapter 53

He'd been here about thirty minutes already, maybe longer, and in all that time his eyes still registered nothing. It was as though they couldn't get used to the intensity of the blackness.

Eddie was both sides of the same coin simultaneously: a little afraid of what was to come, and bored shitless. It was difficult to stay so quiet and so still for so long, not even knowing if things would work out, or if he'd be left here for hours and everything would go to ratshit – or had already gone to ratshit.

They'd managed to get Regan to the hospital, and she was on drips and monitoring equipment, and they'd left her in a critical but comfortable condition, and Eddie had vowed to put all this right. Benson had vowed to make the disturbed evening up to his wife, but this – Regan being poisoned – outweighed his wife's protests by a significant amount.

As well as Benson being dragged away from home, they'd dragged out poor Kenny, too. He'd been slightly less than pleased at having to return to Stan Forbes's house – well, the alley nearby, and process what Eddie had termed an 'accidental death – possibly'. When Eddie had explained to him what had happened, Kenny had laughed so hard he went light-headed and had to sit down. They'd agreed to lock down

Stan's house, and would look into beginning a forensic examination in the following days, personnel permitting.

Clara had been formally released on condition that she be checked over in the A&E department at the Leeds General. Eddie himself had put her in a beat car and had instructed the officers to stay glued to her side to make sure she had a medical examination, and then drop her at a Holiday Inn in Horsforth. "You can probably come back to your family home in a couple of days, okay?"

She'd protested about the medical, but Eddie had insisted. He got in close, and said, "Listen; I want to thank you so much for being there when I needed to get here so quickly. And I have a duty of care to make sure you're not injured, okay? I know you don't want to spend a couple of hours in A&E, but would you please just endure it? For me?"

She'd nodded, said, "Thank you. I'm sorry we've caused you so much trouble."

"Hey, it's been no trouble. I was just grateful you were on hand to get me here quick enough. It's down to you that Regan is still alive." He'd smiled, patted her arm, and added, "I'll be back at your house from about midday tomorrow, and I'll rattle through it fairly quickly, so you could be back home as early as tomorrow evening. How 'bout that?"

"That would be lovely, thank you."

As soon as she'd checked in, and as soon as the police had left her alone, Clara left The Holiday Inn.

Although she wasn't anticipating anything getting in her way, she had a knife and would use it without a second thought. Freedom was everything now – that and the money she had – it was well worth defending with someone else's life if required. She held it now, gripped it tightly, nervous, throat dry.

She peered over the back fence and saw the back yard was still deserted. She assumed there would be a cop up by the front of the house, sitting in his car, maybe playing backgammon or Othello on his phone, watching a film, maybe, watching *porn* maybe – attention somewhere else entirely. The house and the garage totally forgotten by him just as the aliens landed or Miss Biglips got her tits out.

Either way, there was nothing to be wary of, and she calmed slightly, assured by the lack of any light around here – protected by the darkness.

She thought back to the last thing Stan had said to her before he inadvertently fell on the skewer: get the key, and meet at midday. Well, Clara had wasted no time at all, and as soon as she'd managed to shake Eddie Collins and the cops off, she'd gone and got the key, and she'd got Stan's cash too, nearly eighty thousand. A very nice little contribution, and when his house sold, there'd be more. But for now, that, and the thirty thousand she already had would tide her over and give her investment business a healthy shot in the arm and a kick up the arse she'd longed for.

There would also be the opportunity to buy her folks' house too – the mortgage company would look favourably on her, and she could sell that at a massive markup. And that's when Clara's life would truly begin. She was tingling at the thought; her body almost crackled with excitement, and she congratulated herself on the perfect plan.

Well, almost perfect.

She hadn't expected her parents to get caught. But that little event would give her their house, so it wasn't entirely without its positives. The only negative though, as far as she could tell, was her own bad luck in having the same CSI guy examine Mia's scene and her dad's garage. Okay, she admitted to herself, the only fault had been her own – a slight lapse in memory or in planning perhaps. But never mind, she told herself, she would put that right tonight and sleep well ever after.

Clara felt the cool dampness across the top of the wooden fence, winced at the pain in her palm, and slowly pulled herself up and over, sliding down the other side in silence, her feet touching down in soft soil. She took a moment to gather her thoughts, and to calm her heart before hopping onto the lawn and creeping to the garage and the side door.

She'd prepared herself for it to be locked and had the spare key from the kitchen in her backpack. She reached forward and tried the handle slowly twisting it until it clicked. Her heart thudded and she silently pulled the door open. She tightened her grip on the knife – still a little apprehensive. It was absolutely black in here, only the smell of blood and dampness to keep her company.

Eddie heard the door. It clicked before the faintest slice of non-black grew wider as the door opened. A figure filled the door frame and Eddie's heart tripped over itself. The figure came inside, and Eddie could hear the rustling of its clothing. He could see Clara, and heard her pause and remove the backpack. From it she took a light and suddenly the blackness exploded, and Eddie blinked, hoped she wouldn't notice him, and saw her walk across the dried blood on the floor, and reach out for the rope. She took it down, shoved it in the bag, straightened and put it back on.

He took a stride forward and said, "Don't forget the skewers."

Clara shrieked and dropped the torch, and was about to run for the door but Eddie beat her to it, stood in her way. The torch rolled away and stopped against the wall, shining a quarter of a beam of light along the floor. "You'll want the skewers," he said, "otherwise I might think *you* killed Stan after I compare them."

"Eddie," she said, panicking.

"'Oh, Eddie, I don't know what happened, he must've fallen on it.' You're so full of shit, Clara. And the rope. I thought a girl like you, one who has the rest of her life planned out and sewn up, would have thought about it ages ago and removed it. But you didn't, you forgot about it." He stepped towards her. "*I* didn't forget it. And I knew you'd come back for it. Unless, you *had* remembered, and that…"

Clara's hand twitched.

"That's what you were doing here earlier on when you bumped into me."

She said nothing.

"Having a chat with your old Uncle Eddie, eh? Gauging how the case was progressing, marvelling at how no one had spotted the rope here, how it seemed identical to the one that Mia hanged herself with."

"I have no idea what you're talking about, now stand aside and let me leave."

"You can leave when you tell me why you killed her."

"I did not kill my sister."

"You throttled her then hanged her, and you planted a knife from Stan Forbes's kitchen that had Marshall's blood all over it, in your sister's handbag. Before doing that, though, you put her fingerprint ridge detail into the blood on the blade, thereby implicating her in Marshall's murder. How'm I doing so far?" He grinned.

"I'm warning you, you're holding me here illegally, Mr Collins. You have no power of arrest."

"Of course I do. I am allowed to arrest you to prevent you committing a crime, and I *know* you're about to commit a fucking crime, Clara."

"What crime?"

"But do you know what you messed up?"

"I have no—"

"No idea what I'm talking about? Yeah, yeah. Save it for the interview later – Benson loves a challenge." He pointed at her, not with a finger of accusation, but with a thoughtful finger, a 'have you considered this' finger. "You forgot the rope, yeah, we know about that."

"I don't—"

"It's in your fucking rucksack, Clara!" And then Eddie relaxed slightly. "But that aside, you want to know what you forgot? It's fundamental; so surprised you didn't consider it."

Clara bit down on her bottom lip, eyes all the time looking for a chance to bolt for the door while Eddie's attention was elsewhere.

"What's the last thing you're going to touch if you decide to end it all by hanging?"

"May I go now?"

"Think about it, right. The rope is around your neck, and you're looking down at your feet, wondering if it'll hurt, and if so, how long for. How long will you suffer with your weight on your neck before you pass out? Then how long before you die? You've heard it's only ten seconds, but that seems rather short to you. You wonder if it's nearer thirty seconds. Forty. A minute? Could you endure all that pain for a minute?"

"Eddie—"

"And not being able to breathe for a minute, it must be like drowning. Your lungs screaming at you, your chest on fire, panic setting in.

Could you handle it? But you're nearly sure it's only ten seconds. Not long, is it? You test the weight by bending your knees; you want to see what it feels like. The rope tightens a bit and... well, have you ever had your blood pressure checked, Clara? When that cuff tightens, the pressure in your forearm is amazing – it hurts like fuck, and then you can feel your heartbeat booming along your arm and it's like being on fire. And that's what begins to happen in your neck, the heart booming in your ear drums. The pain.

"And then you slip, or your knees finally give out and boom! Your entire weight is on your neck, and panic kicks you in the chest. Your feet slip across the floor, and the need to breathe becomes more massive than anything you've ever experienced in your life, and the booming is violent, you grit your teeth, and you reach for the rope. You grab at it, trying to loosen it just to give yourself a bit of relief, just a sip of cold air, please!"

Clara blinked, shuffled her foot left and right across the garage floor. "That's all very interesting. Thank you. Can I go now?"

Eddie whispered, "If you're Mia, and you've got blood on your fingers from when you supposedly killed Marshall Forbes and dipped your fingers in his blood, and you're dying from hanging, you are going to struggle with that rope. You are going to leave some of his blood on that rope and on your neck. There was none. I took great care removing that rope, and I used ultra-violet light to see where your fingers had been on her skin."

Clara's mouth opened, her eyes were locked on Eddie.

"Mia was already dead when you put that rope around her neck. You'd strangled her with your bare hands, and I got your DNA from her neck. That was your mistake. I also found cotton fibres under her nails because she was clawing you as you strangled her, wasn't she? Huh, and you cleaned under her nails with a swab." Eddie took another step closer to her. "I got that confirmation email this evening, about your DNA on her neck. DI Benson was going to arrest you in the morning. I thought you might be gone by morning."

Clara lunged and brought the knife up, stabbing Eddie in the chest over and over as she pushed him backwards towards the door, rapid little stabs, fast, violent, until both were out of the door and Eddie tripped and fell backwards onto the lawn, she landed on top of him. Then she was off him, panting, ready to run.

Eddie lay on his back, blinking at the night sky, wondering if the constellation he could see was Orion. In truth, he couldn't see anything more than streaks of white light against the darkness, but was doing his best to focus. Warm blood flowed across his left arm and no sooner had he realised that than the pain bit. "You know what your biggest mistake was?"

She didn't reply.

"As soon as you started talking about investments and screwing fifteen percent, or whatever the fuck it was. Greed. Those who are greedy have the greatest need to hide."

Her footsteps raced away.

"Stop," he croaked, "you're under arrest."

There were shouts as Clara disappeared from Eddie's field of vision. Among them was Benson, shouting loudest, desperate to prove that an old geezer can still run with the young ones, can still do battle with them and win. He wasn't too old, and he wasn't too fat, and he wasn't useless.

Eddie tried to sit up and failed, but he rolled over and shouted, "Benson, no, she's got a knife! Benson. No!"

Chapter 54

EDDIE WATCHED HIS BREATH clouding above him and drift away into nothingness. He climbed to his feet as the lights came on, saw the blood gushing down his arm, said, "Fuck," and almost passed out.

There was more shouting from the front of the house, a scream, and then even more shouting.

Eddie heard hurried footfalls across the lawn, coming towards him. "Get a paramedic here, now!" Someone shouted. It was Colin, the PCSO Eddie had Christened Halitosis. He was at Eddie's side in seconds, "How are you?"

"How's Benson?"

There was a moment where Colin just looked at Eddie, seemingly unsure of how to proceed.

Eddie began peeling off the Velcro from the stab vest, thankful she'd only struck flesh once or twice. "Tell me. He okay?"

The garage door clattered against the wall, and Eddie looked up as a cameraman edged out of the narrow door, dressed all in black. He saw Eddie and put his thumb up, "Truly excellent job!"

"Where's Fooky Nell?"

"I'm here."

Eddie turned and saw him approaching from the top of the garden near the house. "I was recording the outdoor part in infra-red, and we've got a white light camera going all the time," he said, smiling, "and it was just wonderful. You wait till Netflix sees this – I'll be famous at last."

"Did you get the garage scenes?"

"Yes, yes, we had IR and daylight cameras in there too. Got it all on tape. You were very good, but weren't you afraid she might stab you in the neck at all?"

The smile fell off Eddie's face.

Epilogue

Eddie clutched a pathetic bunch of flowers. Much to his embarrassment, he'd only remembered to get any at the very last moment, and the only ones they had left at the local petrol station looked like they'd been sprayed with weedkiller. No wonder they were the only ones left, he thought. When he looked around, no one else had even brought flowers, so now he felt stupid for bringing them, and tight for bringing shit ones all at the same time. Even though no one seemed to pay him any attention, he began to blush.

He swallowed, told himself it was the thought that counted. "So fuck you," he added, confirming how bad he was at observing social conventions.

He shuffled along the pew as someone else entered. It was a scraggly, mucky woman with matted hair. She turned to him, and smiled. She was not one of Michelangelo's models, that was for sure, but there was something beautiful about her. Eddie wondered if all that aura bullshit that people speak of might have some truth behind it after all. Yes, she had a beauty, and she nodded at him. Ah, he remembered who she was. "Benson mentioned you to me."

"Did he? How kind."

"He would have been pleased to know you came along, Libby."

"Always had a soft spot for Mr Benson."

"Is it a peat bog in Wales?"

She nodded at the flowers. "Rob a grave?"

He dropped them on the floor and heeled them under the pew, felt like giggling with her, but managed to hold it back.

After the service, people congregated outside the church doors, the vicar nodding, shaking hands, and engaging in conversation with everyone who sidled past him.

Libby tugged on Eddie's arm as he walked to the new graveside, and offered his flowers, "I think you left these behind, mister," she said, and winked.

Eddie grabbed them, tossed them onto the nearest grave and tried to blend into a crowd of mourners by the graveside. And as if this was something out of a movie, the rain began. Eddie pulled up his collar and then Benson was right beside him, "I saw you fling that bunch of weeds. That's desecration, is that."

"Thought you couldn't make it?"

"Well, I'm here now; better late than never." He turned and gave Libby's arm a gentle squeeze, "How are you, dear?"

She smiled at him with something approaching coyness. "Better than her," she nodded at the coffin sinking into the ground. "I thought she was going to make a full recovery. That's what the doctors said, after all."

"Heart finally gave out," Benson whispered. "Poor Daisy."

"Oh," Eddie elbowed Benson, "thanks for telling me you had a stab vest on the night you arrested Clara Chandler."

Benson shrugged. "Why would I? *You* had one on, others had them on. Didn't know—"

"Well, you should have told me."

"Worried about me?" Benson grinned.

"Well how was I supposed to know they even did them in your size?"

Libby snorted.

"Or maybe they didn't. Maybe they stuck two together."

Benson sneered, "Very funny. Hilarious."

"And another thing," he turned to Benson again. "What about my neck? She could have stabbed me in the fucking neck."

"Eh? But she didn't, that's the important thing."

"But she *could* have!"

He nodded, "It was a risk, I admit."

"A risk?"

"It paid off, didn't it, what are you complaining about? You got some good overtime from that job." Benson fiddled with change in his pocket, "Meant to tell you…"

"What?"

"The swabs for DNA you took from Mia's neck and from under her fingernails?"

"What about them?"

"I finally got the results. Inconclusive – mixed profile; not able to get a profile, so unable to provide a name."

"Really?" Eddie said, concerned. "I was sure they'd come back as Clara. Even told her as much." And then he coughed, shrugged, "Well she didn't deny it, did she?" He winked at Benson as the vicar droned on about Daisy and her unfortunate ending. Eddie whispered, "Why are you late?"

"I was at Regan's. She's doing very well, hoping to be back in the next couple of days. And I've been given orders to look after her."

"Oh yeah?" he winked again.

"I took her some flowers. Only mine didn't look like weeds."

"You dirty old dog. I say again, oh yeah?"

"Yeah, and my wife came along too. So there! And she's the one who told me to look after her. Ner!"

"You're a big kid!"

"Oh, and she said the sight of you in your boxer shorts will haunt her forever. What on earth have you been doing to the poor girl?"

Around them was silence as the vicar and the congregation stared at them.

"Sorry," they uttered together. Beside them, Libby giggled behind her hand.

Back in the CSI office, Sid tucked into a plateful of biscuits and read Charles's latest chapter on his desktop screen. This was the penultimate chapter, and the story had worked nicely to a climax with the final denouement due shortly. There were fewer and fewer mistakes for Sid to work through with each new chapter, and Charles was becoming a more confident writer who had a gift for telling a tale.

The door opened and a PCSO entered. "Hi, Sid."

Sid looked up, and was surprised to see, "Skid! How are you?"

Skid marched up the office with a smile on his face. "It's good to see the old place again."

"You only left a couple of days ago. Missing us already?"

"I just came to drop off my old ID card." He slid it onto Sid's desk and snaffled a garibaldi from the plate. "So who's Eddie getting to replace me?"

Sid smirked at the biscuit theft, and shrugged, "Don't know. He's looking for candidates, though."

"You don't think he hates me, do you?"

"Eddie? No, no, don't be daft. Better to find out now and keep your sanity! You did the right thing."

"Ah that's okay, then." Skid finished the biscuit and asked, "how did the sponsored walk go?"

"Raised 187 quid, so I did quite well. Most people stuck a fiver in my tin, but I know Eddie put twenty in there hoping I wouldn't notice. He's a good sort, Mark; I hope you have fond memories of him and working here."

The light was drawing in and Charles had one of those screensavers playing on the TV screen. It was of a log fire burning in a hearth, complete with crackles and whooshes, sparks flying up the chimney. It was great to write by.

And he was right at the end of the final chapter, his old square fingers beating the keys with such rapidity that he couldn't actually follow them any more, just stared at the centre of the keyboard and played the story out in his head, letting the fingers do their own thing.

It had been a strange story of two brothers who never got along, despite living in splendour in Swillington Manor. As they grew older, their intolerance of each other increased to the point where they couldn't be in the same room without a fight breaking out. One brother had warmth and brains, and was popular with the villagers and the gentry alike, and the other had money and greed, but was jealous of his brother's popularity.

The popular brother with the brains was called Emial, and the rich, jealous one, was called Clarance. Clarance was proudest of one of his attributes more than any other – his flawlessness, his perfection.

Clarance constructed a plan to be rid of Emial once and for all. He planned on killing Emial's lover, Mars, and making sure everyone thought Emial was the culprit. But that was only half of the plan. Clarance would kill Emial with his bare hands, and make it look as though he'd taken his own life in a fit of guilt over killing Mars.

It was fool proof.

But it turned out not to be fool proof, after all. Clarance had forgotten about one thing – his flawlessness had made him complacent, that he could forget nothing. Except he *had* forgotten something, hadn't he? His greed and his jealousy had made him the perfect candidate for Emial's killer – the greediest person with most to gain from Emial's death – and all it needed was one person to figure it out and look a little harder, maybe offer a token flaw that Clarance would emphatically deny but in doing so fell into the bigger trap.

Charles looked at the two words he thought he'd never type: The End, and he reached for a tissue with a sense of accomplishment and a teeny bit of pride as well.

Acknowledgments

As with any (ad)venture as large and involved as writing a book, there comes a time when one must stop and ask others for help and advice. I'm very lucky to have some wonderful people in my corner who always seem so enthusiastic when it comes to stories and when it comes to accompanying me on another part of the journey.

You'll know Kath Middleton and I always walk this path together and she inspires me, and gives me the thumbs up or the thumbs down (she isn't shy of telling it how it is!), and then there's Emmy Ellis who designs superb covers, and Zoé-Lee O'Farrell and her superb band of bloggers (thank you so much!) for spreading the word throughout the book world, Dee Groocock for her unstinting support and generosity. There are so many fantastic Facebook groups with lots of friends in each – all contributing by commenting or liking the strange things this man from Leeds posts on there. Not least are those stalwarts in my own Facebook Groups and those who subscribe to my monthly newsletter, too. Thanks, everyone for your kindness and support - it means the world to me.

A special thanks to my eagle-eyed beta and ARC readers whose input makes the book come alive, and makes this part of the journey so much fun. It's one of the best parts of publishing a book.

Lastly, if you're one of those readers who care enough about the story, the character, and the time devoted to knitting them all together, to leave an honest review so that new readers might share your enjoyment, then I bow sincerely at your feet - you keep the book world turning, and you keep me and my author friends tapping the keys.

Beta Readers, thank you...
Lesley Lloyd
Joanna Joseph
Fritzi Redgrave
Alex Mellor
Gail Ferguson
Patti Holycross
Dee Groocock

About the Author

Andrew Barrett has enjoyed variety in his professional life, from engine-builder to farmer, from oilfield service technician in Kuwait, to his current role of senior CSI in Yorkshire. He's been a CSI since 1996, and has worked on all scene types from terrorism to murder, suicide to rape, drugs manufacture to bomb scenes. One way or another, Andrew's life revolves around crime.

In 1997 he finished his first crime thriller, *A Long Time Dead*, and it's still a readers' favourite today, some 200,000 copies later, topping the Amazon charts several times. Two more books featuring SOCO Roger Conniston completed the trilogy.

He's best known for his lead character, CSI Eddie Collins, and the acerbic way in which he roots out criminals and administers justice. Eddie's series is seven books and five novellas in length, and there's still more to come.

Andrew is a proud Yorkshireman and sets all of his novels there, using his home city of Leeds as another major, and complementary, character in each of the stories.

You can find out more about him and his writing at **www.andrewbarrett.co.uk**, where you can sign up for his Reader's Club, and claim your free starter library. He'd be delighted to hear your comments on

Facebook (and so would Eddie Collins) and Twitter. Email him and say hello at **andrew@andrewbarrett.co.uk**

Also by Andrew Barrett

The CSI Eddie Collins series:
The Pain of Strangers
Black by Rose
Sword of Damocles
Ledston Luck
The Death of Jessica Ripley
This Side of Death
Death Warning

Did you enjoy *Death Warning?* Please click on the image below and you'll be taken to a special landing page where you can choose your next Andrew Barrett book from your favourite store. Or visit your local Amazon store and search **Andrew Barrett**. Or take out your mobile phone and your camera app should take you there via this QR code:

Try a CSI Eddie Collins short story or a novella. Read them from behind the couch! Also available as a box set entitled *Short and Curlies*, and includes a special extra novella, *Eye Contact*. **Please click here.**

Have you tried the SOCO Roger Conniston trilogy?

Also available as a boxed set (eBook only)

Please come along and visit the website:

Reader's Club

As a thank you for joining the Reader's Club, I want you to enjoy a couple of free books, a starter library - I call this **Sign up and Read**.

I'll make sure you get a brilliant thriller and a stunning CSI Eddie Collins novella written in first person.

The Reader's Club features a monthly newsletter with details of new releases, special offers, and other goodies, together with news and snippets of interesting items. How do *you* join the thousands of other crime-thriller fans there? Simply click this link to my website (or type it into your browser), **www.andrewbarrett.co.uk**, and sign up today.

Printed in Great Britain
by Amazon